W9-CZY-832

The Arm of the Starfish

BOOKS BY MADELEINE L'ENGLE

The Arm of the Starfish
The 24 Days Before Christmas
The Moon by Night
A Wrinkle in Time
Meet the Austins
And Both Were Young
A Winter's Love
Camilla Dickinson
Ilsa
The Small Rain

THE ARM

ARIEL BOOKS

OF THE STARFISH

Madeleine L'Engle

FARRAR, STRAUS AND GIROUX

The verse quoted on page 124 is from "Two Tramps in Mud Time" from
Complete Poems of Robert Frost. Copyright 1936 by Robert Frost. Copyright renewed 1964 by Lesley Frost Ballantine. Reprinted by permission
of Holt, Rinehart and Winston, Inc.

Please note that the action of THE ARM OF THE STARFISH is not strictly
contemporary; the story should be read as taking place in the near future.

FOR
EDWARD NASON WEST

ΚΑΙ ΟΣΟΙ ΤΩ ΚΑΝΟΝΙ
ΤΟΤΤΩ ΣΤΟΙΧΗΣΟΤΣΙΝ,
ΕΙΡΗΝΗ ΕΠ᾿ ΑΤΤΟΤΣ

The Arm of the Starfish

1

A heavy summer fog enveloped Kennedy International. The roar of the great planes was silenced but in the airport there was noise and confusion. Adam wandered about, trying not to look lost, keeping one ear open to the blaring of the loudspeaker in case his flight to Lisbon should be called or canceled. His bags had long since disappeared on the perpetually moving conveyor belt, and he was too excited to sit anywhere with a book. All he could do was walk about, looking and listening, caught up in the general feeling of tension.

An extra load of business was being conducted over the insurance counters and at the insurance machines. Adam debated between a machine which would give him insurance and one which would give him coffee, and chose the coffee. Holding the paper cup in one hand, and his battered school briefcase in the other, he walked through a crowd of agitated people who had come to meet planes which were now being deflected to Boston and Philadelphia.

The hot, sweet coffee finished and the carton disposed of in a trash can, Adam headed for a row of phone booths, but they were all occupied by frustrated people whose plans had been changed by the July fog, so he decided against trying to call any of his friends. Probably no one would be home, anyhow; they were either away for the summer or busy with summer jobs.

So there was no point in trying to impress anyone with *his* job which had come up suddenly and gloriously after he and his parents had moved to Woods Hole for the summer and he was already set in the familiar routine of sorting and filing for Old Doc Didymus.

Doc might be ninety and doddering, but it was he who had said, the second day Adam reported for work, "Adam, I'm letting myself get dependent on you in the summer and this isn't good for either of us. My young friend, O'Keefe, is doing some rather extraordinary experiments with starfish on an island off the south coast of Portugal, and I'm sending you over to work for him this summer."

Strangely enough it was almost as easy as it sounded, parental permission, passport, inoculations, and a ticket to Lisbon.

Adam, like every biology major, had heard of Dr. O'Keefe, but the scientist was only a name in the boy's mind. To work for him, to see him as a person, was something else again. He was full of questions. 'Young' to Old Doc meant anywhere between eight and eighty, but Adam had early learned that one did not ask Old Doc anything that did not pertain directly to marine biology. Adam's father, who had also worked for Old Doc in his day, knew this, too. He said only, "If Doc thinks you're ready to work for Dr. O'Keefe then it's the thing for you to do, and I'd be the last person to hold you back. O'Keefe has one of the extraordinary minds of our day. Your mother and I will miss you, but it's time you got off and away."

Over the loudspeaker Adam's flight was postponed for the third time. He started for an emptying phone booth, but a woman with three small children beat him to it. The children huddled together outside the booth; the eldest, bravely holding on to the hands of the two littler ones, began to cry, and Adam, to his own indignation and shame, felt a strong surge of fellow-feeling with the child.

He turned quickly away and walked up and down the large, noisy main hall of the air terminal, trying not to be disturbed by the loudspeaker calling, people rising from couches and trying to listen, annoyed men heading for the bar, mothers trying to

4

coax babies into sleep with bottles of milk or juice. The main thing, he finally acknowledged to himself with a feeling of deep shame, was that he'd always had someone's hand (figuratively, of course) to hold, his family's, or Old Doc's, or the teachers', or the kids' at school, and now for the first time (for shame, Adam, at such an age), he was on his own, and just because his flight kept being postponed was no reason for him to start feeling homesick and to look around for another hand to hold.

Adam Eddington, sixteen, going on seventeen, out of high school and set for Berkeley in the winter, had better be ashamed of himself if a crowded airport, heavy with fog and tension, could put him on edge now.

It was after his flight had been delayed again (but not yet canceled) that he became aware of one person in the enormous, milling crowd, a girl about his own age. He was aware of her not only because she was spectacularly beautiful in a sophisticated way that made him nervous, but because she was aware of him. She looked at him, not coyly, not in any way inviting him to come speak to her, but coolly, deliberately, as though looking for something. Twice Adam thought she was going to come over to him; it was almost as though she had some kind of message for him. But each time she turned in another direction and Adam decided that he was being imaginative again.

He started to go for another cup of coffee, then looked back across the echoing hall, and now not only was the spectacular and enticing girl looking at him, she was walking toward him, and as she came closer she smiled directly at him, and held up one hand in greeting. His palm was slightly moist against the handle of his briefcase.

"Hi," she said. "I know you."

Adam gave what he felt must be a rather silly grin and shook his head. "No. But I wish you did."

She frowned. "I *know* I know you. Where?"

Adam was aware that this was a rather outworn opening gambit. However, he felt that this girl really meant it; she wasn't just casting around for someone to amuse her until her plane should be called or canceled. With her looks in any case she could have had any man in the airport with the lift of an eye-brow; Adam saw several men looking admiringly at the naturally fair hair, that particular shining gold that can never be acquired in a beauty parlor, and which shimmered softly down to slender shoulders. She wore a flame-colored linen dress and spike-heeled pumps. A leather bag was slung casually over one shoulder, and Adam no longer felt even the smallest need to hold anyone's hand, except perhaps the girl's, and that would be a different matter entirely. He was overwhelmingly proud that out of this vast conglomeration of people she had singled him out for her attentions.

"I'm Adam Eddington," he said, "and having met you now I'm not likely to forget it."

The girl laughed, with no coyness. "I admit I'm not used to being forgotten. I'm Carolyn Cutter, called Kali. Where are you off to? That is, of course, if we ever *get* off."

"Lisbon first."

"Oh, sharp! Me too. Where next?"

"Well, I'm going to be working on an island called Gaea. It's somewhere off the south coast of Portugal."

As he said 'Gaea' she frowned slightly—perhaps she was thinking of Gôa—but she said, "What on earth kind of work could you possibly find to do in Gaea?"

"There's a marine biologist working there, Dr. O'Keefe. I'm going to be assisting him."

Now the girl definitely frowned. "Oh, so you know O'Keefe."

"No, I don't know him. I've never met him."

Kali seemed to relax. "Well, *I* know him, and if you'd like the lowdown I'll give it to you. How about going into the coffee shop and having a sandwich and a Coke or something? I was counting on eating on the plane and heaven knows when we'll get on *that*. I'm starved."

"Me, too. Great idea," Adam said. He put his hand against the firm tan skin of her bare arm and they started across the hall to the coffee shop. Suddenly Kali stiffened and veered away.

"What's the matter?" Adam asked.

6

"I don't want him to see me."

"Who?" Adam looked around stupidly and saw a middle-aged clergyman holding on to the hand of a gangly, redheaded girl about twelve years old.

"Him. Canon Tallis. Don't look. Hurry."

As Adam ran to catch up with her, she said, under her breath, but with great intensity, "Listen, Adam, please take this seriously. I'm warning you about him. Watch out for him. I mean it. Truly."

Adam, startled, looked at her. Her lovely face was pale with emotion, her pansy eyes clouded. "What—what do you mean? Warning me? For Pete's sake why?"

She tucked her arm through his and started again toward the coffee shop. "Maybe the simplest thing to tell you is that he's a phony."

"You mean he isn't a—a—"

"Oh, he's a canon all right, you know, a kind of priest who floats around a cathedral. He's from the diocese of Gibraltar. But I didn't really mean that." She turned her limpid eyes toward him, and her hand pressed against his arm. "Adam, please don't think I'm mad."

"Of course I don't think you're mad," Adam said. "I'm just— well, for crying out loud what *is* all this? I don't know you, I don't know your canon or whatever he is, I think you've got me mixed up with someone else."

"No," Kali said, leaning rather wearily against the wall. "Let me tell you about myself, and then maybe you'll understand. But first I want to know something: how do you happen to be working for O'Keefe?"

"I'm majoring in marine biology," Adam said. "My father's a physicist, teaches at Columbia, but we've always gone to Woods Hole for the summer and I've worked for Old Doc Didymus there ever since I was a kid."

"Didymus?"

"You've probably read about him in the papers and stuff," Adam said with some pride. "He's one of the most famous marine biologists in the country, and he's still going strong, even if he is ninety. Anyhow, he got me this job. It's a marvelous opportunity for me."

Four people at the head of the line were beckoned to a table and Adam and Kali moved up. Kali looked around at the people ahead of them and behind them, then said in almost a whisper, "Oh, Adam, it's terribly lucky I met you! I've absolutely *got* to talk to you. But there's no point here—you never know who might be listening. Maybe on the plane—. Anyhow, I'll tell you something about myself now, because at this point if you thought I was a kook I certainly wouldn't blame you."

Looking at Kali standing beside him, at the pale radiance of her hair, at her hand resting lightly on his arm, Adam did not think her a kook. As a matter of fact, it didn't make the slightest difference whether she was a kook or not. She was a gorgeous girl who for some unknown and delightful reason had chosen him out of all this crowd, and what she was saying was only a soprano twittering in his ears. Most girls' conversation was, in his opinion. She chattered away, looking up at him confidently, and he sighed and tried to give a small, courteous amount of attention to her words.

He had always, with a degree of arrogance, considered himself sophisticated because he had grown up in New York, because his friendships cut across racial and economic barriers, because he could cope with subway and shuttle at rush hours, because the island of Manhattan (he thought) held no surprises for him. But, trying to listen to Kali, he saw that his life, in its own way, had been as protected and innocent as that of his summer friends who lived year round at Woods Hole, and with whom he had always felt faintly worldly. Kali, it seemed, crossed the ocean as casually as Adam took a crosstown bus. She knew important people in all the capitals of Europe, and yet she talked about them with an open candor that kept it from being name-dropping. Her father had extensive business interests in Lisbon and on the west coast of Portugal; they had an apartment in Lisbon and were intimate with everybody in the American and British embassies. Because Kali had no mother she acted as her father's hostess for all his entertaining. "And we do lots and lots of it," she said. "Daddy's a sort of unofficial cultural attaché, only lots more so. I mean he's ever so much more important. Good public relations and stuff. Fine for business, and fun, too."

As Adam listened, his mouth opened a little in admiration and awe. Her light, rather high voice, fine as a silver thread, spun a fine web about him. He felt that at last, here in the international atmosphere of the great airport, he was truly entering the adult world in which Kali already trod with beauty and assurance. She gave him a sideways glance, and her fingers pressed lightly against his arm. "I do love being daddy's hostess," she said, "and I really do very well by him. I mean I have a flair for it. I'm not bragging or anything; it's just what I'm good at."

Adam could easily picture her being gracious and charming and radiant and having every man in the room at her feet.

There was a group of six young people ahead of them, three boys and three girls. Adam felt that the boys were conscious of Kali's exotic beauty and envious because it was his arm she held, and that the girls were conscious of the boys' consciousness, and annoyed by it—Those jerks, he thought. —I wonder what they're doing here anyhow?

The harassed coffee shop hostess moved through the crowded room toward the line and held up her fingers. "Two?"

"Oh, good, that's us," Kali said. "Come on, Adam."

They were taken to a dark table in the corner. A waitress wiped off the wet rings and crumbs and stuck menus at them. Kali ignored the menus. "I just want a cheeseburger and a Coke. That okay by you, Adam?"

"Sure. Fine."

Kali waved the menus and the waitress away with an airy command that just barely missed rudeness. She leaned over the table toward Adam. "This was luck, getting a corner table like this. I guess we can talk a little if we keep our voices low. This—what's his name?—Diddy—"

"Didymus."

"You're sure he's all right? You can trust him?"

"Of course! We've always known Old Doc. He's—he's like my grandfather."

She pressed the tips of her long, lovely fingers together thoughtfully. "I wonder."

"What?"

"I wonder how well *he* knows O'Keefe. If he's ninety—"

"There are no fleas on Old Doc. You'd never take him for over sixty."

"O'Keefe has a reputation all right," Kali said. "I mean, he's a scientist. That's no front."

"Why should there be a front?"

"Oh, Adam, it's so complicated! We *are* on the same flight, aren't we?"

They were not.

Adam was going Swissair and Kali, Alitalia. She looked at him blankly. "How long are you going to be in Lisbon?"

"I don't think at all. I'm being met there and flown right on to Gaea."

The waitress plunked their orders in front of them, slopping their Cokes. Kali looked at her sweetly. "I'm so sorry to trouble you, but would you mind wiping the table, please? Thank you *so* much." Then she looked somberly at Adam. "This is bad. I've got to see you somehow. Do you think you'll be coming to Lisbon at all?"

"I don't know. I rather doubt it."

"Then I'll get to Gaea. I'll manage. Because I can't—" She held up her hand for silence as the loudspeaker blared. "That's my flight, Adam! The fog must be lifting. Come with me quickly, and I'll tell you what I can."

They left their untouched food and Adam picked up the check. Kali waited impatiently while he paid and got change.

They hurried along the echoing corridor. "Listen quickly," she said. "I can't really tell you anything now, but just watch out for O'Keefe, Adam. He's in thick with Canon Tallis. That's O'Keefe's kid with Tallis now."

"Dr. O'Keefe's!"

"Yes. I *told* you they were in cahoots. He has dozens of kids.

O'Keefe, I mean. O'Keefe and Tallis are against us, Adam. Don't let them rope you in. I'll try to get you to meet daddy somehow or other as soon as I can. I'm not being an alarmist, Adam. I know what I'm talking about. Believe me."

Adam almost believed. In spite of the wildness of Kali's words there was something about her that carried conviction. And Kali, with her sophistication and beauty, did not need to invent stories to get attention.

They reached the Alitalia gate and through the window Adam could see the big jet waiting in the rain that had driven away the fog. Kali took her ticket out of her bag, turned anxiously, and, to Adam's surprise, kissed him quickly on the cheek, saying again, "Believe me."

Adam stood watching as she hurried through the door. People brushed rapidly past him. He looked vaguely for the canon and the redheaded child, but did not see them. Oddly enough he felt excited and elated as well as bewildered. He did not have the faintest idea what Kali had been talking about, or what she was warning him about, but this was adventure, adventure in the adult world. He had graduated, all right!

He stood watching, bemused, as Kali's plane wheeled around and moved like a cumbersome bird down the runway. He could hear the blast of the jet as it slid out of sight into the rain. Slowly he walked from the Alitalia gates to the Swissair waiting room. There he saw Canon Tallis and the tall, gangly child, Dr. O'Keefe's child, standing with silent concentration licking ice cream cones, side by side, each bowed seriously over the ice cream.

2

Adam studied the clergyman and the child surreptitiously. The only extraordinary thing about Canon Tallis was the fact that he was completely bald, even to having no eyebrows, and had the look, somehow, of an extremely intelligent teddy bear. The girl seemed to Adam no different from most children who have suddenly shot up in height and not caught up with themselves in any other way. Only the flame of her hair and the open clarity of her blue eyes hinted that there was something for her to grow up to.

She looked at him over her ice cream cone and Adam shifted his gaze, for he wanted neither the canon nor the child to know that he was observing them. He took a book out of his briefcase and pretended to read it until his flight was called.

He started to the gate, and saw out of the corner of his eye that they were following him.

Because it was the height of the tourist season the plane was crowded. Adam had been assigned a seat by the window in the tourist section, and though the wing partly obscured his view he would still be able to see a good deal. Across the aisle, next to the window, sat the child, the canon beside her, and a lady with lavender hair in the third seat. The places next to Adam were occupied by two businessmen with attaché cases.

It was ten o'clock at night by Adam's watch when they took off. He had flown in from the Cape in the morning, but this was his first trip in a jet, and the pull of the gravities took him by surprise as momentarily he seemed to be pinned back in his seat. Then, with a smoothness he had never felt on a prop plane, they were airborne, rain drenching against the windows. And suddenly there was a star, and then another and another. Adam tried to watch as the plane flew high and clear of the clouds, but the lights in the cabin turned the windows into mirrors so that he saw his own reflection thrown back at him.

He looked warily about the plane, trying not to let his gaze linger on the dark figure of the canon, who was talking to the child, his face quick with interest and intelligence. But was it a malevolent or a benevolent face? Adam could not tell. The child laughed, openly, spontaneously: Dr. O'Keefe's child. Adam gave a shiver of excitement. Already, and before he had even met Dr. O'Keefe, the job promised to be far more than a summer job with a well-known scientist. Adam, crossing the Atlantic for the first time, dazzled by the international atmosphere of the great jet, felt ready for anything.

There was the click and buzz of the loudspeaker, and, while an attractive stewardess demonstrated, a voice explained, in English, French, and German, the emergency use of oxygen and how to put on the life belts just in case the plane should have to be ditched in the middle of the Atlantic. The captain, also using the three languages, introduced himself, and described the flight route and the altitude at which they would be flying. All of this and Adam hadn't even noticed that the NO SMOKING and FASTEN SEAT BELTS signs had blinked off. Feeling a little foolish, he undid his belt, noting that his companions had already unfastened theirs, and tried to relax and look world-traveled. But he was too keyed up for the tautness to leave his body.

Dinner was served, a full and delicious meal in spite of the hour, and Adam, having had none of his cheeseburger in the coffee shop with Kali, ate ravenously. After the trays were cleared the stewardess came around with pillows and blankets, and Adam, like the older men beside him, leaned back in his seat, loosening his tie and belt. He knew it was important to try to sleep as soon as he could because the difference in time would make it a short night. When they landed in Lisbon at eight-thirty in the morning it would still be only three-thirty in New York.

But his mind would not shut off. He found himself remembering a trip to the Hayden Planetarium. He loved the Planetarium and went there often to see the dome come alive with stars. He thought now of a lecturer who had said, "Of course you never see stars like this in New York. If you want to see stars you must go out into the country where there are no lights to dim them. But if you *really* want to see stars then you must be out in the middle of the ocean. Then you can see them as the sailors and navigators saw them in the days when stars were known as very few people know them now."

Adam, wakeful, remembering these words, glanced at his seat companions. Both had their eyes closed, so very gently he drew back the curtains at the window. The lights in the cabin had been dimmed; the window was no longer a mirror, and he saw that the Planetarium lecturer had spoken the truth. Never had there been stars as he saw them now, not at Woods Hole on the beach, nor even out in a sailboat at night. The stars—how many miles out over the Atlantic?—were clearer and more brilliant than anything he could have imagined, glorious myriads pulsing and throbbing about the plane. With his face turned toward the window he dozed, never sleeping soundly, but over and over again opening his eyes to the stars.

Then, very slowly, in the east, straight ahead of him, the sky began to lighten faintly, the stars to seem just a little less clear. A pale red warmed the horizon, but what made it different from sunrise seen from the land, or even from a ship, was the plane's great altitude, and the most extraordinary sight came surprisingly from behind the plane, in the west. They were flying east into sunlight, but the western sky was a strange, deep blue, with a haze of rose spreading out below and pulsing slowly upward.

By now he was completely awake, looking out the window

before him, behind him, below him. The plane was so high that he did not see the ocean as ocean, but as great patches of purply-grey darkness among the scattered whiteness of clouds. As the light brightened, so that he was afraid his seat companions would ask him to draw the curtains, the clouds thickened beneath the plane, though it was flying in dazzling sunshine.

He leaned back in his seat, saturated for the moment with beauty, and looked around the cabin. Most of the passengers were still asleep. A portly gentleman moved stiffly up the aisle past Adam to the washroom. Across the aisle the canon and the O'Keefe child were eagerly peering out the window, the priest leaning over the child, his arm around her. He seemed very avuncular and not in the least sinister, and for a moment Adam wondered if he could have dreamed Kali and her warnings. In the aisle seat next to the canon the lavender-haired lady snored delicately.

Then, at three o'clock in the morning New York time, all the lights were turned on in the plane cabin, and breakfast was served, which, Adam felt, must have been a little hard on those passengers going on to Geneva and Zurich, though he himself was more than ready for food, and the hot, fragrant coffee made him forget his lack of sleep.

He was starting to wonder why they were not beginning the descent for Lisbon when he heard the buzz of the loudspeaker: "Ladies and gentlemen, this is your captain. We have just passed over Lisbon. Because of weather conditions we are unable to land and will proceed to Madrid." The same message was repeated in French and German.

The man next to Adam rang for the stewardess and asked about visas in Madrid; if they were being forced into Madrid he wanted to do some sightseeing; he wanted to go to the Prado.

It would be perfectly all right, the stewardess assured him; if the plane was held in Madrid for any length of time those passengers wanting visas would be issued them.

This struck Adam as an unlooked-for piece of luck; a glimpse of Lisbon and then the island of Gaea were all he had expected to see. A day in Madrid was a wonderful and added adventure.

The Prado, he knew, was a museum; if that was the place to go, go to it he would.

Within a few minutes the clouds dispersed as they started their slow descent, and he could see the countryside of Spain beneath them. It was all he could have hoped for in his most romantic dreams: it was as though the plane had taken them centuries instead of miles out of their way. In the distance were snow-capped mountains. Below him were fields of all shapes and patterns and in all shades of green and brown. He thought he recognized olive trees, but the plane was still too high up for him to be sure. There were hills with ancient forts built around a square; there were hills with turreted castles. He had heard of castles in Spain; now he was seeing them. Suddenly he saw great bare circles of some kind of modern military emplacements; he was not sure what they were; perhaps Nike sites. Strange, bleak pockmarks on an ancient rural landscape, they jerked him out of the middle ages and into the present.

FASTEN SEAT BELTS flicked on. Across from Adam the canon and the child slowly sat back in their seats.

The landing was effortless and the great plane taxied down and around long runways until in the distance Adam could see a large, cold-looking modern airport; there were many men in military uniforms moving about. As soon as the plane had stopped, the rolling steps were pushed up and the passengers herded out and into a waiting bus, although the jet was only a few yards from the terminal. Probably, Adam thought, they're taking us to some other entrance where they can fix up our visas and tell us when we can get to Lisbon.

The bus was all part of the adventure, it was so definitely not an American bus. There was something almost institutional about it, as though it were not a bus for which one ever voluntarily paid a fare to take a ride; it was like a bus in a dream into which people were thrust, as the jet passengers were now, like it or not, and taken to some impersonal destination, probably unknown.

About half the passengers were able to sit on the seats which ran the length of the bus; the rest of them, including Canon

Tallis and the O'Keefe child, and, of course, Adam, stood as the bus jounced the few yards to the air terminal: no more. They were as drenched by the rain that had suddenly started as they would have been if they had been allowed to run the short distance between plane and port, and why they hadn't been Adam could not fathom; but since nobody else was remarking on this he kept his mouth shut.

From the bus they were urged into the terminal where one of the stewardesses smiled with professional cheer and confidence and said, "Wait."

This must be tough, he realized, throwing the whole flight out of schedule; for the plane personnel it was not the adventure it was to Adam and to some of the passengers who were already making sightseeing plans; others were yawning openly and talking about getting to a hotel and catching some sleep. There was also some speculation as to what kind of hotel they were being taken to, and one of the more traveled passengers said that probably it would be the Plaza, since the Swissair offices were in the same building, and that, though there was nothing wrong with the Plaza, it bore no resemblance whatsoever to the Plaza in New York and no one had better expect any such luxury.

The interior of the terminal was as modern and cold and bleak as the exterior, and as filled with men in uniform, though these at least were keeping dry. As Adam looked at their dark, stern faces he felt some of his optimistic sense of well-being and grownupness beginning to fade, but shook himself, remembering that he had not had much sleep for two nights now, and lack of sleep always tended to make him edgy and apprehensive—one reason he never sat up late studying for exams. If he didn't know it he didn't know it.

In the big, chill room some of the passengers sat wearily on wooden benches, others chatted desultorily, making tentative plans. Canon Tallis stood holding the hand of the child, who was beginning to look white with fatigue, but neither of them spoke. It seemed a long time before one of the stewardesses reappeared and said that they would now be given visas and would then be driven to a hotel in Madrid. She herded them into two lines, telling them to have their passports ready for inspection and stamping.

Adam asked her anxiously, "I'm being met in Lisbon. Will they be notified there?"

"Certainly, sir, but we'll be glad to send a telegram for you. To whom?"

"I'm not sure who's meeting me. Could you just notify Dr. O'Keefe on Gaea? My name's Adam Eddington."

"Of course." She made a note, smiled again, and excused herself charmingly.

In the other line, with his passport already being inspected, stood the canon, and Adam realized that the older man had overheard him and was now looking at him in an intent and curious way. As the priest took his passport and the child's and walked off toward the exit he turned and looked back at Adam.

The lines moved quickly. The passport was given to one man, who checked it. Then the passenger was moved along to another man who stamped the passport with the required visa and returned it. It was all brisk and uncomplicated.

Until it was Adam's turn.

The officer at the window took Adam's passport and flipped casually through it, then turned back to the beginning and began to go slowly over each page. Finally, in heavily accented English, he said, "Your name, please."

"Adam Eddington." Then the boy spoke in Spanish, since he had had four years of it in school, and Juan, one of his closest friends was a Puerto Rican, school track star and prize chemistry student, whose family spoke no English. "Aquí tiene usted todo escrito en el pasaporte." —It's all there, right in the passport.

The officer looked at him sharply. "You have been in Spain before?"

"No, sir," Adam said.

"Then why do you speak Spanish?"

"I learned it in school."

The officer looked at him unbelievingly. "Americans do not make a study of languages."

"Oh, yes, sir. Some of us do." Adam made the mistake of smiling as he remembered Juan's initial struggles with English.

The officer stared darkly at Adam with hard black eyes; his hair, too, was black, wavy, and highly polished. His chin had a dark shadow on it that would never disappear no matter how recently he had shaved. Looking at him Adam began to feel distinctly uncomfortable. Maybe speaking Spanish had been the wrong thing to do, but he had only intended to be polite.

After giving Adam the silent treatment for almost a full minute the inspector returned to the passport, his eyes flicking from Adam's photo to his face to the photo again. Finally he said, in deliberate English, "Your destination?"

Adam did not try Spanish again. "Well, Lisbon."

"And from there?"

"Gaea."

A cold flicker seemed to come into the man's eye. "Why Gaea?"

"I have a job there for the summer with a Dr. O'Keefe."

"O'Keefe," the inspector said thoughtfully, tapping Adam's passport against his teeth. Then he slapped the passport sharply on the palm of his hand and stood up. He spoke to two other officials who were behind him, but in Spanish so swift and low that Adam could not catch it. He turned to the boy: "Be so kind as to come with me."

"Now, look here," Adam said indignantly, "what business is all this of yours? I was supposed to land in Lisbon, not Madrid. The only reason I'm here is the fog, and I didn't have anything to do with that. If you don't want to give me a visa to go into Madrid, that's your business. But I'm not trying to get a job or anything in Spain and I don't see why any of this has anything to do with you."

The inspector listened impassively. Then he jerked his head. "Come," he repeated.

Adam opened his mouth to protest again, but something in the inspector's visage made him keep quiet. Stomach churning, he followed the inspector past the line of passengers, through the airport hall, down a corridor. Until the corridor turned he could feel the eyes of the other passengers on him. He had a moment's impulse to shout at them not to let him be taken away like this, but he controlled himself. It was probably something not quite right about his vaccination certificate, at which the inspector had glared for several seconds, or something silly and simple like that.

The inspector led him into a bare room painted a dark, oppressive grey. There was an unshaded light glaring from the ceiling, a desk with a chair before and behind. The one small, high window was barred. Adam, his knees suddenly feeling weak, went to one of the chairs and sat down.

"Stand," the inspector snapped.

Adam stood. "What is this—" he started to protest again, but the inspector cut him off.

"Silence."

Adam shut his mouth.

The inspector went with deliberate pace across the room, behind the desk, sat down. He looked at Adam again from head to foot, as though he did not like at all what he saw. With a gesture of his dark chin he indicated that Adam might sit.

This time Adam decided that he was happier standing on his own two feet.

"SIT," the inspector barked.

Adam sat.

For a full minute the inspector looked at him in silence. Then he said, "Why are you working for Dr. O'Keefe?"

"Well—it's—it's just a summer job," Adam said. "I've just graduated from school and I'm going to Berkeley—that's in California—in the winter."

"So why a summer job? Why is this necessary?"

"Most of us kids have to work in the summer to help out some with our education. Besides this was a big opportunity for me."

"Opportunity? How?"

Adam tried not to let his eyes falter as the inspector pinned him with his stare. He thought of saying that one does not treat law-abiding American citizens in this way, but decided that it might just get him into more difficulty, so he said nothing.

Because of the placement of the chairs the sharp light fell directly on Adam, but the inspector did not entirely escape the glare which glinted against a gold tooth in his stern mouth and threw back a tiny gleam of light. "Opportunity, *how?*" he asked again.

"Well—to work with Dr. O'Keefe—and I've never been in Europe before—"

"And now that you are here you intend to do what?"

"Well—just work for Dr. O'Keefe."

"What kind of work?"

"I don't know exactly. Just whatever I can to help out, I suppose."

"Such as?"

"Well—there may be experiments with starfish or something I could check on."

The inspector looked at him sharply, as though the boy had said something unexpected. He opened his mouth to speak but was stopped by a knock on the door. He snapped, "Come in."

The door opened and in came one of the uniformed men, followed by Canon Tallis, looking grim.

Adam suddenly remembered with horror all of Kali's warnings. He realized that they had seemed part of an adventure that was somehow make-believe; he had not taken them very seriously.

He took them seriously now.

3

The canon did not look at Adam, but went straight to the inspector, bowing and saying, "Good morning." Then, in precise British accent, he said, *"But yield who will to their separation . . ."*

There was a pause as the inspector looked at the canon. His visage, too, was grim. Finally he replied, *"My object in living is to unite . . ."*

The two men remained looking at each other, not speaking, until the inspector got up from the desk, nodded at the canon, came around to Adam, and handed him his passport. "I find your papers are quite in order after all," he said. "You may go. I believe the bus is still waiting."

The official who had escorted the canon opened the door, making a respectful obeisance. The canon looked at the inspector, bowed slightly, turned to Adam, saying, "Come."

Adam followed him. The priest moved with the ease of familiarity through the maze of passages until they were at the glass doors. Outside the bus was sitting greyly at the curb. The driver opened the doors. The canon got in. Adam climbed in after him. Someone had given the redheaded child a seat and she was asleep, her head down on the shoulder of a middle-aged, motherly-looking woman, who looked at the canon, saying, "She's all tuckered out. Let her sleep."

The priest smiled at her. "Thank you, Martha."

Adam knew that he, too, ought to say 'thank you,' since in some way the canon had been responsible for the escape from the inspector's inquisition, but the boy's mind was in such a turmoil that he could not speak.

It was obvious that the passengers, who had been kept waiting in the dark bus all this time, were intensely curious. A young man turned to Adam. "What on earth happened? Why did they drag you away like that?"

The canon answered quickly for him. "Just the usual passport confusion. There's one in every busload. You'll get used to it."

Now at last Adam said, "Thank you very much, sir." But he was not sure just how grateful he was. Although the canon had an easy and relaxed expression, reminding Adam once again of the intelligent teddy bear, there was still the memory of the grim look with which Tallis had greeted him in the inspector's office.

The bus started with a grinding of gears and a series of jolts. Adam felt surprisingly weak in the knees and would have liked to be able to sit down, but he clutched the aluminum pole firmly and braced himself so that without bending down too far he could look out the window. The trip into Madrid somehow surprised him. Spain seen from the air had been, except for the emplacements, everything that he had pictured it in his imagination; the outskirts of Madrid were a strange and unexpected conglomeration of old and new. There were many bleak housing developments like the projects in New York or those pictured in articles about Russia. Ugly apartments crowded upon beautiful old houses with walled gardens. Some new buildings were finished as far as the scaffolding, but seemed abandoned. Outside both the old buildings and the new laundry was flapping in the breeze. There were many billboards, well over half of them advertising American products, Pepsi-Cola, Coca-Cola, toothpaste, Singer sewing machines. The city itself was modern, commercial—buses, trolley cars, taxis, booths advertising the

National Lottery, priests, nuns, young people on bicycles, old women with long black skirts and black shawls over their heads, girls with bright skirts high above their knees, newsboys calling, lottery boys calling—Adam's mind whirled. The impressions were coming too thick, too fast, events had been too confusing from the moment he had reached the fog-bound airport in New York for him to assimilate and sort out any of it.

Canon Tallis reached down and wakened the child. "Poly. We're here."

She opened her eyes and yawned as the bus drew up in front of the Hotel Plaza with another sickening jerk that almost threw Adam and all the standing passengers off their feet. As they surged toward the exit Canon Tallis said to the boy, "I'll see you."

A pleasant Swissair representative was waiting for them and herded them quickly out of the bus and through the revolving doors into the hotel. The Hotel Plaza, at least, seemed to hold no startling surprises for Adam; it was very much what he had imagined a middle-class European hotel would be like.

The passengers were lined up at the desk, where their passports were collected. Adam's was given no more, no less attention than anybody else's. They were assigned rooms. The man from Swissair explained that, because of the fog that gripped Lisbon now as it had New York the day before, they would not be able to leave Madrid until five in the afternoon, when weather conditions were supposed to improve. Precisely at five they were all to be in the lobby of the hotel and would be driven back to the airport where a plane would be waiting for them. Meanwhile they were free to sleep or to do some sightseeing around Madrid.

Adam went up in the elevator to his room not knowing exactly what he was going to do. He was wavery with the desire to sleep, but he was determined not to waste the day. He decided that a shower and some food would refresh him, and then he would find a bus or trolley to take him to the Prado and maybe some other places of interest.

His room, a small one with an enormous bathroom, faced the

back. If the view from the front of the hotel was definitely twentieth century, the view from the rear flung him into the Middle Ages. He looked down into a courtyard filled with strutting black geese. In the center was a stone fountain. The rooftops, in a confused jumble of levels, were warm red tile. The houses were oyster white, with crooked, unmatched windows. The geese strutted about, their heads jerking awkwardly in and out of the downpour. An old woman, almost completely covered by an enormous black shawl, came out of a door and threw the geese some grain, toward which they scurried, gabbling. The woman stood, one hand holding the shawl about her face, watching them; then she disappeared into the house.

Adam felt his eyes gritty with sleep. If he didn't take that shower and get some more coffee and some food he would succumb to the temptation to lie down on the brass bed, and that he was determined not to do. Who knew when he would ever have another day in Madrid?

The water was hot and he steamed happily, then turned on the cold; he was shivering under its stinging needles when he became aware of a tapping on his door. He turned off the shower and called out, "Just a moment, please."

The hotel towels were fluffy and white and voluminous enough to wrap around him as a kind of bathrobe. Some instinct—or was it Kali's warnings?—made him call, before he opened the door, "Who is it?"

A pleasant British voice replied, "Canon Tallis."

Adam fought down a desire to say, 'Go away. You're dangerous. Kali warned me.' But after all the canon *had*, by no matter what devious means, rescued him. So he said, "If you'd wait a minute, please, sir, I'm just out of the shower. I'll throw on some clothes."

He dried and dressed as quickly as he could, then cautiously opened the door. Canon Tallis was standing, hands behind his back, staring upward through the ceiling at some inner vision. He smiled, the faint ridges where he should have had eyebrows rising slightly, followed Adam into the small room and sat on the one chair. Adam sat on the bed. The canon looked at him for a moment; Adam was getting distinctly tired of being looked at.

"So you're the young man who's going to be working for Dr. O'Keefe this summer." It was a statement, not a question.

Adam responded with a terse "yes." He was giving out no information. He began to wonder if Old Doc might not be getting senile after all, letting him in for this kind of thing. And as for his parents, they had no right to allow him to go off into the unknown like this. Of course there had been correspondence between his father and Dr. O'Keefe, and a couple of transatlantic phone calls, but Adam felt that none of the disagreeable things that had happened should have been allowed by parents who took a proper concern for their offspring. He forgot that he had been elated at first by Kali and her warnings.

"Tired?" Canon Tallis asked.

"No." He bit the word off and did not add *sir* or *father* or whatever it was one was supposed to call an English canon.

"Not much sleep last night."

Adam could not help adding, "Nor the night before."

"Planning to catch up on it today?"

"No," Adam said briefly. "I'm going to the Prado." Then, because his training in courtesy had been thorough, he added in a more reasonable voice, "I've never been in Spain before and I don't know when I'll get another chance. I didn't think I ought to waste it."

Canon Tallis nodded. "Poly's taking a bit of a nap, but then we're going to the Prado ourselves. Meanwhile I need a cup of coffee and a bite to eat. How about you? Dr. O'Keefe's a friend of mine, and maybe I can brief you a bit. Also I want to ask you a favor. I find I am going to have to stay in Madrid for a few days on business that would be very dull for Poly. She's the O'Keefes' daughter and a bright child, and perfectly capable at this point of traveling alone, but I'm responsible for her, and I feel rather badly about cutting her little vacation short, so I thought, since we've happened to run into each other, that I'd ask you to be kind enough to let her travel back to Lisbon with you."

What was there to say? There was no possible grounds for refusal of this perfectly reasonable request, so Adam nodded with a mumbled, "Yes, sir."

The canon stood up and yawned amply. "Two sleepless nights haven't given you the best preparation in the world for seeing the Prado. Nevertheless you may find it rather impressive in its own modest way."

When they reached the lobby the priest, instead of heading for the revolving doors, went to the desk. "Passports for Canon Tallis and Adam Eddington, please," he said in fluent Spanish. There was a brief wait, during which Adam felt himself getting nervous again. But the passports were handed to them without question.

"Be careful of it," the canon said. Adam did not mention that the advice was unnecessary. "Let's just go into the dining room here, shall we? No point in getting soaked again before we have to."

They went into an almost empty dining room with white-naped tables, and the canon ordered café au lait and an omelette.

Adam told the waitress, "Está bien para mi, también."

As she left the canon said, "You speak excellent Spanish."

"I had it in school," Adam found himself explaining again.

"Any other languages?"

"A bit of French and German."

"Portuguese?"

"No."

"Too bad. Russian?"

"No. I'd have liked to, but they stretched a few points for me with the ones I took."

"Poly's our linguist," the canon said. "She speaks all of those, plus Gaean. Now she wants to tackle Chinese. Sometimes it's a bit hard to hold Poly down." He seemed to be looking at Adam as though searching for something. "Poly's the oldest of the O'Keefe children, and she helps her mother a great deal. This is the first real vacation she's had. I had to give a couple of lectures in Boston and it seemed a good chance for her to get away. Then I was to have gone to Geneva for a few days and I'd planned to take her with me there, too. Too bad this fog had to come up and spoil her little treat for her. I must ask you, Adam, please to stay close to her. It is not that Poly isn't capable of taking care of herself. But there are some—shall we call them undesirable characters?—who are far too interested in Dr. O'Keefe's experiments. I will see to it that you both get on the plane, and Dr. O'Keefe will be at the airport to meet you. But please do not let Poly out of your sight. Will you promise me that?"

"Well—yes, of course," Adam said. "But I don't understand."

The priest looked at him thoughtfully. Adam looked back. —I'm going to do some of the staring, too, he decided. Grey eyes looked steadily into grey. Finally the canon said, "Adam, I wish I could tell you the things that would make you understand. When you start working for Dr. O'Keefe you'll realize for yourself the importance of his work, and its implications. But for now I must simply ask you to trust me, as I must, in my turn, trust you." His face again looked grim, though it was a different kind of grimness from that in the stark and frightening room in the airport.

—But I don't trust you, Adam thought. Not after Kali. Not after you seemed to be so in cahoots with a fink like the inspector. People you can trust simply aren't *in* with secret police kind of people.

The waitress brought their coffee and omelette, and crisp, crunchy rolls each wrapped separately in tissue-like paper. The omelette was delicious, though the coffee was bitter, and stronger than any Adam had tasted before. He watched the canon take the hot milk pitcher in one hand, coffee pot in the other, and pour simultaneously, and so he did the same for his second cup and found it considerably improved.

Finally, leaning back and lighting a cigarette, the canon said, "There. That's better. I hear that you have the makings of a fine scientist."

"Well—it's what I'm interested in," Adam said. "Marine biology."

"Yes. I saw the letter Dr. Didymus wrote Dr. O'Keefe. You will, I trust, like working with Dr. O'Keefe, Adam. He's a very great man, far greater than Dr. Didymus, fine though he is—"

"Old Doc—" Adam started indignantly.

"Old Doc would be the first to acknowledge it," the canon said sternly. "If he didn't think you had the makings of—somebody worthwhile, he would never have sent you over here."

Adam flushed with pleasure, then remembered Kali's warnings, superimposed on a few Grade B movies. —Flattery, he thought. —He's trying to get around me with flattery. And just because he looks like Winnie the Pooh. . . . Yukh: I've got to watch it.

Canon Tallis pushed back his chair. "Let's go wake poor Poly up, and then we'll be off to the Prado. You'll come with us, of course." This, again, was a statement, not a question.

Adam's first instinct was to say, "Of course I won't." But then he thought, —If I go with him I can keep an eye on him. And if I have to drag this kid to Lisbon with me I might as well see what she's like, too.

So all he said was, "That will be fine, sir."

They went up in the elevator together to the top floor. As he reached for his keys the canon whistled the first few measures of a melody. Behind the closed door the melody was returned. Adam recognized the tune, but in the fatigue and confusion of the moment he could not place it. Canon Tallis unlocked the door.

Poly was sitting on the edge of the bed, reading. She looked up, indignantly. "You locked me in."

4

"No, Poly darling," the canon said. "Just others out."

"Oh. Oh, okay, then."

"Adam, this is Poly O'Keefe. Poly, this is Adam Eddington, your father's new laboratory assistant."

Poly stuck out a lean brown hand and shook Adam's. Her grip was firm and confident. "Hello, Adam. Actually my name's Polyhymnia. Isn't that an awful name to give anybody? And it's all Father Tallis' fault. He's my godfather and he christened me. It's surprising that I still love him, isn't it? I tell you all this so that you'll know that if you ever call me anything but Poly I'll jump at you and kick and scratch like a wildcat."

"All right: Poly it will be," Adam said.

Canon Tallis said, "Get your coat and hat, Pol."

Poly looked out her window, which faced front on the modern street. "Nasty, stinking, foul old rain," she said, crossly, wheeled and took a navy blue burberry and a beret out of the closet.

They stopped off on Adam's floor while he picked up his trenchcoat, then went out into the street where the canon hailed a taxi with his furled umbrella.

"A lot of good it does us *that* way," Poly remarked.

They got in the taxi and the canon began pointing out places of interest. "If we have time this afternoon we'll go to the Plaza Mayor and you can walk around a bit."

"That's where the Spanish Inquisition started," Poly said, "and bullfights, and all kinds of icky stuff. It always gives me the shivers. Do we have to go there, Father?"

"Don't you think Adam ought to see it?"

"Oh, I suppose so. But I always seem to hear screams still quivering in the air. And smell blood." She looked defiantly at Adam. "I am *not* morbid."

"It's all right," Adam assured her. "I think that places hold atmospheres, too."

"You're nice," Poly said. "I shan't mind flying to Lisbon with you after all. At least Father said that that's what I'd be doing if it's all right with you."

"It's fine with me," Adam said. She was a queer kid and he couldn't very well hurt her feelings. Something in the tone of his voice, though, seemed to make her dubious, so he added, "Now I won't have to worry about recognizing your father."

Poly laughed, a warm, deep chuckle. "I look *exactly* like daddy. Stringbean aspect and all. Some of daddy's assistants have called him a long drink of water. That's me."

"The red hair and blue eyes, too," Canon Tallis said, "and with a little bit of luck the looks of your mother and maternal grandmother."

"Oh, I don't really care about being beautiful," Poly stated. "At least not yet."

As they neared the Prado, which was a longer drive than Adam had anticipated, Canon Tallis explained that although the museum was now in the city of Madrid, it was not too very long ago that it had been out in the country in the middle of fields.

It was not at all what Adam had expected of one of the most famous museums in Europe. Not only was it utterly unlike the Guggenheim or even the Frick, which was only natural, it also bore no resemblance whatsoever to the Metropolitan, either in the building itself, or in the display of pictures. He was amazed to find it an enormous, dirty, badly lighted place, the light even

31

worse than usual now because of skies dark with rain. In room after room there was a great jumble of masterpieces, El Grecos, Murillos (many of these looking like cheap religious Christmas cards), Velásquezes, Goyas, Raphaels, lesser known painters, unknown painters, early work, middle work, later work, good painting, middling painting, bad painting, finished and unfinished painting, all thrown at the wanderer in one great saturating splash. Canon Tallis was obviously familiar with every inch of the place, separating, sorting, explaining, ostensibly to Poly, but also for Adam.

Poly stood in a roomful of El Grecos and turned round and round, slowly. Then she stopped in front of a large painting of St. Andrew and St. Francis, the two of them standing together in obvious and direct communion. "I'm staggered," she said, "absolutely staggered, Father. Why haven't I seen it before?" She contemplated the picture again for a time in silence, assuming a junior version of Canon Tallis' stance, her legs braced slightly apart, her hands behind her back. "Of course it's impossible," she said.

"What?" Adam asked.

"That they should be there, like that, standing, talking together when they lived eleven hundred years apart. But I'm so glad they are. It does make time seem unimportant, doesn't it?" She turned to Canon Tallis and smiled. "I'm sorry I was horrid about not going to Geneva with you. But we'll do it another time, won't we?"

"Yes," he said gently. "Yes, we'll do that, Poly."

Just as Adam felt super-saturated, they paused for lunch in the museum cafeteria. This, at least, Adam found not unlike the cafeterias in the Met or the Museum of Natural History, except that it was much smaller, and most people automatically ordered a bottle of wine with lunch.

Here, for some reason, the canon and Poly switched into Spanish, so Adam joined them. Poly smiled at him warmly, "Oh, good, I'm so glad you aren't one of these Americans who refuses to speak anybody else's language. You speak awfully well."

"Thank you."

"Adam, do have a hamburger. Spanish hamburgers are the funniest things. The meat even is different. People who want some good Amurrican food order them and then go into a state of shock. Then they say it's bad meat cooked in rancid oil." She grinned at the canon and slapped her own hand lightly. "I'm being judgmental again, aren't I? I'm sorry. But do try one, Adam. I find them absolutely *cordon bleu.*"

The hamburger was indeed unlike an American hamburger; Poly's milkshake, too, bore little resemblance to anything Adam had had at home. He and the canon had coffee; without it Adam by now could not have stayed awake, and fatigue multiplied the already existing confusion in his mind. Poly, like the hamburger and the milkshake, was unlike any American child Adam had ever met, but she had evidently spent most of her life abroad. It was obvious that she adored Canon Tallis, and he, in his turn, seemed to love her deeply, but Adam was still very unsure of the canon. After all, a man in ecclesiastical garb could get away with murder—well, perhaps not murder, exactly—a lot more easily than anybody else.

After lunch they wandered around the museum for a while longer. Adam's legs were beginning to ache with fatigue. He now felt only irritation at some of the pictures which were so badly hung that they could hardly be seen for the glare; at others Adam found he was squinting, one eye closed, his nose almost touching the canvas. In many of the rooms were smocked art students copying paintings. The canon stopped by a young girl who was copying a baroque Annunciation. She turned around and smiled at him, brilliantly and warmly, in recognition. He pressed one hand briefly against her shoulder, but neither of them spoke, nor did he seem to consider introducing her to Adam or Poly. They moved on into a large rotunda full of statues watched over by a uniformed guard. As Adam and Poly followed the canon in, the guard moved over to them quietly, saying in English,

"*My avocation and my vocation—*"

"*—As my two eyes make one in sight,*" the canon replied.

The exchange was so swift, the voices were so low, that no one but Adam, and perhaps Poly, was aware that anything had been said.

Adam's retentive memory, the envy of his friends at school, came to his rescue now. For a moment he seemed to be back in the secret police room in the airport with the grim-faced canon speaking to the inspector.

—They rhyme! Adam thought suddenly. —What he said with the inspector then, and with the guard now. I don't remember the words, but I'm sure if I could get them and put them together and make four lines of them, they'd rhyme. An ABAB rhyme scheme.

He looked at the canon. The canon looked at him. Neither of them spoke.

—It's familiar, Adam thought. —It's vaguely familiar. Maybe something I had at school. If I could only figure out what it was I'd know more what I think about him.

The canon pulled out a very plain gold watch with a Phi Beta Kappa key on the chain. Something clicked in Adam's mind. —But he's English. He shouldn't have a Phi Beta Kappa key. Not unless he went to an American university as an undergraduate. Not likely. So then he *must* be a phony, the way Kali said. Unless—well, it *could* be honorary, like Churchill's. I don't know.

His eyes flickered back over the canon. For the first time Adam noticed that the plain black of the priest's clothing was broken by the tiny red sliver of the French Legion d'Honneur ribbon in his lapel. This was possible. Old Doc had one, too.

"Time to go," Canon Tallis said briskly.

Perhaps because of Poly's words Adam was not too happy with the Plaza Mayor. Then again it may have been simply the rain which dripped down the collar of his trenchcoat, though Canon Tallis tried to shield the three of them with his big black umbrella as they walked slowly about. The Plaza Mayor was a great, beautiful square, cobblestoned, with magnificent buildings, horses sadly pulling wagons, arches leading to narrow, winding streets with shops and restaurants and laundry hanging

34

out even in the downpour: perhaps it was the sullen stream of rain which was responsible for the dark aura that Adam felt as he looked across the vast, echoing space of the square.

It was almost five when they got back to the hotel, and Adam went up to his room to collect his things. When he opened his briefcase, which he had not taken to the Prado, he was quite sure that someone had gone through it while he was out, that his books were not as he had left them. His first thought was to rush to Canon Tallis with this disturbing news. Then he realized, with a sudden jerk of the stomach, that the trip to the Prado might have been engineered by the canon simply to get him out of the room.

Adam went through the briefcase again, carefully. Nothing had been taken, but he was quite certain that its contents had been examined and then replaced as accurately as possible. —When I get to Lisbon, he thought, —I'll make some excuse at least to telephone Kali. If I see her again now maybe I'll be able to sort things out.

Downstairs the Swissair man and almost all the other passengers were already assembled. Those who had been going on to Geneva and Zurich, with the exception of Canon Tallis and Poly, had left, so it was a smaller group gathered together in the lobby. The perpetually pleasant Swissair man told them that the bus was waiting, that they would be taken to the airport and flown to Lisbon, and would be there in time for dinner.

Since the canon was staying in Madrid instead of going on to Geneva, as originally planned, or even to Lisbon, there seemed to be some question about his being allowed to go in the bus with them to the airport. Adam felt like saying that he could take care of Poly perfectly well by himself, but at this point he thought it wiser not to cross the older man who was talking in a quiet but most determined way to the Swissair man, who finally smiled and nodded, shook hands with the canon, and then ushered the passengers out into the rain and onto the bus.

At the airport the Swissair man, still smiling, but beginning to look tired and harassed from all the questions being thrust at him, took them into the dining room where he told them to order refreshments, compliments of Swissair. Adam sat at a large, round table with Poly and Canon Tallis and five other passengers, so that conversation was perforce general, and mostly about the weather. Bits of gossip flitted from table to table as the Swissair man would appear, speak to one group, then hurry off: the airport in Lisbon was still closed; the airport in Lisbon was open; the airport in Lisbon was open but might close at any moment; the airport in Lisbon was closed but might open at any moment. Strangely enough the downpour in Madrid never seemed to be any concern.

After a little over an hour had gone by the Swissair man came hurrying in and told the entire group, in a voice now slightly hoarse, that they would be served dinner since the airport in Lisbon was definitely still closed down.

There was a small, smug, middle-aged couple at Adam's table who decided that they would like to stay on in Madrid and were furious when the Swissair man wouldn't pay for their hotel or passage to Lisbon unless they traveled with the rest of the group. Adam was embarrassed by their rudeness, and ashamed that they were American. Poly leaned sleepily against Canon Tallis who sipped at a small glass of Tio Pépé.

The Swissair man disappeared again and the table was quickly set and a full dinner served, soup, omelette, chicken, fruit, cheese. Adam discovered that he was starved. They were finishing their coffee when the Swissair man appeared again, beaming like the Cheshire cat. A Spanish plane would take them to Lisbon where the airport was at last open. He hurried off; in a few minutes the plane was called and everyone trooped to the gate where they were completely unexpected. Canon Tallis was trying to sort out the situation with the Iberian Airlines official when the Swissair man came panting up. Wait! A plane was being flown in from Geneva for them.

It was well after ten when they were finally herded through the gate. Canon Tallis stood watching after Poly and Adam as they paddled out into the rain and onto the bus, stood watching until the bus was driven off. This time it was more than a few yards to the plane. The bus began to gather speed and although the rain was letting up and the atmosphere was lighter it was not long before the dark figure of the canon had disappeared.

Poly turned anxiously to Adam. "You *will* stay right with me, won't you?"

"Yes, if you want me to. Why? Are you nervous?" Adam asked, hoping to get some information out of her.

Poly contemplated him as the bus jolted along over the wet ground. Finally she said calmly, "I have never traveled alone before, and, after all, I am still a child."

Adam felt like crying, —Okay, child, why are *you* holding out on me, too?

But if he ever wanted to get anything out of Poly it would not do to antagonize her now. Granted she was an odd kid, but she was obviously a bright one, and he liked her, and he knew that she liked him, despite the deliberate evasiveness of her last answer. Sooner or later she would talk to him, as long as he didn't push her. Most people did seem to talk to Adam, which may have been one reason he wasn't more surprised at Kali's confidences or at anything else that had happened.

Giving him a wary look Poly put her hand in his as they left the bus, and held it firmly until they were safely in the plane. "A caravelle," Poly said. "You don't mind if I sit next to the window, with you on the aisle, do you, Adam? It's just because I like to look out."

"Is that the only reason?" he asked her, stowing her small blue case and his briefcase under their seats.

"Isn't it reason enough?" she asked as he sat down beside her.

It was to be a short flight, they were told, about forty-five minutes. After they had been in the air less than half an hour Poly said, "I have to go to the washroom, Adam."

He moved his knees to let her go by. At the aisle she stopped, started to say something, walked on for a couple of rows, then came back. "Watch after me, Adam, please," she said tensely, then hurried up the aisle and disappeared into the washroom.

Adam had looked over the passengers and a more normal lot, he felt, could not have been found. The original group was all

American, vocal, and eager to be on the way. Only a handful of new passengers had been added, and none of these looked in the least sinister or even curious. The only figure who was even faintly colorful was a rabbi with a long, luxuriant growth of brown beard. He had a look of quiet dignity, and sat, isolated in contemplation, until he turned to a book which Adam could see, by straining, was something by Martin Buber.

Poly's small voice as she had turned back toward him made him a little tense, but after all she was only a kid, and a girl, and girls are apt to be hysterical, and that doggoned canon had evidently frightened her about something. He shook himself and settled back to read an article on starfish which Old Doc had stuck into his hand that last day in Woods Hole. Adam could usually concentrate but his eyes now kept flicking to the face of his wristwatch. After Poly had been gone a couple of minutes he began to look back toward the washroom door every few seconds. After the hands showed that five minutes had passed he put the starfish article aside and did nothing but look at the washroom. After another minute he felt a distinct queasiness in the pit of his stomach, and went to the back of the plane.

The steward looked at him, saying courteously, "The other washroom is empty, sir."

"Yes," Adam said. "I'm traveling with a little girl and she's been in there several minutes and I'm afraid she may not be well."

The steward tapped lightly on the door. Nothing happened. Adam knocked, rather more loudly. "Poly!" he called.

Nothing.

"Not so loud, please, sir," the steward said. "We don't want to disturb the other passengers. Just a minute and I will unlock the door from this side."

He took out a key and after a certain amount of manipulation the door swung open.

The washroom was empty.

5

"You must have been mistaken, sir," the steward said.

"I saw her go in."

"Then she must have left without your noticing it."

Wildly Adam looked round the plane, but his hope of seeing Poly safely in her seat vanished. "Find her for me, then," he said, angrily.

"What does she look like?"

"A tall, thin child, about twelve. Red hair and blue eyes."

The steward went methodically up and down the aisles, even looking into the pilot's cabin. When he came back to Adam he spoke soothingly. "Are you absolutely certain, sir, that any such child came onto the plane?"

"Get the stewardess to check the records," Adam suggested.

The steward summoned the stewardess, speaking in Spanish. "This young idiot," he said, "seems to think he brought some kid on the plane with him, and now he's lost her. He has a wild idea she's been flushed down the toilet or something. Just another American crackpot. But check your records." Turning to Adam he said, in English, "Her name, please."

"Polyhymnia O'Keefe."

Adam stood, seething, until the stewardess looked up from her papers. "No O'Keefe got on the plane."

39

Adam burst into Spanish. He had learned a good deal of picturesque language from Juan and his family and he let it all out now. Up and down the cabin passengers roused from snoozing and turned their heads in curiosity.

Adam thought he saw the steward press some kind of signal. In any case the FASTEN SEAT BELTS light flashed on and the stewardess moved briskly through the cabin, seeing that the passengers, many of whom had risen at Adam's flow of invective, were seated and their seat belts snapped on.

The steward turned to Adam. "We are going through some turbulence, sir," he said, though this time in Spanish, seeming not at all abashed that Adam must have understood his words to the stewardess. "You will have to go to your seat."

Adam did not move. "*I'm* going through turbulence all right. I was put in charge of the child and I am responsible for her. I saw her go into the washroom."

"Sir." The steward sighed in resignation at Adam's idiocy. "No child came onto the plane with you. You saw us check the passenger list. I must insist that you sit down, and in Lisbon— are you being met, sir?"

"Yes," Adam snapped.

"Then perhaps you should see a doctor." The steward's hands shot out with unexpected suddenness and strength, grasped Adam's arms, and forcibly propelled him down the aisle. He was put into his seat with a quick shove, and the belt tightened around him.

The loudspeaker coughed. "This is your captain. We are now beginning the descent to Lisbon."

The stewardess walked up and down the aisle, adjusting a pillow here, asking a passenger to put out a cigarette there. The steward stood lounging by Adam's seat.

"Listen," Adam said, "if you don't believe me, the blue case under the seat belongs to Poly. How did it get there if she didn't come onto the plane?"

The steward spoke gently. "There is no blue case under the seat."

Adam looked down. His briefcase was there, but not Poly's

little blue bag. "Hey!" he called wildly, looking up and down the plane. "I *did* get on with a redheaded kid, didn't I?"

The steward's hand pressed against the boy's mouth as he explained apologetically to the passengers that Adam wasn't well, that a doctor would be found as soon as they had landed in Lisbon, that there was no cause for alarm. No one need worry. Over the steward's hand Adam looked frantically at the passengers, but nobody said anything or moved to rescue him. He heard one woman say, "I thought I saw a child, but maybe it was at the hotel with that priest. I'm so tired I just don't remember which way is up."

The steward removed his hand. If Adam had thought it would do any good he would have started a physical battle with the man. But that course would, at this point, seem to lead into worse trouble than already surrounded him.

"If you will stay quietly where you are until we land," the steward said, "everything will be all right." He walked back the length of the plane to his post.

Again Adam looked up and down the cabin, though he did not move in his seat or turn his head more than necessary. Surely they must have heard him; surely someone must have noticed Poly and would come to tell him so.

The rabbi was sitting with his hands in his lap, his book evidently put away in his briefcase. His head was back against the seat rest and he appeared to be contemplating the ceiling. To Adam's surprise he began to whistle thoughtfully.

Adam almost jumped out of his seat.

It was the melody Canon Tallis had whistled for Poly at the Hotel Plaza.

He kept his eyes fixed on the rabbi, but the rabbi continued to look upward. Although Adam still could not place the melody it was familiar enough to him (had he sung it in school? in choir? was it something his parents knew?) so that he in his turn could whistle a measure. The rabbi stopped. His eyes moved slowly from the ceiling. He turned, looked at Adam, nodded almost imperceptibly, then turned away and studied the ceiling again.

Adam was too upset and confused to look out the window as the plane descended toward Lisbon. He kept looking up and down the cabin, with his gaze coming to pause again and again on the rabbi. But the rabbi did not move. Adam felt, after a while, that he should not stare, that he should not let the other passengers, and certainly not the steward, know that he had had any kind of communication with anybody in the plane since Poly's disappearance.

He was startled to feel the touch of wheels upon runway, to know that they were earthbound again. The loudspeaker buzzed and the passengers were told the disembarking procedure. It would all be very simple. Except, of course, for Adam.

The FASTEN SEAT BELTS sign blinked out, though the NO SMOKING sign remained lit. The passengers rose and took coats and bags and began moving to the door. Adam pushed forward as quickly as he could, almost knocking into the rabbi who was just ahead of him. As they waited to get out Adam touched the dark sleeve gently and the rabbi moved his head just enough to let Adam know that he was listening.

"I *did* have the child with me, didn't I?"

The rabbi gave an almost imperceptible nod.

At this quiet confirmation Adam was again able to think coherently. By the time he reached the exit he knew what he was going to say and do. He spoke to the steward with cold control. "I will have to report this to the authorities. I have taken your name and that of the stewardess."

The steward shrugged indifferently. "As you like, sir. You will be yourself again soon, I am sure."

The stewardess simply smiled blandly at him as she had at the other passengers, saying, as though there had been no trouble, "I hope you enjoyed your trip."

Adam brushed by her and down the steps after the rabbi.

At the passport counter, despite, or perhaps because of his hurry, Adam found a number of passengers ahead of him; he was in the middle of the line. He looked ahead and saw the rabbi collecting his passport and disappearing. Adam was shocked and disappointed at this complete abandonment. For a moment he had felt that the situation was under control, that everything would be all right as soon as the proper authorities were spoken to. Now he felt blind panic.

The line here in Lisbon moved more slowly than it had in Madrid. When Adam's turn came he handed his passport across the counter saying, "I want to report a missing child. I got onto the plane with a twelve-year-old girl and she went to the washroom and never came out."

The official looked at him incredulously. "But sir, that is impossible."

"Yes," Adam said. "Nevertheless it happened."

"Why didn't you speak immediately to the steward or the stewardess?"

"I did. They were not very helpful."

"Oh, but sir, the personnel is always—"

Adam interrupted. "They said the child had not come on to the plane with me."

The official relaxed. "Well, then, sir—"

"But she *did* get on the plane with me. If you will get in touch with Canon Tallis in Madrid—"

"Yes?" the official asked helpfully. "His address, please? Or perhaps you know his phone number?"

Adam realized that he had no way of knowing where in that enormous city the canon might be. He thought quickly, then said, "I don't know where he is staying, but if you call the English church they would be able to tell you there."

"Sir," the official said, shaking his head sadly, "I'm afraid I cannot possibly help you. I will see that you are conducted to my superior, and you can tell your story to him." H summoned a young boy in a page's uniform, and spoke to him in rapid Portuguese. Adam had hoped that Spanish and Portuguese would be close enough so that he would be able to understand, but they were not.

The page said, "Kindly follow me, sir." Adam started to move away from the window when a voice said, "Don't forget your passport."

Startled, and furious with himself for having almost done exactly that, Adam wheeled around and there was the rabbi, together with a tall, blue-eyed, redheaded man. The resemblance to Poly was plain; it could be none other than Dr. O'Keefe who came up to the window and spoke in slow, clear English. "Mr. Eddington's passport, please. He has had an unfortunate experience and is a little—upset. I will take care of everything."

Adam started to turn on Dr. O'Keefe in indignation, but something in the older man's expression stopped him. The official at the window handed Adam the passport, saying, "Certainly, and my sincere thanks, Dr. O'Keefe."

Adam found himself hustled out of the airport and into a waiting taxi. As the door was slammed and the taxi pulled off he realized that he was alone with Dr. O'Keefe; the rabbi had again disappeared. "But Poly—" he started.

"Not now," Dr. O'Keefe said. Adam looked at him and could see that the older man's face was white with strain. His complete quiet and control was costing him an enormous effort. After a moment, as though to break the silence, he said, "We managed to get your bags. Fortunately you had them well labeled. They're in the trunk of the taxi."

"Where are we going?" Adam asked.

"The Hotel Avenida Palace. We will have to stay there until—"

"Sir," Adam started, "sir . . ." and then stopped because he found that he could not go on.

Dr. O'Keefe said quietly, "You are not to blame yourself for this in any way. It was nothing you could have prevented. We thought getting Poly away would be the best thing. But—" again he broke off.

Adam saw little of Lisbon as they drove in, though, in order to gather himself together, he turned his face toward the window as though he were looking out. Lisbon was, even to his confused eyes, completely different from Madrid. Madrid was a cold city, Lisbon a warm one, full of buildings painted sun yellow, deep blue. There were squares with fountains, statues, gardens, a sense of space and color everywhere.

44

The Avenida Palace was an old hotel, a beautiful building which at any other time would have delighted Adam; but he was now so tired with the events of the past hours as well as with lack of sleep that he followed Dr. O'Keefe like a small child. A porter took his bags out of the taxi's trunk, and Adam went with Dr. O'Keefe into the hotel.

"Your passport, please, Adam," Dr. O'Keefe said, and registered for him. The passport, as in Madrid, was retained, but Dr. O'Keefe explained that this was routine procedure, and, unless there were trouble with the police they would get it back shortly.

They were taken to a great square corner room with four shuttered and curtained windows. There were twin beds, an octagonal table with easy chairs, a desk, a crystal chandelier. The bathroom was large and all of marble.

"We look out on the Place dos Restauradores and the Rue Jardim do Regedor," Dr. O'Keefe told Adam as the page put down the suitcases. "There's a rather interesting view of the Fort up on the crest of the hill." He gestured to one of the curtained windows, but made no move to pull back the draperies. He locked the door carefully, checked the cupboards.

"Poly—" Adam started desperately.

Although Dr. O'Keefe's rigid control had not lessened, he dropped, now that he and Adam were alone, the public manner, answering with the one word, "Kidnapped."

"But—"

"But why? Old Doc may have told you something of my research."

"Just that it was interesting, and—unusual."

"I've stumbled onto something. Something that *is* unusual, desirable to many people, and important. It was wise of Old Doc not to tell you anything about it. What you don't know, you can tell no one. Therefore, if you will forgive me, I will not tell you yet. But Poly knows too much for her own good. Therefore, Adam, I will have to ask you to stay here in this room until I return. Are you hungry?"

"No, sir."

"But tired, I imagine."

"Yes."

"Then this will be a good opportunity for you to sleep. You should answer the telephone if it rings. But under no circumstances open the door, and when I go please double-lock it from the inside. The best thing you can possibly do now is to catch up on your sleep. When I find Poly and we get to Gaea I will be able to explain things more fully to you."

Adam said, "But, sir, what are you going to do?"

"There are only certain things I *can* do. First I'll go to Interpol—the International Police. But there is only so much, at this point, that *they* can do. Then the Embassy. Then to a man I know and trust in the police here. But for Poly's sake nothing must be done wildly or without thought. Don't be worried if I'm not back immediately."

Adam nodded numbly, taking courage from the fact that there was not a hint of a suggestion that Poly might *not* be found.

When the older man had left he undressed and took a long, hot bath, followed by a shower, as though to wash off the evil aura of the steward and stewardess who had tried to make him believe that Poly didn't exist. He put on his pajamas, turned down one of the twin beds, and got in. The telephone, a rather old-fashioned instrument, stood, silent, on the table between the beds. Adam looked at it, felt his eyelids sag. He had thought, while bathing, that he was much too upset to be able to sleep, but the moment his head touched the pillow his exhausted body took over and he blanked out.

He did not know how long he had been lost in sleep, sleep so deep that it was dreamless, when he became aware at the edges of his consciousness of a soft but persistent tapping on the door. He had no idea where he was, his sleep-drugged body feeling that he was back in Woods Hole and that his mother was trying to rouse him to get him to Old Doc's on time. "All right, Mother, all *right*, I'm *up*," he mumbled irritably.

The tapping continued.

Finally it penetrated into Adam's mind enough so that he

knew that he must drag himself out of his stupor and do something about it. He pulled open his eyes to absolute darkness. His room at Woods Hole, many-windowed and curtainless, had always been full of light. He could not be there. Where was he? Slowly his tired mind began dredging up the events of the hours since he had first gone into the airport in New York, though it was several moments before he was able to waken sufficiently to remember that he was in Lisbon, in a hotel called the Avenida Palace, that the windows were heavily shuttered and curtained, and that this accounted for the sultry darkness. He fumbled around until he found the bedlamp and turned it on, a bulb of wattage that would be thoroughly inadequate for reading but did suffice to show him the face of his watch. It was almost four o'clock. In the morning or in the afternoon? He looked across to the other twin bed and it was empty. In this closed-in room there was no telling the hour of day or night.

The tapping on the door persisted, never getting louder, just going on and on, like a branch in a light breeze knocking constantly against a window.

It should have made him afraid. Alone in this dark, timeless place with someone—who?—softly trying to penetrate his consciousness and then his room, he should have been weak with terror. But he was too tired to feel anything but regret for his lost sleep.

"Wait!" he called, shoving back the sheet, getting out of bed, crossing to the nearest window, dragging back heavy folds of curtain, opening creaking white shutters. A welcome breath of cool, damp air came in. Street lamps shone waveringly onto dark, rain-wet pavement.

Four in the morning, then.

He went warily to the door, put his hand on the knob, then drew back as if the door were hot, and called softly, "Who is it?"

He half expected to hear the voice of the steward from the plane, or even Canon Tallis; but it was a girl's light voice. "Adam, it's Kali. Let me in."

Adam felt weak with relief, but just as he started to unlock the door his hand drew back again. "Just a minute." He stood there in the dimly lit room, trying to marshal his thoughts. He was still not all the way out of sleep; his mind circled and would not focus.

"Adam, what's the matter?" Kali's voice came softly, urgently.

"Just a minute," Adam said again. If he could have slept a little longer he would know better what to do. In spite of the urgency of the moment he could not control an enormous yawn. Finally a question that seemed reasonable came to him. "How did you know I was here?"

"O'Keefe always stays at the Avenida Palace. Adam, let me in. I have to talk to you. We have work to do."

"Just a minute," Adam said for the third time. He went into the bathroom and splashed cold water on his face, over and over again, until his thoughts began to clear.

If Kali was right, then Canon Tallis was wrong.

This was the primary fact he had to work with.

It was not difficult for him to believe that Canon Tallis was wrong. But if Canon Tallis was wrong, then so was Dr. O'Keefe. This, too, was perfectly possible to believe. Hadn't Dr. O'Keefe acted in a rather strange way at the Lisbon airport? Wasn't this whole setup at the Avenida Palace peculiar? But then: if Canon Tallis and Dr. O'Keefe were wrong, then so was Polyhymnia, and right or wrong, Adam was responsible for Polyhymnia.

He went back to the door. "Kali."

"I'm *waiting*, Adam."

"Why are you here, and at such an hour? It's the middle of the night."

"I'm here because of *you*, of course. And I had to come while O'Keefe was out."

"How did you know he was out?"

"I was at a party at the Embassy with daddy, and he came in."

"To the *party*?" Adam's voice soared and cracked as though he were an eighth grader again. If Dr. O'Keefe, with Poly vanished, could go to parties, then there was no doubt on whose side Adam had to align himself.

But Kali said, "To *see* someone, silly. I don't suppose he'd even been invited to the party. Adam, I can't help you if you keep me out here in the hall. Someone's bound to come along."

"How are you planning to help me?" Adam asked.

"Don't you want to find the redheaded kid?"

"Why should I need to find her?"

"Because you know as well as I do that she's been kidnapped. Adam, I'm not going to stand out here any longer. Either you open the door and let me in, or I go and you can just get out of this mess on your own."

You should answer the telephone if it rings, Dr. O'Keefe had said. *But under no circumstances open the door.*

"Wait," Adam said sharply to Kali. Never had his mind functioned at such a snail's pace. He usually made decisions quickly; sometimes too quickly. At school he had been president of Student Council and often decisions had been forced on him, and occasionally decisions that seemed on first sight to go counter to the rules.

'Rules are made for people, not people for rules,' he had once said in defending one of his actions. 'If you accept any position of authority you have to know when to break or circumvent a rule. It's the knowing *when* that's important.'

But now he was in no position of authority.

No. But one of responsibility. He was still responsible for Poly. She had been in his care when she disappeared.

He pounded one fist into the palm of his other hand. Then he unlocked the door.

6

Kali came in. She was dressed for evening, and Adam drew in his breath sharply because he had forgotten how beautiful she was. Her shimmering hair was drawn softly back with a fili-greed gold tiara. Her dress, of a material that Adam, being a boy, could not place, was the color of champagne. Her feet were in gold sandals. She gave him a scowl which managed not to wrinkle her brow. "And about time, too," she said, going over to the octagonal table and sitting in one of the easy chairs. "Now tell me everything."

Adam sat on the side of his rumpled bed. "You seem to know everything already."

Kali sighed with resignation. "I know your plane was re-routed to Madrid. I know you didn't get to Lisbon till tonight. I saw O'Keefe come in to the Embassy and go off with the Ambassador. I happened to walk by the door of the library, looking for the ladies' room, when O'Keefe mentioned his child. That was a lucky break, hearing that; it gave me some idea of what we're up against and how I can help you. Get dressed and I'll take you to daddy."

"To help me find Polyhymnia?"

"Of course."

"But why me? Why didn't you go right to Dr. O'Keefe?"

Kali sighed again. "Adam, you are really very slow. It's in O'Keefe's own interest that the child be gone. Don't you see he's in on the whole thing? What we have to do is get her to daddy. Then he'll take care of everything."

"Okay, I'm slow," Adam said, "but even on not enough sleep that's logic nohow contrariwise. Why under the sun would Dr. O'Keefe be in on the kidnapping of his own daughter?"

Kali got up and went to the one uncurtained, unshuttered window, and stood looking out. "Adam, my sweet, you aren't in your little backwash of a Woods Hole now, or your ivory tower of school. This is Lisbon. Lisbon."

"Yes," Adam said. "I'd figured it might be."

"Has it never occurred to you that we do *not* live in one world? That there are certain nations interested in the private businesses of certain other nations? If this primary fact has never occurred to you, living in New York—and for heaven's sake, kid, haven't you ever even taken a tour through the UN?—it can hardly escape you in any of the capitals of Europe. Don't you know we're in a war, Adam? Aren't you aware of it?"

Adam had taken College Boards in Modern European History. But that was history.

Kali continued: "Of course his going to the Embassy was a front, and a rather clever one, I must admit that. But never make the mistake of thinking O'Keefe's a fool. He isn't. What he wants to do is keep the child out of the way until. . . . And he's ruthless, Adam. If something happens to her then something happens to her. When I think of daddy and me—Well, O'Keefe gives me the shudders. Now come on, Adam. Get dressed and let's go. I hope I have made myself clear."

"As mud," Adam said. "But I'll get dressed. Let me take a quick shower. It'll help me wake up a bit." It seemed he had been doing nothing but take showers to wake up since the bus had taken him to the Plaza Hotel in Madrid.

When Adam and Kali emerged onto the sidewalk dawn was beginning to lighten the sky; the dim street lamps became even dimmer. The rain had stopped but the air was wet and heavy. A dark limousine was waiting in the courtyard of the hotel and Kali walked quickly toward it. A uniformed chauffeur climbed out and opened the door for them.

"Take us home, Molèc, please," Kali said. She sat back in the upholstered seat as though she were very tired. "I don't know why I'm taking so much trouble about you, Adam, I really don't."

"Well, why are you, then?" Adam demanded.

"Not for your own sake, I assure you. At least not to start out with, I wasn't. But you're like a half-grown puppy. There's something endearing about your clumsiness. I have to admit that I *am* doing it for you, too. But that's wrong, of course."

"Wrong?"

"Adam, we simply *cannot* let people matter to us or we won't get anywhere. Letting people matter is nothing but sentimentality."

—Then I have become rather quickly sentimental about Polyhymnia, Adam thought. —Only there's something wrong here. 'Sentimental' is not the right word. If only I could have slept a few hours longer.

He tried unsuccessfully to stifle a yawn.

Kali put a hand on his arm. "I'm sorry I had to wake you up. But you do see, don't you, how desperately urgent it is?"

Yes, he saw, though there was something wrong with this, too.

The limousine drove a narrow and winding way. Some streets were barely wide enough for the car. Others were as steep as San Francisco. They went under arches, into streets wide enough for buses, under more arches into alleys, finally drawing up before a whitewashed wall. The chauffeur, Molèc, got out and opened the door, and Adam climbed out after Kali. She opened a gate in the wall and went down a steep flight of steps to a pale pink house with a deeper pink door which she unlocked. As she shut the door behind them she held her finger to her lips and took Adam down a softly carpeted hall.

The room into which she led him was already beginning to fill with light which flooded in from a great sweep of windows overlooking the harbor and the dawn. The view was so enormous that at first Adam did not notice the room itself, a room striking in stark blacks and whites. The long wall of windows was curtainless, but the opposite wall was hung with black velvet. Against the background of velvet was only one thing, a picture, an unframed portrait (for the great sweep of velvet was the frame) of the most handsome young man Adam had ever seen. It was a young man with the bearing of an angel, hair the same pale gold as Kali's, heavily fringed eyes, the mouth slightly opened as though in eagerness to meet life.

"Adam," Kali said, and he turned from the portrait to follow her across the black marble floor.

Silhouetted against the dawn was the dark figure of a man who stood, motionless, staring out across the bay, a man big in both height and bulk.

"Daddy," Kali said, and the man turned around.

Because he stood between Adam and the light he was still only a silhouette as he stretched out his hand in greeting. "Adam, you're safely here." He took the boy's hand in a grip of steel. His voice was high, and light for the bulk of his body, but it, too, had the quality of steel, the steel of a spool of fine wire. He dropped Adam's hand and crossed to a desk made of a great slab of black-and-white marble, and sat in a black leather chair, leaning back so that at last the light struck his face. It was a powerful face: there were pouches of fatigue under the dark eyes, and the thin lips were closed in tight control. He impatiently pushed back a strand of thinning, pale gold hair. Involuntarily Adam glanced at the portrait.

"That's daddy," Kali said, with pride. "Wasn't he beautiful?"

The man laughed. "Yes. Nothing of Dorian Gray about Typhon Cutter, is there, Adam? I am marked by the inroads of time. Time and experience. And this is something you lack, is it not?"

"I'm getting it," Adam said, warily.

"And learning from it?"

"I hope so."

Typhon Cutter looked thoughtfully at the portrait. "The

years make their marks on ordinary, hardworking mortals, and I can assure you that my work is hard. And now you have become part of it." He looked from the portrait to Adam, and Adam looked back, saying nothing, swaying slightly with fatigue.

Typhon Cutter picked up a black marble paperweight and appeared to study it. He crossed his legs, and as he did this Adam realized that although the great body was ponderous with weight, the arms and legs were thin and bony, but again giving the effect of steel. Typhon Cutter, sitting at his desk in a black satin dressing gown, was one of the most extraordinary men Adam had ever seen.

"Tired?" Cutter asked in his surprising tenor voice.

"Yes, sir. I haven't had much sleep."

Typhon Cutter motioned to a stiff ebony chair on the opposite side of the desk. "You may sit there as long as you stay awake. I'm sorry not to be able to let you sleep, but there's no time now for anything but business. And we *do* have business, you and I."

In a daze of fatigue Adam staggered to the chair. Typhon Cutter leaned across the desk and snapped his fingers in the boy's face. "Wake up."

"I'm sorry," Adam mumbled.

"Kali, see about coffee."

"Yes, daddy." In quick and loving obedience Kali slipped from the room.

"Now, Adam."

"Sir?"

"How much has Kali told you?"

"That you'll help me to find Poly—Dr. O'Keefe's daughter."

Typhon Cutter nodded, for a moment speaking almost absently. "Yes. We'll cope with that." Then, sharply, "Wake up. What else?"

"About what, sir?"

"How much has Kali told you? Perhaps you may have thought that she seemed a little wild, or even a little hysterical, but she never does so without cause."

"I didn't think she seemed hysterical, sir."

"Good boy. I assume she warned you about Tallis and O'Keefe?"

"Yes, sir."

"Did you take her warning seriously?"

"Mr. Cutter, I'm too confused to know what to think. I'm too tired."

Again the fingers were snapped in Adam's face. "Wake up. Why did you come with Kali now, then?"

"Because I have to find Polyhymn——"

"Yes. All right, Adam, try to stay awake while we get down to business. You are to be working as laboratory assistant to O'Keefe this summer."

"Yes, sir."

"O'Keefe is a great scientist. In that respect you are very privileged."

"Yes, sir," Adam responded automatically, knowing that each time Typhon Cutter paused he was expected to make a response to prove that he was awake, that he was listening.

"Do you know what your work will be? I mean by that, do you know the experiment O'Keefe is involved in?"

"I believe it's the regenerative process of the arm of the starfish, sir."

"Explain yourself."

"Well, if a starfish loses an arm it can simply grow one back."

"How?"

"That's the point. No one knows. I mean, the starfish is still pretty much a mystery even to the people who know most about it."

"That is true. I, for instance, know as much about the starfish as any layman, and I am the first to admit that this is not much. But I fancy you'll find that the starfish is less of an enigma to O'Keefe than to anybody else in the world."

The door opened and Kali came in followed by a white-jacketed servant bearing a silver tray which he set down on the desk. Typhon Cutter waited until the door was closed again, then picked up a silver coffeepot and poured. He handed a cup across the desk to Adam. "I don't know how you usually drink it, but this time it will have to be black. You *must* wake up."

"Sorry, sir."

"All right, Adam. Now tell me something. If O'Keefe is learning new things about the regenerative process of the arm of the starfish, why is this of such importance?"

"Well, sir, in the evolutionary scale man comes pretty directly from the starfish."

"Go on."

"Well, man is a member of phylum Chordata, and we developed directly from the phylum Echinodermata, or the starfish. We both had an interior spinal column and the same kind of body cavities."

Typhon Cutter pressed his thin, strong fingertips together, nodding in satisfaction. "Good. Good. Of course one goes on the assumption that if O'Keefe is willing to employ you, you must have a certain amount of intelligence. Let us proceed to the next step. What is the implication of O'Keefe's experiments?"

"Well, sir, that anything he finds out about starfish might also apply to people."

Kali perched on the arm of her father's chair. "Why? Just because we have the same great great great grandpappy? I should think you'd need more than that."

"You do," Adam told her. "We have the same kind of complex nervous system, and we're the only ones who do—echinoderms and chordates—people and starfish."

"So?" Typhon Cutter asked.

"So if someone could find out how the starfish regenerates then maybe this knowledge could be used for man. But—"

"No buts," Typhon Cutter said. "Don't try to evade what you've said. The implications are so staggering that most people will tend to turn away from them or refuse to face them. You're a bright boy, Adam, and a brave one, or you wouldn't be here in this room, now. You can be of great help to mankind if you will."

56

Adam's mind was gritty with fatigue, but he said, "I think I have to know how I am to help."

"A perfectly reasonable attitude. Kali has perhaps told you something about me?"

"That you have business concerns in Portugal—"

"And—" Typhon Cutter reached across the desk and poured more coffee into Adam's cup.

"That you know a great many people at the Embassy."

"There's the key, boy. My business is—business. And a very lucrative one, I might add. But it is also more than business. Just as you are in a position to be useful to me, I am in a position to be useful to the Embassy. More than that, I have been asked by Washington to assist the Embassy and to keep my eye on a group there whose loyalty is not entirely unquestioned. There is nothing I care about more than my country and I hope I am not wrong in assuming that you feel the same way."

"Well, of course, sir—" Adam started, and stopped. Abruptly. Listening.

From somewhere deep in the house he thought he heard a faint, thin wail. A child's wail.

7

Typhon Cutter held up his hand. "It's all right, Adam. She's here. We have her, safe and sound."

"But—"

"Wait." The word lashed at Adam like the flick of a whip. "You will see her in a few minutes. But there are certain things you must know first. Drink your coffee. Wake up."

The wailing continued.

"She is all right," Typhon Cutter said. "She has only had a frightening experience. She is caught in a web of events that she is too young to understand, and she is being used as a pawn. You will take her back to her father, but you will not say from where."

"But—"

"Be quiet. Listen. I have told you that O'Keefe is a great scientist."

"Yes."

"But, like many other great scientists his wisdom does not extend beyond his work. You yourself know of scientists who have been spies, who have sold their country down the river."

"Well, yes, but—" Abruptly the crying stopped. *"Please,"* Adam was determined this time not to be cut off. "Why is Poly here? How did you get her?"

Typhon Cutter held up his hand, speaking tolerantly. "Hold it, boy. One thing at a time."

"But how did you get her? Did you get her from the plane?"

"Not very likely, is it? Has it occurred to you that you may not be the only one interested in her safety?"

"Her father is! He must be out of his mind with worry."

"Oh?" Typhon Cutter gave a thin laugh. "I hardly think so. It was her father and his inconsistencies we were talking about when you interrupted me." He paused, as though to give the boy a chance to say, 'Sorry,' but, as Adam was silent, he continued, "Let us simply say that we managed—and with no little difficulty, I might add—to rescue her."

"From whom?"

"Don't you know?"

"No, sir. I don't."

"Then you'll have to find out, won't you? I can hardly spell it out for you more clearly."

"But—"

"This is not, at the moment, the point. The point is what it means—what *all* of it means—to the United States. To do O'Keefe justice, I do not think that he would betray his country deliberately. But I have been instructed to see that he does not do it even inadvertently. I am asking you to help me."

Adam nodded, and took another swallow of coffee.

Typhon Cutter looked at him and smiled tightly. "It has come to my attention that I am sometimes compared to a spider. I do not find the comparison entirely invidious. It is my intention to spin a net and to pull it tight around anyone who does not put the interests of our country first. As for you, my boy, the moment you were chosen to work for O'Keefe you became important. You were important enough to be watched by both sides—our own, and the enemy's—from the moment you entered the airport in New York. I sent Kali as my personal emissary. I have every faith in my daughter; she has never let me down. I hope that I will be able to say the same thing about you. You *do* care for your country, don't you, Adam?"

"Of course, sir."

59

"Then you must do as I say." The thin cry came again, and ceased. "I have told you that O'Keefe's child is being used as a pawn. For the moment she is safe. She does not know where she is, and she is being blindfolded. This is for her own protection as well as ours. And yours. You are far more useful to us alive than dead, my boy, and I think perhaps you are not quite aware of how many people are aware of *you*, and the fact that you are going to Gaea. If you will do as I say I think that I can protect you. If not—" Typhon Cutter shrugged.

—I am half dead with sleep, Adam thought. —I don't understand anything. I don't want to understand. I want to sleep.

Typhon Cutter's high voice probed like a needle into his fatigue. "Are you going to help us, Adam?"

"I—"

"Think. Think about the child."

"I am."

"If you could not trust me, do you think I could trust you with the child?"

"But she's not your child."

"No, she's a pawn of dangerous, ruthless men. As I have said, I do not think that O'Keefe is fully cognizant of what he is doing. But there are others. Men like the egregious canon."

"Well, what about him, sir?"

"Do you think highly of someone who would deliberately send a child onto that plane?"

"But if she hadn't gone into the washroom—"

"Don't be naïve, boy. That simply made it a little easier."

Adam looked at Typhon Cutter. Yes, there was indeed the resemblance to a spider. Then he thought of Canon Tallis, the body portly but firm, the piercing grey eyes, the bald head. . . .

—But you can't go by people's looks, he thought groggily. —Just because I prefer teddy bears to spiders. . . .

"Why does Canon Tallis have no eyebrows?" he asked without thinking.

"I believe he does what he can to broadcast some story of losing all his hair after some extraordinary physical bravery in Korea; this kind of thing does happen occasionally, I believe.

However, I am inclined to doubt it. Tallis, you will find, likes to take the easy way and to receive credit for daydreams. If he has done anything braver than kowtow to the bishop of Gibraltar I have yet to hear of it. Now Adam: I know that you are tired and so for the moment my instructions will be simple. You are to take Poly back to her father at the Avenida Palace. You will be driven to a central point from which you will be able to find your way to the hotel without trouble. I cannot risk taking you directly there, since my chauffeur, Molèc, who is one of my key men, would be recognized. You will tell O'Keefe that you were half asleep when you opened the door to loud knocking, that you were grabbed and blindfolded, that you were taken you know not where, and interrogated. Since you knew nothing— and what you know *is* nothing, I assure you—there was very little you could tell. You were not in any way abused. You were put into a car, and when you were ungagged and unblindfolded you stood on the street with Polyhymnia O'Keefe. Understand?"

"Yes, sir."

"Take her immediately to the Avenida Palace. From there I presume you will proceed to Gaea. Kali or I—probably Kali— will get in touch with you there and give you further instructions. In the meantime you are to learn as much about O'Keefe and what he is doing as possible. Since you will be working with him directly on the starfish experiments this ought to be a good deal. Don't be afraid. The Embassy knows where you are. If you do as you are told you will be perfectly safe. If you do *not* do as you are told I cannot answer for the consequences."

Swaying, Adam finished the bitter dregs of his coffee. —But I have *not* done as I was told, he thought. —I opened the door. I let Kali in. And whether I did right or wrong I don't know. Whether this man is right or wrong I don't know.

His eyelids started to droop.

Typhon Cutter rose. "Take him to the car, Kali. The child is already there."

"Am I to go with them, daddy?"

61

"No. Molèc will take care of it. Goodbye, Adam. Remember what I have told you. We will be in touch with you soon."

"Yes, sir," Adam said. "Goodbye."

As he and Kali reached the front door she stopped and turned to him, putting one hand lightly on his arm. "Adam—" Then her arms were around him, her face tilted upward, her lips against his.

Kali was not the first girl he had kissed, but now he was no longer a schoolboy; he was a man. His arms tightened around Kali's slender body.

She turned her face away. "We have to go now, Adam." Holding his hand, she took him out of the house, and up the steps to where the limousine was waiting for them. The chauffeur murmured something to Kali, who turned to Adam, saying, "You are to sit in front with Molèc. The O'Keefe child mustn't know you're in the car until you're let out." She paused, and then whispered, "Adam, oh, Adam darling, you must *not* move or speak or in any way let her know you're in the car. Molèc will silence you if you do, and Adam, you wouldn't like it."

The chauffeur opened the front door of the car and shut it on Adam with efficient quietness, climbed in behind the wheel, looked darkly at the boy, and put his finger in warning against his lips.

Kali echoed the gesture, then turned her hand and put the tips of her fingers against her lips.

There was a grinding of gears and the car moved off.

Molèc drove swiftly, skillfully, turning, winding, so that Adam was convinced that no matter how complex the pattern of Lisbon's streets might be Molèc was deliberately making them more confusing, so that the boy would never be able to retrace his steps.

As they moved deeper into the awakening city there were more people abroad and Adam heard the hawking of lottery tickets. Molèc swerved around a cumbersome, double-decker bus, down a dark alley lightened only by high-flapping laundry. As Adam turned to make sure that Poly was truly in the back seat the side of Molèc's hand came down with a sharp thwack on his knee. The pain took him by surprise but he managed not to cry out, though tears rushed uncontrollably to his eyes and he blinked in fury, gritting his teeth. He tried to listen for any sound from behind him, but could hear nothing. He became certain that Poly was not in the car. Out of the corner of his eye he glanced at Molèc. The face under the visored chauffeur's cap was set and sullen; the hands on the steering wheel were enormous and covered with curling black hair. Perhaps Molèc was a useful person to have working for one, but he gave Adam no sense of confidence in the present situation. He had a feeling that it would not displease Molèc to bring that massive hand down in a clip on the back of his neck, that causing pain would incite rather than deter the chauffeur. Adam determined not to move or make a sound no matter what happened.

"Ritz," Molèc grunted suddenly, and pulled the car over to the curb in a quick stop. As Adam saw the great modern bulk of a luxury hotel ahead of him the chauffeur leaped from the front seat with the powerful swiftness of a Doberman Pinscher and opened the door to the back. Adam turned to see him snatching a blindfold and gag from Poly and thrusting her out of the car and onto the street, where she gave a strange, strangled moan.

"Go," Molèc said between his teeth.

Adam did not need urging. He pushed the handle of the door down and out, and, as he slammed it, Molèc shot off down the street. Adam caught Poly as she started to fall.

"Adam," she cried in a choked gasp. "Adam."

He held her firmly, disregarding the stares of people walking down the narrow mosaic sidewalk and having to step around them into the street in order to pass. "Are you all right? Poly, are you all right?"

The child gave a great, shuddering sob and managed to stand on her own feet, though Adam continued to support her with his arm. "It's all right, Poly, you're all right now," he kept saying.

Poly continued the great, choking sobbing breaths, and her hand clutched Adam's frantically, although he could see that she was making a great effort at self-control. Her set, white face was disturbingly reminiscent of her father's.

"Poly," he said, "I'll get a taxi and we'll go to the Avenida Palace."

Poly shook her head, and managed to say through shudders, "Not a taxi, it isn't safe. We're right at the Ritz. Take me in. I know the concierge."

"But your father's at the Avenida Palace."

"We can't go there alone. They might . . . Please, Adam, take me into the Ritz."

In order to calm her Adam nodded in assent and, with his arm still holding her, for he was not at all certain that she was able to walk alone, led her down the hill the short distance to the hotel.

"Good, it's Joaquim," Poly said, as they came up to the doorman. Her voice came stronger, and she said, sounding almost cheerful, what Adam recognized as "Good morning" in Portuguese. In the great lobby she turned left to the concierge's desk. Behind it sat a man reading a newspaper.

"Arcangelo!" Poly cried, her voice rising in a note of hysteria.

The man looked at her, said something in Portuguese, said "Wait," in English, and picked up his phone, breaking into Portuguese again. In a moment another uniformed man came into the concierge's booth, and Arcangelo left, without a word, to join Adam and Poly. "Upstairs," he said, and walked ahead of them to one of the elevators.

"But we shouldn't—" Adam started, as the elevator doors shut on them.

"Wait," the concierge said again.

There was no point now in telling Poly that they should be going, whether by taxi or on foot, to the Avenida Palace. There was no point in telling Poly that they might be walking into some kind of trap. There was no point in doing anything but keeping his mouth closed and seeing what happened next. Never before in Adam's life had situations constantly been taken out of his hands as they had ever since he had left the known safety of Woods Hole. Never had his personal decision seemed to mean less, his intelligence and his will shoved so to one side. Indeed the only decision he seemed to have made in this entire adventure was to open the door of the hotel room at the Avenida Palace to Kali, and whether this was the best or the worst thing he had done he still had no way of knowing.

The concierge led them down a wide hall and unlocked the door to one of the rooms, holding it open for them. Poly entered, taking Adam perforce along with her. They were in one of the most luxurious and beautiful rooms he had ever seen, but very different from the ancient grandeur of the Avenida Palace. Here everything was modern and costly; a great window wall of glass looked over the park, but the concierge quickly swept the gold brocade curtains across, then turned on the lights, which, again in contrast to the Avenida Palace, were soft but powerful.

Arcangelo shut out the light of day at the Ritz with gold brocade. In the Avenida Palace Dr. O'Keefe was barricaded with white shutters and dark green damask. Only Typhon Cutter, standing at the window that overlooked the harbor, seemed to have no fear of being seen. Or was that the entire explanation?

The beds were covered with the same rich material as the curtains; there was a chaise longue padded with pale green velvet, and pale green velvet easy chairs at the round table in a small alcove. The floor was carpeted in what seemed to Adam to be gold velvet; modern paintings hung on the walls; the telephones, one for each bed, were lemon yellow.

Poly let go his hand, flung herself at the concierge, shouting, "Arcangelo!" and burst into loud sobbing. He held her closely, not speaking, rubbing gently between her shoulder blades, kissing the top of her head, waiting until the sobs had spent themselves. At last she looked up at him, saying, "We must speak English because of Adam. Or Spanish, if you like. He's fine with Spanish."

"Not Spanish," Arcangelo said absently, still soothing her.

"French might do," Poly babbled. "I think Adam's all right with French."

"English will do, *meu bem*," Arcangelo said gently. "Hush,

now, Polyzinha, hush." He cupped her chin in his hand and looked at her, at the red marks showing where the blindfold and the gag had been. "What have they done to you? What has happened?"

"Hold me, Arcangelo," Poly said. "Tell him, Adam."

Arcangelo sat down on one of the pale green velvet chairs and pulled Poly up onto his lap; her long legs dangled to the floor but she leaned against him as though she were a very small child. He looked inquiringly at Adam, and now Adam was able to look back at the concierge, at a dark, powerful man, perhaps in his fifties, though it was difficult to tell, with a nose that looked as though it had been broken.

The story Typhon Cutter had prepared was for Dr. O'Keefe; it did not work here in this luxurious room at the Ritz for a Portuguese concierge whom Poly treated as though he were a beloved uncle.

"Tell him, Adam," she said again.

"It was on the plane from Madrid to Lisbon. Poly went into the washroom and didn't come out, and when the steward opened the door she wasn't there." He looked at Poly. "What happened?"

She shuddered again, and reached frantically for Arcangelo's hand.

"Not if you don't want to," he said gently.

She shook her head against the blue of his uniform. "No. It's all right. He came in and grabbed me. The steward. He put his hand over my mouth before I could yell. He had some kind of canvas sack with air holes in it, and he put me into it. The washroom was so small that I couldn't fight or kick and he was strong, and he stuck something sweet and sickly-smelling on my nose and it made me all sleepy. He gagged me, too, did I tell you? And it was all dark and horrible and I was too much asleep to try to wriggle or anything and I think I was just dumped on top of the luggage. And then I was in a car and then in some-body's house, I don't know where, because the curtains were drawn. They took off the gag and gave me something to drink and it put me all the way to sleep and then I woke up and I tried to get out but the door was locked and I started to cry. And then that man, the one who drove us, Adam, came in and told me to be quiet and I wouldn't get hurt and I knew he meant business so I was quiet, and he just sat there and watched me, and I sat there and watched him, and I had a headache, and he wouldn't talk or tell me where I was or anything, and then he put the gag back on, and blindfolded me, and told me not to move or I'd get hurt, so I didn't move even when I felt the car start. Arcangelo, please call the Embassy for me." She climbed down off the concierge's lap and went and sat on one of the beds near the phone. "Get them, 'Gelo, and ask for Joshua Archer. I don't want the switchboard people here to hear my voice."

Adam felt that he ought to assert himself, now that Poly's tears were spent and her hysteria gone. "Polyhymnia," he started firmly, but she interrupted him.

"You promised *never* to call me that."

Adam sighed. "Poly. I don't know why you want to call the Embassy, but I think the thing for us to do is to get back to the Avenida Palace to your father. Or, if you want to use the telephone, call the hotel and ask to speak to him."

Poly looked at him as though she were a teacher trying to explain something to an unexpectedly stupid student who fails to understand a very simple problem. "Adam, daddy won't go back to the Avenida Palace without me. He might be at the Embassy. If he isn't, Josh will know how to get hold of him and what to do. We can't go back to the Avenida Palace alone anyhow, and Arcangelo can't get away to take us. Please call, 'Gelo."

Sighing again, Adam waited while the concierge asked for the American Embassy, then for Mr. Archer, then, several times over, evidently to different people, for Mr. Joshua Archer. Finally he held the phone out to Poly.

"Josh," she said. "Yes, it's me. I'm at the Ritz. . . . Yes, he's here . . . well, he was in the car with me when we were dumped here. . . . I was blindfolded, I don't know. . . ." She looked accusingly at Adam. "Were you at the Avenida Palace with daddy?"

"Yes," Adam said.

"Why didn't you tell me?"

"You've hardly let me finish a sentence, you know," Adam reproved her.

Poly scowled at him. "If you were at the Avenida Palace with daddy why did you leave?"

"I can't tell you now," Adam said. "Poly, I'm half dead with sleep." This was not only clever evasion. It was hot now that the sun was higher in the sky, and the air-conditioning unit in the room was not turned on; the heat pressing down on Adam seemed to be pulling on his eyelids. "I haven't had any sleep for three nights," he said.

Poly turned back to the phone. "Where's daddy? . . . Can you get to him to tell him I'm all right? . . . Okay. . . . Okay, Josh. . . . Yes, Arcangelo'll answer. . . . Okay, Josh, 'bye." She hung up, turned back to Adam, demanding, "*Why* haven't you had any sleep?"

Adam spoke with heavy patience. "The last night I was in Woods Hole there was a party that lasted until the kids put me on the plane for New York. Then we didn't sleep much on the plane to Madrid. That's two nights. Then last night I'd just gone to sleep when I was waked up."

"How were you waked up? How did you get in that car with me?"

Adam looked around the luxurious room. "I can't talk to you now. I have to sleep. I have to think."

"Do you want some coffee?"

"I've had coffee. Coffee can't keep me awake any longer."

"Do you want a shower or something?"

"I've had a shower. All I want to do is go to sleep."

"Are you hungry?"

"Polyhymn—— Poly—all I want to do is *sleep*."

Poly looked at Arcangelo. "Can he sleep here?"

Arcangelo nodded.

"We have to wait until Josh calls back. He could sleep for a while, anyhow."

Arcangelo rose and pulled the golden coverlet down off one of the beds. In a fog of sleep Adam flopped down, not feeling the softness of the mattress, not even aware of his cheek touching the fine linen of the pillow. Through a haze of sleep he seemed to hear the phone ringing, to hear voices, but he could not rouse enough to listen. He was engulfed in a black sea of slumber.

8

He woke up slowly, not because anybody was knocking at the door or in any way trying to disturb his rest but because he had at last, finally, had enough sleep. For a moment, remembering nothing, he stretched, his eyes closed, his body languid, his mind soothed by his body's comfort. Then the events of the past three days came sliding back into his relaxed and unsuspecting brain, so that his body stiffened with the shock of recollection, and his eyes flew open.

He was still in the golden room at the Ritz. Poly and Arcangelo were nowhere to be seen, but a fair young man was sitting on a green velvet chair, reading. As Adam moved, the young man's gaze flicked alertly toward the bed.

"So you're awake," he said.

Adam sat up, every muscle tense and wary. "Who are you?"

"Joshua Archer, of the American Embassy, at your service."

"Are you the Ambassador?"

The young man laughed, easy, spontaneous laughter. "I'm not sure the Ambassador would appreciate that. Hardly. I'm the lowest of the low."

Still lulled with sleep Adam thought that Joshua Archer must be a friend of Kali's and Mr. Cutter's, one of their Embassy crowd. Then he remembered the call Poly had made Arcangelo put through to the Embassy. How was it possible that both Kali and Poly should assume the protection of the Embassy? He looked warily at the young man. "You're the one Poly called?"

"Yes."

"Where is she?"

"On Gaea with her parents. They phoned the Embassy when they reached the island, and the Embassy in turn was kind enough to call me here."

"It seems to me," Adam said slowly, "that I heard the phone ring several times."

"You might have." The young man leaned back in his chair and smiled pleasantly at Adam. Adam stared back and waited. Joshua Archer was a nicely made young man with a lean face, but nothing in any way conspicuous about him. All Adam saw was light brown hair, greyish eyes, a Brooks Brothers–style suit, a young man who looked like any nice, normal American. Adam's scowl and stare deepened; the only thing he felt might single Joshua out from anyone just through college and starting to make his own way in the world was a look of sadness lurking in the eyes, and this Adam did not consciously identify; all he knew was that there was something about the young man's steady gaze that invited confidence, and this very fact put him on his guard.

"Well?" the young man said, still smiling.

"Well?" Adam asked back.

"Would you like something to eat?"

"Yes. I suppose so. Thank you."

The young man came over to the lemon-yellow phone by the second bed, and called, speaking in Portuguese, so that Adam did not have any idea what was being ordered, or even, indeed, if the young man were really calling room service. Perhaps he was reporting that the dumb kid, Adam Eddington, was finally awake; perhaps he was getting something else awful lined up for Adam's further confusion. If the boy had not had such a full and uninterrupted sleep he would probably have felt very sorry for himself. As it was, he simply tensed up so that he would be ready for whatever happened next.

Joshua Archer went back to his chair and continued to smile questioningly at Adam. Adam became more and more uncomfortable. Finally he said, "What time is it?"

Joshua Archer looked around the room. The golden draperies were still pulled across the windows and no light filtered through. "Around nine in the evening. You went to sleep yesterday morning, so you've had about thirty-six hours. Feeling better?"

"Yes, thanks."

"The bathroom is there," Joshua said. When Adam returned he continued, "Now the problem is what to do with you. You *are* rather a problem, Adam."

"Sorry."

"The Ambassador was all for sending you back to Woods Hole immediately."

Without stopping to think Adam responded bitterly, "You mean I should crawl right back into the Hole I crawled out of?"

Joshua laughed again. "Is it as bad as all that?"

"It might help if someone would tell me just what is going on."

Joshua's voice was smooth as silk, his face as expressionless. "Didn't Typhon Cutter?"

"What about him?"

Joshua shrugged. "Oh, nothing much. Or is there?" Adam was silent. "The last time I saw him was at a party at the Embassy the evening Poly was kidnapped."

"Oh?" Adam asked politely.

There was a knock. Joshua shot a sharp glance at Adam, then unlocked the door. Arcangelo came in rolling a dinner cart. He looked at Adam but he did not smile and he did not speak. He wheeled the cart over to the table and spread a tablecloth, put out silver and plates. From covered dishes a delicious smell rose. When the dinner was set out he looked over at Joshua, who simply nodded. Arcangelo glanced again at Adam, then left, closing the door quietly behind him. Joshua locked the door from the inside, came back to the table and sat down, beckoning to Adam. "Come on. You'll feel better after you've had some food."

"I'd feel lots better if I knew more about what was going on."

Joshua looked at him thoughtfully. "Yes, we all would. But I can't be open with you unless you'll be open with me."

Adam was sitting on the side of the bed still in his travelling suit, which was by now thoroughly wrinkled. He leaned down and reached for his shoes, put them on. As he walked, rather stiffly, to the table, he said, "I'm sorry, but I'm so confused that I don't think I can be very open with anybody." He pulled out his chair, deliberately trying to curb his instinctive liking for Joshua. "I'm just a dumb American kid and the things that have been happening are beyond me."

Joshua ladled some interesting-smelling soup into Adam's dish. "Fair enough. We'll try to clear up what we can. Mind if I ask you a few questions? You don't have to answer if you don't want to, but I'd appreciate it if you'd try. Then I'll know better what to do next. Do you want to go back to America?"

Oddly enough Adam wasn't even tempted. He was in the middle of this thing, and it was a mess, and he hated it, but he knew that he could not deliberately walk out on it until he knew what it was all about. "No."

"Then what do you think you should do?"

Adam swallowed some of the soup; it was delicious and delicate, with a faintly sour, sorrel taste. "I think I should go to Gaea to work for Dr. O'Keefe the way Dr. Didymus wanted me to do."

"And Dr. O'Keefe?"

"What about him?"

"Do you think he wants you?"

"That was the understanding when I left Woods Hole."

"But things have happened since then. Do you think he can trust you?"

"Why not?" Adam asked warily.

"He told you not to open the door of your room at the Avenida Palace, didn't he?"

73

"Yes."

"Yet you opened it."

"Yes."

"Why?"

"It seemed to me that it was the right thing to do."

"Why?"

"I was alone, and Poly was kidnapped, and I was responsible for her."

"Did you think opening the door would help you find her?"

"Yes."

"Why?"

"I just did."

Sighing rather absently Joshua removed the soup plates—Adam had not quite finished his soup—and put them on the serving cart. Raising the metal dome from a platter of fish Joshua asked, "Did you just open the door of your own accord and go blundering off in the dark in the middle of the night to look for Poly? Or was someone on the other side of the door? Did you let someone into the room?"

Adam did not answer and Joshua deftly placed a sauce-covered fish on his plate, then handed him a bowl of little, wrinkled olives. Adam took an olive and it was tender and delicious. With the pit still in his mouth he said, "I don't think I can tell you." He looked at Joshua and fought down the temptation to spill everything out to him. Putting the olive pit on his plate he said, "I'd like to tell you. It's just that I have to know more about what's what."

Joshua nodded. "Yes. I see that. From your point of view this is perfectly reasonable. But under the circumstances this entire situation is too potentially explosive for me to be able to do anything until I know more about what happened from the moment you opened that door. I am going on the assumption that you opened it to someone. Unless I can find out where you went and who you were with I shall have no alternative to sending you back to the States." With an expert stroke of his knife he removed the backbone of his fish.

Adam asked, "Do you know what happened up to the time I opened the door?"

"Yes. I have talked at length with Poly, with her father, and, on a closed Embassy line, with Canon Tallis in Madrid. I completely understand how confusing all of this must be for you. And Father Tallis is inclined to trust you, and he's a perceptive old boy. I have a lot of faith in his judgment. He's never blinded by sentimentality. If I'd put Poly in your charge and you'd let her disappear I'd have you on the next jet to New York. Sorry, Adam. I know it wasn't your fault. All I mean is that I'd have blamed you, fault or no, out of my own guilt, and Canon Tallis didn't."

Adam said excitedly. "But then you see why I *had* to open the door, why I *had* to try to find Poly. It was the only way I knew."

"Yes," Joshua said thoughtfully. "I see that. Okay. After we've finished dinner we'll go to my flat; your luggage has been taken there. You can change into fresh clothes, and then maybe it might be a good idea if we go to the Embassy. If there's anyone you'd like to talk to it can be arranged from there."

"Who would I want to talk to?"

"Canon Tallis?"

Adam shook his head.

"Your parents?"

"I don't want them upset."

"Dr. Didymus? I think it might help if you talked to him."

"I don't know," Adam said. "I just don't know."

"Eat your fish," Joshua told him. "Brain food, my grandmother always used to say."

"You mean you think I need it?"

Joshua laughed. "Don't we all." He removed the fish plates to the serving tray, and helped Adam to meat, rice, carrots. "Still hungry? I've never managed to get used to two seven-course meals a day, so I get around it by not eating any lunch. It's been a couple of days since you've eaten, hasn't it?"

"It probably has," Adam said. "I don't remember. But I *am* still hungry, and this is very good." Then, feeling that perhaps he had been too friendly he picked up his knife and fork. If only he did not have this instinctive feeling that Joshua Archer was someone to be trusted he could be more objective. But if Typhon Cutter and Kali were right then Joshua was the last person in the world to trust.

"Adam," Joshua said, "have you seen Carolyn Cutter since you went into the coffee shop with her at the airport in New York?"

"How do you know I saw her then?"

"I happen to know it from several sources," Joshua said. "The one that might interest you most is Typhon Cutter. He mentioned it at the dinner table at the Embassy."

"You mean the night Poly was kidnapped?"

"Yes."

"You're *sure* Poly is all right?"

"I told you she's on Gaea with her parents."

"How do I know that you're telling me the truth?"

"You don't. You're just going to have to follow your instincts about me one way or the other."

Adam glowered across the table. "But I don't trust my instincts any more, Mr. Archer."

"Call me Josh."

"Okay."

"What's wrong with your instincts?"

"They're just not working," Adam said. "I *do* have a feeling that somebody has to be right and somebody has to be wrong, but I haven't a dream who is which."

"Would it help any if I tell you that I trust you?"

"I don't know. All I can tell you is that if I needed to be taken down a peg I've been taken."

"Because Poly was kidnapped while you were in charge of her?"

"That," Adam said, "but mostly because I can't trust my own decisions or my own thoughts. I used to be pretty sure of myself. I thought I could handle just about any situation."

"You handled some pretty rough ones in New York, didn't you?"

"Well," Adam said, "yes. How did you know?"

"Dr. O'Keefe was kind enough to let me see his dossier on you."

"How did *he* know?"

"His work is too important for him to take any chances. You weren't aware that you were being investigated?"

"No. I guess I wasn't. I thought Dr. Didymus' recommendation was all that was needed."

"Not even Old Doc's word is enough for something as vital as this. What I liked best of what I read about you was the time you and your Puerto Rican friend—Juan, wasn't it—"

"Yes."

"—the time the two of you managed to stop a rumble from starting. Maybe that's what makes me trust you, makes me know that you're fighting on the same side I am. But I think I'd trust you even if I didn't know anything about you. Have some salad?"

"Yes, please." Adam watched while Joshua served. "Could I ask you a question?"

"Fire ahead."

"You say you know I went into that coffee shop with Kali—"

"Yes."

"She told me her father has businesses here."

"That's right. He does."

"And that he knows lots of people at the Embassy."

"Correct."

"Do you know him?"

"Slightly. I'm not important enough for him to bother with."

"What do you think of him?"

"That he's a very clever man."

"Do you trust him?"

"As far as I could throw the bathtub."

"Is this instinct, or do you have reasons?"

"Both."

"Could I know the reasons?"

Joshua seemed to ponder. Finally he said, "He cares more about money than he does about anything else. Money and power. And he doesn't care who's sacrificed as long as he gets them."

"Is Dr. O'Keefe powerful?"

"Not in his own mind, certainly, and only because his mind can run circles around any other mind I've ever met. But power is always subordinate with him. Manipulating people is the last thing in the world he'd want."

"So what do you think about power?" Adam demanded.

"Power corrupts," Joshua quoted. "Absolute power corrupts absolutely."

Adam sighed.

Joshua stood up. "You don't want any dessert, do you? We'll have coffee at my place. I've made my decision about you, Adam, whether you trust me or not."

For a moment Adam felt only relieved that the decision had been made, that it had been taken out of his hands. Then he knew that if Joshua Archer were to try to send him back to America he would have to escape him somehow and go back to Kali and her father.

But Joshua said, "I'm going to take you to Gaea."

9

*

They left the hotel without speaking to anybody, without giving in keys at the desk, without further communication with Arcangelo. Joshua turned to the right and they walked briskly for about ten minutes through the sweet summer darkness. They stopped before a narrow house faced in gleaming blue-and-white patterned tile. "Ever seen the Portuguese tile before?" Joshua asked absently, not waiting for Adam to respond. "It's quite famous." He put his key in the door. "I have the top floor. Modest, but mine. I love this stairway. Pink marble. Beautiful, isn't it?"

"Yes." Adam followed him up three flights.

At the top was a blue painted door, which Joshua also unlocked, saying, "Gone are those innocent days when I didn't worry about keys. I got awfully tired of having my things gone through. So 'Gelo very kindly helped me fashion a lock that is impossible to pick or duplicate."

"Who is Arcangelo?" Adam demanded.

"My very good friend." Joshua flicked a switch and in the ceiling a crystal chandelier sparkled into life.

Adam looked around. They were in a fair-sized room, a room that smelled of tobacco and books. It was, indeed, more of a library than a living room, as there were books not only on all four walls but piled on tables and windowsills. Adam saw in a quick glance a record player and shelves of records, a sagging couch covered with an India print, an old red rep easy chair, a large desk that looked as though it had been discarded from an office. It was a good room, the kind of room Adam had dreamed of having some day. He looked at a Picasso print over one of the bookshelves, a sad-eyed harlequin on a white horse. The harlequin reminded him of someone, and suddenly he realized that it was Joshua himself.

Joshua pointed to an open door. "Bedroom and bath. Go in and make yourself at home. Your stuff's all in there. I'll make us some coffee. I don't have a proper kitchen, just a hot plate, but it does."

Adam nodded and went to the bedroom. It was a small, bare room, furnished only with a narrow brass bed, a chest of drawers, a straight chair. The walls were white and absolutely bare. The room was cold and austere in comparison to the cluttered warmth of the living room.

Adam washed his hands and face. He was not being sent back to America. He was going to Gaea. He could not help liking Joshua. But if he should see Kali again how would he feel? So far he had managed to tell Joshua nothing of any importance, and Joshua did not seem to be going to pursue his questioning.

—Play it cool, Adam, he seemed to hear a voice in his ear. Kali's voice.

As long as nobody knew that it was Kali who had come to him at the Avenida Palace, that it was to Kali's apartment he had gone, that he was expected to work for Typhon Cutter as a—what had Mr. Cutter said? Patriotic duty, wasn't it?—then he had not yet committed himself to either side. And as long as he didn't commit himself he couldn't do anything too terribly wrong. Could he?

—I wish things were black and white, he thought savagely. —I wish things were *clear*.

He remembered his math teacher back at school, a brilliant young Irishman, telling of his personal confusion when he first began to study higher mathematics and discovered that not all mathematical problems have one single and simple answer, that there is a choice of answers and a decision to be made by the mathematician even when dealing with something like an equation that ought to be definite and straightforward and to allow of no more than one interpretation. "And that's the way life is," the teacher had said. "Right and wrong, good and evil, aren't always clear and simple for us; we have to interpret and decide; we have to commit ourselves, just as we do with this equation."

As though reading his thoughts Joshua came and lounged in the doorway. "Don't hold off too long, Adam. The time comes when you have to make a choice and you're not going to be able to put it off much longer. Unless you've already made it?"

"I don't know." Adam rubbed his face with a clean, rough towel.

"The trouble is," Joshua said, "that I can't guarantee you anything. If you decide to work with Dr. O'Keefe I can't in any honesty tell you that anything is going to be easier for you than it has been for the past few days. I *can* tell you that nobody expected things to start breaking quite so soon, or we wouldn't have let you come. You were never supposed to be in any kind of danger. It was pure coincidence that it was this summer that Old Doc decided you were worth sending to Dr. O'Keefe to be educated. Of course neither Canon Tallis nor Dr. O'Keefe believe in coincidence. I'm afraid that I do, and that we're often impaled upon it. Then, on the other hand, I can't help wondering if it *was* pure coincidence that made Canon Tallis finish his work in Boston at just the moment he did so that he and Poly were on the plane with you."

"But if he was lecturing there," Adam protested, "he'd know when he was going to be through."

"Oh, did he tell you he was lecturing? Well, probably he was," Joshua said somewhat vaguely. "The main thing is that if you're worth educating then I suppose you ought to be up to facing whatever there is to face, oughtn't you?"

"What is there to face?" Adam sat at the foot of Joshua's bed.

Joshua did not answer his question. Instead: "Maybe it'll help you if I tell you that it wasn't easy for me, either. I don't know about you, Adam, but I can't look forward to pie in the sky. I'm a heretic and a heathen, and I let myself depend far too much on the human beings I love, because—well, just because. I guess the real point is that I care about having a decent world, and if you care about having a decent world you have to take sides. You have to decide who, for you, are the good guys, and who are the bad guys. So, like the fool that I am, I chose the difficult side, the unsafe side, the side that guarantees me not one thing besides danger and hard work."

"Then why did you choose it?" Adam demanded.

Joshua continued to lean against the door. "Why? I'm not sure I did. It seemed to choose me, unlikely material though I be. And it's the side that—that cares about people like Polyhymnia O'Keefe." He wheeled and went back into the living room. In a moment the sound of music came clear and gay, Respighi's *The Birds*, Adam thought, following him into the living room. Joshua grinned. "It's the fall of the sparrow I care about, Adam. But who is the sparrow? We run into problems there, too. Now let's have our coffee."

He picked up a battered white enamel percolator from the hot plate on one of the bookcases. "Want to go to the Embassy when we're through?"

Adam watched Joshua pour the dark and fragrant brew. "Why? Do we have to?"

Joshua handed him a cup, indicated sugar and milk. "No. Not if you don't want to."

"I'm not sure it would make things any clearer." Adam put three heaping spoons of sugar in his coffee. "I don't want to telephone anybody. I mean, why bother Old Doc? I think he feels about me kind of the way you feel about Poly, if you know what I mean, so it would just be upsetting to him to have me ask him to help make up my own mind. I mean, I have to do it myself, don't I?"

"When you get right down to it, yes," Joshua said.

"And the whole idea of the Embassy business is very confusing to me. I mean, you working there, and then both the O'Keefes and the Cutters seeming to know everybody, and everybody thinking the Embassy's on their side and it *can't* be on everybody's side. I think I'd rather stay clear of any more confusion for a while."

"Okay," Joshua said. "I follow you. I thought it might help, but I see your point. What about your passport, by the way?"

Adam felt the by-now-familiar jolt in the pit of his stomach. "I suppose it's still at the Avenida Palace. I'd forgotten all about it."

Joshua reached in his breast pocket and handed the thin green book to Adam. "Here. But it's something you'd better remember from now on. Think you could do any more sleeping?"

"You wouldn't think I could, would you?" Adam asked, yawned, and laughed.

"Good. Let's just have our coffee and maybe listen to a little music and go to bed. I'll take the sofa in here; I'm used to it. In the morning we'll go to Gaea. I hope you won't mind flying with me. Actually I'm a pretty fair pilot."

Without knowing why Adam realized that he would feel perfectly safe with Joshua at the controls of plane, boat, or car. It was an instinct that the wariness acquired in the past three days could not shake, no matter how little at the moment he trusted his instincts.

Although Adam protested briefly at the idea of taking Joshua's bed he found to his surprise that he was very happy to get undressed and stretch out. In the living room he could hear Joshua puttering around, changing records, cleaning up the coffee things. The last thing he was conscious of was the strains of a Mozart Horn Concerto. Then Joshua was shaking him; sunlight streamed in through the open, uncurtained bedroom window; and the smell of coffee came from the living room. Joshua, unlike Dr. O'Keefe or Arcangelo, seemed to feel no need to close himself in behind shutters or draperies; or was it just in knowing when and where?

They had coffee, bacon and eggs, all of which Joshua somehow managed with ease on his single hot plate; then they took a taxi out to the airport. This was not the huge state-owned field at which Adam had arrived, but a small, private field with a couple of rickety-looking hangars. The waiting room was a Quonset hut, with a few desks behind which sat the inevitable uniformed men, a row of phone booths, and a speaker system loud enough for Grand Central Station, so that each time a voice came through it the few passengers waiting in the hut were almost blasted out of their seats.

Joshua walked in his usual casual, almost lounging way over to one of the desks, where he stood smiling and speaking fluent Portuguese to the uniformed man behind it; they seemed to be old friends and after a few minutes Joshua turned, smiling, to Adam. "Everything's just about ready for us. Five minutes to wait, that's all. Okay?"

"Sure." What would Joshua have done if he'd said, 'Nope'?

Joshua led him over to an uncomfortable but empty wooden bench and began to talk lightly about Embassy life, of his own job of filing and checking and being general errand boy, all of which, he said, could perfectly well be done by a ten-year-old. Every once in a while he would have to stop as his narrative was punctured by the braying of the loudspeaker. Adam almost laughed as Joshua would shut his eyes against the blast, his sensitive ears seeming to quiver in pain. Adam's own ears pricked up as he heard, "Jhoshuajh Archair. . . . Jhoshuajh Archair. . . ." followed by a message in Portuguese.

"I seem to have a call from the Embassy," Joshua said, sighing. "Please wait right here for me, Adam. Please do not move, I beg of you."

Adam gave a rather lopsided grin. "I won't open any more locked doors."

"Good boy." Joshua ambled off, never seeming to hurry, but covering the distance to the telephones in an amazingly short time.

Adam leaned back on the bench, stretching his legs. Perhaps it was catching up on his sleep that was responsible for his feeling of calm and certainty. —I can't help it, he thought. —I couldn't feel this way about Joshua if he weren't all right. And Poly. They've got to be the way I want them to be. And Dr. O'Keefe and Canon Tallis. I'm making up my mind to be on their side whether I want to or not. It's making itself up for me. Just the way Joshua said it did for him.

"Adam."

He jerked upright, his thoughts knocked out from under him. Standing before him was a man in ecclesiastical garb.

But it was not Canon Tallis. It was a younger man, taller, extremely handsome, with a head of luxuriant black hair.

"Adam?"

Adam looked but he did not speak. It probably was, it *must* be a friend of Canon Tallis'. But even if his mind was being made up for him there was no being certain of anything any more. Even if it was somebody who knew his name.

"It *is* Adam Eddington, isn't it?" the man asked, in one of the most mellifluous voices Adam had ever heard.

He could hardly pretend to be a deaf mute. "Yes."

"I'm Dr. Baal." Adam looked somewhat startled, and the man repeated, "Dr. Eliphaz Ball, rector of St. Zophar's, the American church here in Lisbon." A hand was held out toward Adam, a white, clean, well-manicured hand. The grip was strong, man-to-man.

"How do you do, sir?" Adam murmured.

Dr. Eliphaz Ball, smiling pleasantly, sat down beside him. "Your young friend, Joshua Archer, and my friend, too, I am happy to say, has had to go back to the Embassy. Poor lad, when his superiors call he must jump, no matter what previous engagements he may have hoped to fulfill. So he's asked me to see to it that you get to Gaea. I'm afraid I'm no pilot myself, but I've made arrangements for one of the local men to hop us over." Dr. Ball's beautiful voice was smooth and pleasant, his manner easy, as he smiled at Adam. "Poor laddie, we're all more sorry than we can say for everything that has happened to you. It must all have been more than confusing. But once you get to Gaea and settle down to work with the good doctor you'll be able to relax and forget all the unpleasantness. Thank God our darling Poly was returned unharmed, the precious child."

Adam looked at the handsome, friendly face of Dr. Ball and was not happy. For some reason his instinct was telling him not to trust Dr. Ball, but he no longer trusted his instinct. For a brief moment he contrasted the doctor with Canon Tallis. Canon Tallis was brusque, stern, businesslike, formidable. He would never have called Poly a precious child, but Adam knew that it was to the canon that Poly was precious. He knew it. At least he went along with his instinct that far.

"I'm afraid we'll have to hurry," Dr. Ball said. "I think we can manage your bags between us, don't you?"

Joshua had told Adam not to move. Adam had promised to open no more locked doors. "I'm sorry," he said, courteously, "but I'm afraid I'll have to wait here for Mr. Archer."

"But my poor dear boy, I've just explained to you that poor Josh has been called back to the Embassy, and has put you in my charge."

Adam shook his head stubbornly. "I'm sorry. I have to wait here."

The velvet smoothness of Dr. Ball's voice did not alter, nor the friendly look fade from his features, as he said, "Adam, don't you think you've caused the O'Keefes enough trouble already?"

"I'm sorry," Adam said for the third time. "I don't mean to be difficult, but I have to wait."

"Poor lad, I hadn't realized just quite how confused you are, in spite of what Joshua told me. Joshua is not coming back. Please try to understand this. He has been called to the Embassy. Do try to realize that it is absolutely essential for me to get you to Gaea at once. Won't you be a good boy and come with me?" Adam shook his head. "It will be so much easier for both of us if you'll come of your own free will." Adam shook his head again. Dr. Ball sighed and cast his eyes up to heaven. "Dear Lord, be patient with the boy." He looked down at Adam. "I'm sorry, truly sorry, laddie, but I'll have to take you with me. Please do understand that it's for your own protection."

He glanced behind him, snapped his fingers lightly, and a burly porter moved up to stand beside him.

Adam braced himself. With a wild and irrational stubbornness he was determined not to move from the bench where he had promised to wait for Joshua.

A second figure appeared beside the porter.

It was Arcangelo.

Adam did not move. Arcangelo spoke in a low voice to the porter, who looked at Adam, at Dr. Ball, shrugged in a vague kind of apology, though Adam could not tell to whom, and trotted off to a baggage cart. A shadow seemed to cross Dr. Ball's brow, but his pleasant expression did not change. He smiled again at Adam, showing his even, white teeth. "We do seem to be running into problems, don't we?" He turned to Arcangelo. "And who are you, my good man?"

"A friend," Arcangelo said.

"Of whom?"

Arcangelo jerked his head in Adam's direction. Then he pointed across the room. Adam looked and saw Joshua coming toward them. As swiftly as he had appeared, Arcangelo left.

Dr. Ball put his hand on Adam's knee. "What an unfortunate incident. I will speak quickly, Adam. I am a friend of Typhon Cutter's."

"He wanted me to go to Gaea," Adam said.

"I am aware of that. Why do you think I am here? I was sent to help you. And to help you to help your country."

"Thank you." Adam turned his eyes to see Joshua's progress across a floor that now seemed endless.

"Not a word to Archer. We'll get a message to you as soon as possible." Dr. Ball's hand pressed harder against Adam's knee. Joshua reached them. Dr. Ball removed his hand, rose, and greeted Joshua. "My young friend, the charming Mr. Archer! How fortunate to meet you here this morning! And how is life at the Embassy?"

"Splendid, thank you, Dr. Ball," Joshua said coolly.

"Keeping you busy?"

"Enough."

"I've had a delightful time talking to your young protégé here. Do take care of him for us."

"I'll do that," Joshua said.

"And give my warmest regards to the O'Keefes."

"Certainly."

"A brilliant mind, O'Keefe's. Brilliant. Our country needs more men like that."

"Right," Joshua said.

"I trust I'll see you around the Embassy, my boy."

"Very likely."

"Do have a safe and pleasant trip. Small craft warnings are out, I believe." Still smiling, Dr. Ball moved off.

Without a word Joshua picked up one of Adam's bags. Adam picked up the other and his briefcase and followed him out of the Quonset hut and onto a runway. A small plane was waiting several hundred yards away. Trotting behind Joshua, Adam could see only a tense, angry line of jaw.

—He said he trusted me, Adam thought resentfully,—so what right does he have to go jumping to conclusions now?

As they came up to the plane Adam saw that it was an old, single-engine, British Hawker Hurricane converted to a two-seater. Arcangelo was standing beside it. Silently he handed Adam, then Joshua, leather jackets, goggles, helmets, and helped them up and into the seats. Joshua, still without speaking (and silence from Joshua, unlike silence from Arcangelo, seemed completely out of character), turned around and showed Adam how to strap himself in, then clipped on his own webbing. Suddenly his face relaxed and he looked at Adam and grinned. "Feel like something out of a World War II movie?"

"Kind of," Adam said. And then, "This guy Ball—"

"Wait till we get going. Silence is golden and all that stuff." Joshua's experienced hands moved over the controls; the engine coughed, choked, finally caught. The blades of the slowly circling propeller merged into a swift blur. Joshua leaned out and waved down at Arcangelo who waved back, then turned and walked toward the Quonset hut. The plane slowly taxied along the runway. "She's a bit bumpy," Joshua shouted above the noise of the engines. "Hold on tight."

Adam held on. After a moment he closed his eyes and gritted his teeth. The plane seemed to buck and strain, to refuse to leave the ground: how could it possibly expect to fly at such an advanced age? The only fit place for it was a museum.

Bounce. Bounce. Jerk. Bounce. A jerk that threw Adam back against the seat. Then a straining upward and a pleased laugh from Joshua. Adam opened his eyes.

They were nosing up, up, higher, higher. They circled the small airport. As Adam looked down he could see Arcangelo leaving the Quonset hut, getting into a car, and driving off.

This seemed to be what Joshua was waiting for. He turned the plane away from the port, away from the land, nosed further and further up. Ahead of them over the rooftops Adam could see water.

"Okay, kid," Joshua shouted back to him. "Everything under control."

Adam shouted in return, "I hope that's not the overstatement of the year."

"I never go in for famous last words," Joshua called. "Don't mind talking in bellows, do you?"

"I'm a good bellower," Adam bellowed.

"Good. Me, too. Nobody listening in but sea gulls. We're over the Tagus now." Adam leaned over and looked down at the rim of Lisbon sprawled along the river. "That's the Jeronymos Monastery," Joshua called back. "It's just about my favorite piece of architecture in Lisbon, except for the Saô Juan Chrysostom Monastery which is even better. I'll take you there someday." He flew along the coast, pointing and calling. "There's the Belém Tower. Famous Portuguese Manueline architecture. Moorish influence heavy. Makes you think you're in Africa, doesn't it? Lots of Portugal will." And, a moment later, "That monstrosity is the monument to Henry the Navigator, but I've become very fond of it. Now what about Ball?" he asked without transition.

"Who *is* he?"

"Rector of St. Zophar's."

"Friend of yours?"

"I never make friends with the pious."

"What about Canon Tallis?"

Joshua snorted. "He's not pious."

"Did you send him to me?"

"Who? Canon Tallis?"

"No. Dr. Ball."

"Did he tell you I had?"

"Yes," Adam shouted, glad at last to be able to be open about something. He looked down and they were flying over the harbor which was speckled with ferries, small fishing vessels, pleasure craft. "Does he really have a church and stuff?"

"That's right. Very popular gentleman of the cloth. Ladies swoon."

"You don't?"

"I'm no lady."

"Is he a friend of Canon Tallis'?"

Joshua roared. "Hardly."

"But I thought—"

"Adam, my son," Joshua howled over the sound of the engines, over the blasting of the wind, "don't expect any group of people to be all of a kind. The church is no exception. And it is not only because I am a heathen that I say this. So what did the old black crow say to you?"

"That you'd been called back to the Embassy and had sent him to take me to Gaea."

"And you didn't bite," Joshua said. "Good boy."

"I thought you thought I had." Adam looked away from Joshua, over the side of the plane, down at the open water of the Atlantic. Land was only a dark shadow behind them, almost lost in haze. The water was unusually dark, with occasional brilliant flashes as it was caught by sunlight.

"Because I got all furious?" Joshua asked. "Not at you. I thought you'd had about all you could take and I could have strangled him with my bare hands. There wasn't any phone call for me from the Embassy or anyplace else, by the way. He'd bribed somebody to page me to get me out of the way."

After a pause Adam said, "I think I'm shocked."

"Because he's a churchman and stuff?"

"I guess so."

"I had that kind of being shocked knocked out of me when I was in knee pants. Also thinking that anyone in my government's employ necessarily has the interest of my country at heart. This is one of the few reasons I'm of any use in the Embassy. Don't let it get you, Adam. People don't compartmentalize. One bad guy in a group doesn't make everybody else bad, and one good one doesn't make everybody else good."

At that moment the plane dropped. Adam flew up from his seat and was kept in the plane only by the webbing of his harness.

"Whoops," Joshua called, pulling at the stick and nosing the plane up again. "We're going into a spot of turbulence. I can't get above these clouds; we'll have to go through them."

He opened the throttle and the little plane shot into a great, churning white mass. Adam remembered Dr. Ball's smug comment about small-craft warnings. The plane jolted and jerked, dropped and steadied, so that Adam's stomach leapt from his toes to his mouth and back. The noise of the engine seemed accentuated by the swirling cloud, by the unexpected pockets of air into which they fell like a stone.

Adam felt absolutely calm at the same time that he knew that he was as frightened as he had ever been in his life. With each jerk and leap he expected the plane to plummet into the ocean, but Joshua always managed to steady it.

In front of him Adam heard an unexpected sound. It was Joshua. Joshua was singing, his head flung back, his mouth open, bellowing the joyful last chorus from Beethoven's *Ninth Symphony*. Joshua, Adam realized, was enjoying the battle with the cloud. Beside this supreme happiness Adam's own fears fled. Holding on tightly to his seat, trying not to be thrown about any more than necessary, he watched the young man rather than the blind fury of the cloud.

And then suddenly they were through it and into the blue and gold of the day again. The plane choked and steadied. Joshua turned back to Adam and grinned. "Scare you?"

"At first."

Joshua patted the controls fondly. "She's a good old crate. I'll get you there in one piece. I hope."

They plunged into another cloud and dropped headlong toward the ocean.

10

It was not precisely a relaxing trip, but Adam caught Joshua's exhilaration; he held on tight and the thought that they might not reach Gaea left him.

"This is better than the roller coaster at Palisades Park," he shouted.

"Rather!" Joshua called back, then burst into song again.

Adam did not know how long a routine flight to Gaea ought to last; it took Joshua, battling through the clouds in the little plane, the better part of two hours before the sky cleared again and there below them was the green of land with a great, curving, golden beach. "Gaea," Joshua called. "Hold on tight, Adam. Tide's out, all's clear, and I'm coming down on the beach."

Joshua accomplished the landing with skill and grace. The wheels touched the hard-packed sand gently and rolled along the water's edge to a smooth stop. He sat for a moment over the controls, breathing deeply, flexing his hands, deliberately relaxing. Then they unstrapped themselves, took off helmets, goggles, leather jackets. As Adam climbed out he realized that his legs were stiff and that, unconsciously, he must have been bracing them against the footboards during most of the trip.

"That was a great ride," he shouted, though the noise of the engine had stopped. "I loved every minute of it."

Joshua stretched, a great wide gesture of well-being. "I love to fly. Heaven, as far as I'm concerned. Adam—"

Adam was looking about, at the ocean, the sand, the dunes, and beyond the dunes to scrub and pine. "Hm?"

Joshua was looking at him directly, questioningly, bringing him back from the excitement of the flight to this moment of the arrival on Gaea, so different from the arrival he had anticipated when he left Woods Hole.

"Josh," he asked, "this Eliphaz Ball creep: what was he up to?"

Joshua stared out to sea, his eyes squinting a little against the brilliance. "I'm not sure. My guess is that he wanted to—well, you might call it indoctrinate you—before you had a chance to talk to Dr. O'Keefe. To get you firmly sewed up in the Cutter camp." He paused, again looking at Adam questioningly, then said, "Before I take you to the O'Keefes do you want to tell me who you opened the door to at the Avenida Palace?"

Adam, too, stared out to sea, his eyes almost closing against the radiance of sun and water. "I haven't told you, have I?"

"No."

"Oh, Joshua—" Adam started, then trailed off.

"You can't make only part of a decision," Joshua said gently. "You have to go all the way."

"I *have* decided," Adam said.

"I know you have."

"Do you know *what* I've decided?"

"To work for Dr. O'Keefe."

"How do you know that?"

"Because you wouldn't come here to work as his assistant and work against him in any other way."

A cloud moved across the sun; its shadow slid murkily over the beach, draining the gold from the sand; the blackness was reflected in Adam's mind. He looked down at his feet, the city shoes darkly incongruous against the damp sand. "Do I have to work *for* him in order not to work *against* him? You don't understand, Joshua. Or *I* don't understand. I don't see why I have to take sides at all. I know I couldn't work against you, and if that means not working against Dr. O'Keefe, then I won't work against him. But I didn't come over here to take sides about anything. I came to assist a scientist in some experiments in marine biology because that's what Dr. Didymus wanted me to do. You said yourself he didn't know about anything else."

Joshua shoved his hands into his pockets. The cloud moved past the sun and the sea was again dazzled with brilliance. "That's quite true, Adam. But you *are* involved, whether you want to be or not. In the end you'll have to take sides, and it'll be easier for you if you don't keep putting it off."

Adam scowled. "It would help if somebody would tell me what I'm supposed to be taking sides about."

"Adam," Joshua said with heavy patience, "if you're as bright as you're supposed to be you ought to know without my telling you that it's because Dr. O'Keefe has, in his work, come across certain far-reaching discoveries that certain irresponsible people are trying to steal."

"But you can't keep scientific discoveries secret," Adam protested.

"You have to try to keep them from being misused."

"You can't do that, either."

Joshua gave a rather wry smile. "That sounds more like jaded old Josh than a kid fresh out of school who ought to have all his illusions intact. If you'd been working for a scientist who was in charge, say, of antibiotics for a hospital, would you have sat back while self-interested men stole them, diluted them, and sold them for high black-market prices to doctors who gave them to children who died in agony as a result?"

"I've read *The Third Man*," Adam said, "and I've seen it on the Late Late Show."

"So don't you see that it's not a joking or a casual matter? You *cannot* be uncommitted, Adam, believe me, you cannot."

Adam's jaw set stubbornly. "I have to be clear about things."

Suddenly Joshua shrugged, and wheeled around from the ocean, kicking at the thin remains of a broken golden conch

95

shell. "Okay. Forget it. Come on. We have a three-mile hike to get to the O'Keefes'."

Adam's scowl settled into stubborn sullenness. He did not understand his own blind lack of decision, but he knew that he hated having Joshua disappointed in him, and he knew that Joshua was disappointed. He was striding across the sand to the dunes; on the crest was a dead and rusty palm toward which he headed. One branch of palm, brown fronds drooping like feathers, seemed to point inland. There was nothing for Adam to do but follow, feet slipping as they reached the deep, soft sand at the foot of the dunes.

Supporting himself on coarse tufts of beach grass Joshua climbed the dune, standing, waiting until Adam caught up. Then he started ahead, moving slowly through what seemed to be no more than an animal track in the undergrowth. Thorny branches stretched across their way, and these Joshua held aside for Adam. Forest creepers looped from tree to tree, and although machete scars showed that the path had recently been cleared, the creepers were tenaciously starting to block the way again. Joshua untangled them, pausing occasionally to see that Adam was behind him. Above them were intermittent flashes of brilliant color, scarlet, orange, gold, and the alarmed shrieks of birds. Shadows moved constantly as the leaves stirred in the slightest breath of air. Joshua was caught in a shifting pattern of shadows, so that his sandy hair, his white shirt, his tanned skin flickered with green, purple, gold.

After a half mile or so of jungle they reached a clearing, a wide savannah of golden grasses. At the edge of the clearing a cloud of multi-colored butterflies hovered. One brushed against Adam's face, startling him so that he jumped. A herd of small animals was grazing placidly in the distance, but ran pelting through the grasses and into the underbrush at the scent of human beings. At the far side of the savannah was a grove of palms, and beyond this a hill, which Joshua climbed without slackening his pace. At the top of the hill there was a plateau where monolithic slabs of stone caught the full blast of the sun, glinting with gold. A large flat slab like a table or altar stood in the center, with smaller stones circling it. Joshua went up to the table stone and put his palm on its sun-baked surface, asking in a low voice, "Not going to be a Mordred, are you, Adam?"

"I've read King Arthur, too," Adam said. The sun beat down on his bare head; his upper lip was beaded with sweat.

Joshua looked at him, seemed about to say something in reply, instead straightened up and spoke in his conversational, social-young-man-of-the-Embassy voice. "This is the highest point on the island. Over there, to your left, you can get a glimpse of the Hotel Praia da Gaea. It's getting a bit of a reputation as a resort in spite of the heat. Sunbathing and tennis, and dancing at night if there's enough breeze. Straight ahead, where you can see a kind of promontory, is the native village. They're a gentle people, a mixture of original islander and Portuguese, with a touch of African thrown in. Some people think these stones were brought here by their remote ancestors and represent a kind of primitive religion. On your right, through the trees, that flash of white is the O'Keefes' house and laboratories. By the way, Dr. O'Keefe happens to be doing his work here with the blessing of the President of the United States, though not many people know this, or are supposed to know."

"Why are you telling me?" Adam asked.

Joshua answered quietly, "To try to counteract some of the things I am going on the assumption you have been told."

"By whom?"

"The people you were with from the time you opened the door at the Avenida Palace to the time Poly fell into your arms on the sidewalk in front of the Ritz." There was no longer any censure in his voice. "Until the hotel was built a year ago there was complete privacy here and ideal conditions for Dr. O'Keefe's experiments. After this summer it will probably be necessary for him to move again. Pity."

"Joshua, don't hate me," Adam said.

"I don't."

"I promise you I—are you going to be staying here in Gaea at all?"

"No. I have to fly back to Lisbon tonight."

"In—in *that?*"

"Wind's quieting down. It won't be a bad flight."

"Is there any way I—I could get in touch with you if I needed you?"

"Yes. I'll give you my phone number at home and my special extension at the Embassy. They're both pretty classified, so keep them to yourself. I don't think you're apt to need me. A few days with the O'Keefes will clear things up for you. I was wrong to try to push you. This is all very new for you. I had no right to expect you to leap into understanding."

"I'd still like to have those numbers," Adam said.

Joshua pulled a small pad out of his shirt pocket, a stub of pencil, and wrote. "Here. But please don't lose them. Keep them with your passport."

"Okay."

Joshua took another sweeping glance around. "All right. Let's go."

A footpath, only slightly wider than that leading through the scrub, took them down from the hill. The sun was heavy and hot and pressed on Adam with tangible weight. It seemed that they were walking far more than three miles. Then, suddenly, they were at a series of low, rambling, dazzling white bungalows, joined together by breezeways.

Joshua whistled, the melody Canon Tallis had whistled in Madrid, the melody the rabbi had whistled on the plane.

"What *is* that?" Adam asked.

Joshua grinned. "The Tallis Canon, of course."

Without being able to control himself Adam burst into laughter. "Of course! What an idiot I am! I *knew* I knew it. We used to sing it in choir when I was a kid." Now that memory had returned he did not see how he could have forgotten. The simple melody Thomas Tallis had written in the sixteenth century had been one of the choirmaster's favorites, and singing it in canon had been like singing a round, so the boys had enjoyed it, too. But Adam's choirboy days had ended in the seventh grade, so perhaps it wasn't too strange that Thomas Tallis' canon had not been remembered.

Joshua joined him in laughter. "Polyhymnia's idea. Naturally." He sobered. "That's the way things come clear. All of a sudden. And then you realize how obvious they've been all along."

Before Adam needed to reply a bevy of scantily dressed children came bursting around the corner of the bungalow and Joshua, calling, hurried to meet them. Behind the children, carrying a baby, came a tall, strikingly beautiful woman, smiling in greeting. Children were climbing all over Joshua, inspecting Adam, and then Poly came running out of the bungalow, holding the hand of a very small child she had evidently been tending, since he was dressed only in a torn white undershirt, and she carried a diaper in her hand.

"Josh! Adam!" she cried joyfully. Joshua was kissed with exuberance, then Adam. "You're late! We've been waiting for ages and ages!"

"We ran into a bit of weather," Joshua explained. "Mrs. O'Keefe, this is Adam Eddington."

Mrs. O'Keefe shook hands warmly, laughing. "Poor Adam, this must seem a formidable welcome. But it *is* a welcome. We're all happy to see you, and that you'll be with us this summer. Poly's told us so much about you. Come on in and I'll show you your room. Are his things still in the plane, Josh? Good. I'll ask one of the boys to ride over and get them." She explained to Adam, "It's twice as long by the beach, but you can't ride a horse through the brush. I expect you found it rather scratchy walking. We're much more primitive on our part of the island than they are at the hotel, but we like it." She led Adam along a breezeway and into the largest of the bungalows. They went into an enormous white room with comfortable and shabby-looking chairs and sofas. One wall was filled with books, another was all windows looking out to sea. At one end was a huge fireplace faced with the same lovely blue-and-white tile Adam had seen in Lisbon. The floor was rose-beige marble. Everything was light and open and clean, and a soft ocean breeze blew through.

"The living room," Mrs. O'Keefe said, "obviously lived in."

She went through an arched doorway into a hall off which Adam could see a series of cubicles. "We don't go in for large bedrooms, but everybody has his own. This is the boys' section. Then the doctor and I have our room, and then there's the girls' wing. Your room is nearest the living room. It's a tradition in our family that the rooms go up in age, the youngest being nearest our room. Of course each time we have a new baby the rooms have to be shifted, but that's part of the fun for the children."

She preceded Adam into the first of the cubicles. There was a gayly embroidered spread on the bed, a chest of drawers, a chintz-covered armchair with sagging springs. A small, empty bookcase waited by the bed with a lamp on it, and a bouquet of beach grasses in a glass jar. "Poly's offering," Mrs. O'Keefe said.

Adam looked at Mrs. O'Keefe's tranquil, lovely face. "Is Poly really all right?"

"Yes, Adam. She's fine. And she's very fond of you." Was there a question in the way this was said?

"She wasn't hurt at all?" Adam asked. "You're sure?"

"Quite sure. Only frightened. And you mustn't blame yourself. You had no way of knowing that there was any danger when Tom—Canon Tallis—put you on the plane."

"Is his name really Thomas Tallis, like the composer's?"

"No. It's John. But his last name really *is* Tallis, so of course he gets called Tom. Do you know the Tallis canon?" Again: was there more to her question than the words?

"Yes, but I'd forgotten what it was until just now. Joshua was whistling it and I asked him. It was very stupid of me; we used to sing it in choir."

"Like to sing?"

"Sure, but I've been a bass now for quite a while, and a sort of rumbly one."

"Oh, splendid, we need a bass."

Out of doors Adam could hear the children calling and laughing and then they trooped into the house and in and through the living room. "May we come in?" Poly called. "Adam hasn't been properly introduced."

"Maybe he'd rather wait and get his breath for a few minutes first."

"No." Adam smiled at the crowd of children clustered in the doorway. "I'd like to be introduced."

"May I do it?" Poly asked her mother.

"Go ahead."

"We'll go down in age this time," Poly stated categorically. "After Father Tom gave me my horrendous name mother and daddy wouldn't let him name any of the rest of us, so don't worry. Charles comes next; he's ten, and we're the redheads; we'd given up on having any more carrot tops till we came to the baby, but we haven't come to her yet as far as introductions are concerned."

A stocky, freckle-faced boy in tan shorts and a white shirt shook hands with Adam.

"Hello, Charles," Adam said.

"Sandy comes next." Poly paused for handshaking, "and then Dennys. This is Peggy. She's four; and Johnny; he's two. And there's the baby on mother's shoulder. Father Tom was determined he was going to name her, and if he had it would have been something awful; he has a weird sense of humor. We all call her Rosebud, because that's what she is, aren't you, Rosy? But she was baptized Mary. Lots better than Polyhymnia, don't you think? Isn't it, Rosy?"

The baby opened her toothless mouth in an ecstatic smile and held out her dimpled arms to Poly. The soft fluff on her head was rosy gold and she did indeed have the look of a tiny, perfect bud. Looking at the baby and the other children Adam felt a pang of envy: it would have been nice to have brothers and sisters.

"Not now, Rosy," Poly said. "Mother, may I take Adam out to the lab to daddy?"

"No, Poly, let Josh do it. Come help María get some lunch ready."

"But Josh already is *in* the lab."

"We'll just point it out to Adam, then. It's not very difficult, Pol."

For a moment Poly scowled; then she took the baby from her mother, holding it up and gently rubbing noses, which apparently delighted Rosy, who crowed with soft laughter.

"Come, Adam," Mrs. O'Keefe said. "I'll show you the way."

The bungalows, the boy realized, formed three sides of a square, with the fourth side a cement sea wall. The center bungalow contained living room, dining room, and kitchen. The right arm was bedrooms, the left the lab. Through all of the rooms the salt sea wind blew, and the sound of the slow breakers was a constant background. Adam left the living quarters and walked through the breezeway into an enormous cluttered room; it had the messy maze of tubes, retorts, pipes, files, bottles, acid-scarred counters with which he was familiar in Old Doc's lab, and the same smell of the sea beneath and around the acrid odors of chemicals and Bunsen burners. One wall was lined with tanks, and Dr. O'Keefe and Joshua were looking soberly into one of these.

Adam cleared his throat. "Dr. O'Keefe—Josh—"

The men turned from the tank, which Adam could now see contained two lizards. The sunlight was caught and reflected in Dr. O'Keefe's hair, in the brilliant blue of his eyes. Joshua might be able to slip, unnoticed, in and out of a crowd. Dr. O'Keefe would always stand out. Now he smiled at Adam, and his smile had much of the open warmth of Poly's. Adam realized that up to this moment he had seen the older man only at night, only when his face had been pulled tight with anxiety.

"Adam. Good to have you back with us." He made no reference to the Avenida Palace, to Adam's disobedience. "This afternoon I'll show you the setup of some of our experiments, and how you can help me with correlating. Too near lunchtime now, and I'm hungry. Take him for a quick swim, Josh, while I clean up, and after we've eaten we'll set to work." It was a suggestion, but it was also an order.

Joshua looked at him sharply. "Macrina?" he asked.

Dr. O'Keefe gave a barely perceptible nod of assent.

*

11

*

"My bathing trunks are in my suitcase," Adam said.

"That's all right," Joshua told him. "There are plenty in the bathhouse. Come on." He led the boy through the big room, into a smaller room, also lined with tanks, and then into a cement-floored room with several showers in stalls. A pile of bathing trunks lay on a wooden bench. Bottles of solution and extra lab equipment were stored in corners.

"Help yourself," Joshua told Adam, sorting through the bathing suits and coming up with zebra-striped trunks. "My favorites. Aren't they repulsive?"

Adam took a pair of plain navy trunks, disregarding several violent-looking outfits.

Joshua laughed. "One of the native bath attendants at the hotel is a friend of the cook's. Whenever someone leaves the island, forgetting his trunks—bathing suits, too, for that matter —he brings them over to us. It's very handy."

They emerged from the dim coolness of the bathhouse onto a cement ramp leading to the sea wall, into a blast of sunlight. At the wall stood Poly, in a faded red woolen bathing suit which clashed with her hair.

"Hi!" she called. "I thought maybe you'd take Adam for a

swim before lunch and I didn't want to miss out. What about
. . ." she paused and looked questioningly at Joshua.

Joshua nodded. "Your father said yes."

"Oh, good! May I call her?"

Joshua sighed, looking troubled. "Of course. She comes better for you than for the rest of us."

—I have no right to ask questions, Adam thought. He
jumped off the sea wall into the deep sand which burned
against the soles of his feet so that he hurried, stumbling, across
the beach to the damp, hard-packed sand cooled by the waves.
Poly was already splashing through the shallow breakers; she
threw herself down and started to swim, diving under the waves
until she was beyond the pounding of the surf. Adam and
Joshua followed. Adam had spent much of each summer in the
water, but he had to swim almost to the extent of his energy to
keep up.

"Is this okay?" he called to Joshua as Poly continued to
cleave her way swiftly and cleanly through the water, out toward the open sea.

"Yes," Joshua called back. "Poly's not allowed to go out this
far alone, but she's a natural swimmer and this is as safe a section of beach as you'll find anywhere. They've had trouble with
sharks at the hotel, and with undertow, too." He dove under
the water, sending up a stream of bubbles.

After a few more yards, Poly stopped, rolled over onto her
back and floated for a moment, catching her breath, then
started to tread water. She glanced back at Adam, as though
about to say something, then seemed to change her mind.
Looking out to sea she began to make a series of strange,
breathy noises, which she repeated over and over again.

"Look." Joshua pointed out toward the horizon.

Adam thought he saw a flash of silver, then another flash.
Then there was the unmistakable joyous leap of a dolphin, coming in toward them.

"Watch," Joshua said.

The dolphin came, leaping through the air, plunging into
the water, leaping again, until it had almost reached them.

Then it swam directly toward Poly, who swam to meet it with a glad cry. "Macrina!" She, too, seemed to leap out of the water, and then she was flinging her arms about the dolphin in the same way she had greeted Joshua and Adam, and the two of them were rolling over and over together, splashing, Poly shouting, the dolphin making a high-pitched whistle that was a greeting as radiant as Poly's own.

The dolphin started swimming in a slow, graceful circle, with Poly swimming beside her. "Show me your flipper," she commanded.

Obediently the dolphin rolled on its side, waving a sleek, wet flipper. It was a perfectly ordinary dolphin flipper, but Poly kissed it with exuberance, crying, "Oh, Macrina, darling, you're wonderful!"

For a moment Macrina seemed to nuzzle up to her. Then she leaped in a great shining arc and plunged under the water out of sight. It was evidently her goodbye because Poly turned away, back toward Adam and Joshua.

"Does he know about Macrina?"

"Not yet," Joshua said.

"I don't know a *thing* that's happened since Adam went to sleep in the Ritz," Poly complained. "Every time daddy talked to you on the phone he went out to the lab and wouldn't let me come in. He wouldn't even let me talk to Father Tom."

"You're a very inquisitive child," Joshua said. "We'd better swim in now, Poly. You know your father doesn't like to be kept waiting for lunch."

"But isn't anybody going to tell me anything?" Poly wailed.

"Adam's done practically nothing but sleep," Joshua said. "Come on, race you."

It was a close race, Joshua first, then Poly, last Adam. Poly grinned in satisfaction at beating him. "You swim very well, Adam," she said condescendingly, standing on one leg in the shallow water, shaking her wet hair out of her eyes, then jumping up and down to get the water out of one ear.

"That, my dear Miss Polyhymnia O'Keefe," Joshua said, "is

how to lose friends in one easy lesson. When you're a few years older you'll know better than to beat a young man in a race."

"Like Diana with the golden apples," Poly said. "'Come on, kids, I'm starved."

In the bathhouse they showered, sluicing off the salt, then dressed, still half-wet. Poly and Joshua were filled with such gaiety that Adam found himself relaxing, thinking, —If Dr. O'Keefe asks me about opening the door I'll tell him.

He could not feel, bathed in Poly's and Joshua's high spirits, that there could be any danger here.

As they went in to the central section of the house Charles was standing in wait, calling, "*Hurry,*" and they went directly to the dining room. The dining table was round and the rest of the family was already seated, Johnny in a high chair, and Rosy nearby in a playpen. Mrs. O'Keefe called Joshua to sit at her right, and Adam was taken in hand by Poly who pulled him into the chair by her. Dr. O'Keefe said grace, and then Mrs. O'Keefe and Poly got up and served lunch, helped by a tall, lithe woman with straight black hair and dark skin. The meal consisted of an enormous tureen filled with tiny shellfish, still in their shells, bits of meat and sausage, and the broth in which it had all been cooked.

"One of María's specialties," Mrs. O'Keefe said. "Peggy, how about getting us a couple more bowls to put our empty shells in?" She watched after the little girl, who went to the sideboard and brought two blue bowls to the table. "Joshua, when are you leaving?"

"Low tide."

"About eleven tonight, then. So we can get in some singing before you go."

Joshua laughed. "If Adam can stay awake. I've never seen such a man for sleeping."

Poly defended Adam quickly. "But he was *tired,* Josh, he hadn't had any sleep for three nights."

For a moment there was an uncomfortable silence. Then the phone rang. María looked inquiringly at Mrs. O'Keefe, who said, "It's all right, María, I'll get it," excused herself, and went into the living room, returning to say, "It's for you, Adam."

"But—" Adam started in surprise, pushing back his chair.

"It's Carolyn Cutter," Mrs. O'Keefe said.

"Oh." Adam stood up. "Excuse me." He went into the living room and picked up the phone.

"Adam," came Kali's light, high voice. "I've come to Gaea for a few days, and I'm at the hotel. Isn't that splendid?"

"Yes," Adam said, politely.

"Adam, you don't sound glad to hear from me."

"Well, I am." But he was not.

"Are you where we can talk? I mean are you private or are you surrounded? If you're surrounded just say yes."

"Yes."

"I thought so. Your voice sounds all funny and closed in. Do you think you could escape and come over to the hotel for dinner tonight?"

"I just got here," Adam said, "so I wouldn't think so."

"I was afraid of that. Don't worry, Adam, it'll be all right."

"What will?"

"Everything. I do know it must be awful for you. Come tomorrow night, then. I'll have daddy call and make it all proper and everything. We can't talk now, so I'll say goodbye." Without waiting for him to reply she clicked off.

Adam walked back to the dining room and sat down again, murmuring, "Excuse me."

"I don't like that girl." Poly offered him an orange from a bowl in the center of the table.

Mrs. O'Keefe shook her head, warningly. "You don't know her, Poly."

"I've met her at the Embassy when I've been there with Joshua. I don't like her."

"Poly." Her father looked at her sternly.

"Oh, okay, I'm sorry, but I don't. What did she want, Adam?"

Mrs. O'Keefe said, "If she'd wanted to tell you, no doubt she'd have called you to the phone instead of Adam."

"She wanted me to come to the hotel for dinner tonight."

Poly wailed, "But you're not going!"

"Poly!" Dr. O'Keefe said.

"No, of course I'm not, Poly. Not my first night here."

"Well, thank goodness. I'd have gone green with jealousy."

Dr. O'Keefe rose. "Ready to come to the lab, Adam?"

"Yes, sir." The boy excused himself to Mrs. O'Keefe and followed the doctor out.

In the big lab Adam sniffed hungrily at the odor of fish and chemicals and burning gas in the Bunsens, for there was safety for him in this smell. It was home, it was comfort, and it was, for the moment, escape from confusion. In this familiar room the decisions he had to make would be about what went on in the tanks of starfish, and not choosing between spiders and teddy bears, or between two groups of people, both of whom seemed convinced that they spoke for the American Embassy and therefore for America.

Dr. O'Keefe sat down at a large and ancient rolltop desk. The sunlight struck his hair, firing it. The eyes that looked at Adam were the clear and open blue of the sky. There was, in the smile, the warmth and welcome Adam had come to respond to and to love so quickly in Poly.

Dr. O'Keefe looked around the lab, at the tanks of starfish, at the scarred working counter. "It's a good lab," he said. "I've learned a lot here. I'm sorry to be leaving."

"Because of the hotel?"

Dr. O'Keefe leaned back in his creaking chair. "Yes. This will be our last summer here. It's time to move on." He took up a pipe and filled it slowly. "Sit down."

Adam perched on a rather wobbly stool and waited while Dr. O'Keefe lit his pipe, drawing on it thoughtfully, as though thinking what to say. In the tanks the water murmured and there was the occasional scrabbling sound of an animal moving around.

"We came to the island," Dr. O'Keefe said at last, "because it was, at the time, one of the few places left in the world where I could bring up my family and work undisturbed. We've almost finished what we came for. What we have to do now is to finish it quickly and get out in time."

"In time?"

"When the resort hotel was built here about a year ago it wasn't just because the world is running out of new playgrounds, and it wasn't just one of Typhon Cutter's business ventures—though, as usual, it's been a successful one. It was largely—no false humility here—because of me. Everything I've done in this lab for the past months is now open knowledge." Adam looked at him in a startled way, and Dr. O'Keefe explained. "Therefore everything that's done in this lab is nothing that couldn't have been done by any scientist anywhere in the world: China or Russia, for instance. The important part of my work is neither kept nor recorded here. All right, Adam, enough for now. Let's start you on the tanks and what's going on in them. Your job is to take care of the tanks and keep the daily reports."

Dr. O'Keefe pushed back his chair which gave a loud and protesting squeak. Adam followed him to the first tank in which were several perfectly normal-looking starfish. "Funny," Dr. O'Keefe said. "Here we come from the same family tree and we know so little about these creatures. Presumably," he gave a wry smile, "they know as little about us. Somewhere, a few billion years ago on the evolutionary scale, we chose to develop in different directions. I wonder why?"

"Well," Adam remembered unwillingly his interview with Typhon Cutter, "I suppose Darwin would say it was survival of the fittest and stuff. And mutations."

"Just happenstance?"

"Well, in a way, sir. We developed the way we did because we began to use our forepaws as hands, and stood up on our hind legs."

"Just by accident?"

"Well, I don't know, sir. Dr. Didymus used to talk a lot about free will and making choices and stuff."

The doctor nodded, then pointed to the starfish in the tank. "Do you know how one goes about working with them?"

"Well, it's not easy, sir, because if a starfish feels that an arm is being hurt or threatened in any way he drops it and grows another. So if you want to work with starfish you have to put an anaesthetic solution in the water."

"Standard procedure, yes, and where we've made our first changes. Now, what happens to an isolated arm that drops off?"

"It can't regenerate. There always has to be a piece of central disc, or the starfish can't regrow."

"So one wonders, doesn't one, what is in the central disc that isn't anyplace else? What would your idea be?"

"Well, sir, Dr. Didymus says it's been shown that nerve is very important in regeneration."

"Right. So what we have been doing is taking nerve rings from around the mouth of the animal and transplanting them to isolated arms."

"Wow!"

"Not so spectacular. Not even a very new idea. But it works."

Adam looked not at the starfish in the tank but at Dr. O'Keefe's face, his own face reflecting the doctor's interest and excitement. "What happens?"

"The arm produces its own central disc, and after about four months the familiar five-rayed form is back again. Look. The starfish here have all developed from arm fragments. Perfectly normal, ordinary starfish."

"Wow," Adam said again.

"They've been here a year and we'll continue to observe them until we have to leave the island. You *do* see the implications of all this?"

"Well, yes, sir. If it could be applied to people—"

"Yes. But not too soon. The dangers are so horrifying they hardly bear thinking about. If unscrupulous men got hold of this it would be like letting loose the power of the atom for devastation, for death instead of life. The tiniest thing in the world is the heart of the atom, and yet it's the most powerful. What we are learning from the starfish is just as powerful, and, like the core of the atom, can be either destructive or creative. Misused—it could be like dropping the bomb on Hiroshima." He moved on to the next tank. "Here we transplanted nerve rings about three months ago and you can see that regeneration is well on the way. In this tank we started two months ago but you can see that the starfish is going to grow, that life is going to win. Now here in the first tank you might think nothing is going to happen, but if you'll look carefully you'll see that regeneration has begun."

Adam stared eagerly into the tanks, his excitement at what Dr. O'Keefe was saying pushing the thought of Kali's unwelcome phone call out of his mind. "Why hasn't anybody done this before?" he asked.

"I'm sure other scientists have. Now here in these tanks are frogs and lizards. It's quite openly known that augmented nerve supply stimulates arms to grow on frogs and legs on lizards. The files are here, and I'll show you the file not only for each tank, but for each animal, and it will be your job to keep these up to date daily."

"Yes, Dr. O'Keefe."

"This kind of work interests you, doesn't it?"

"Yes, sir. It excites me more than anything in the world."

"But the exciting things always have implications that we don't foresee. Always, Adam."

"I wish they didn't," Adam said.

"As Poly would remark, if wishes were horses, beggars would ride. Poly has the makings of a scientist, and she's been working with me on this all along. As a matter of fact, I have to keep her out of the laboratory. It's better right now for Poly to help my wife than to work with me here, so I seldom allow her out here until after the younger ones are in bed."

"Is that why she was kidnapped?" Adam asked.

"Because she knows what I'm doing? Yes. But also I think the idea was to use her as a hostage. Then, when you opened that door at the Avenida Palace something new came into the picture. You became more important than Poly. At least this is my guess." He looked at Adam, but Adam looked down at his feet. Dr. O'Keefe sighed.

Adam, still looking down, mumbled, "But you said that none of this was really secret."

"It's not. Most of my lab isn't in a building at all. What's done in here is only the beginning, the going back and working out reasons and proofs. It's the other things, the things that are not here, that are really important. Did you see Macrina when you went swimming?"

"The dolphin? Yes, sir."

"She'll almost always come for Poly. Poly's greatest talent is for loving. She loves in an extraordinary way for a twelve-year-old, a simple, pure outpouring, with no looking for anything in return. What she is too young to have learned yet is that love is too mighty a gift for some people to accept."

"Does she—does she love *every*body?" Adam asked, rather desperately.

The doctor laughed. "As you may have noticed at the table Poly is quite capable of dislike, reasonable or no. Being judgmental is something she knows she has to fight against. But when Poly loves, it simply happens. She loves her family, all of us. She loves Tom Tallis. She loves Joshua. And she loves you, Adam."

At last the boy looked directly at the older man. "Sir. I love Poly, too."

Dr. O'Keefe returned the gaze. "Do you, Adam?"

"Yes, sir. I don't quite know why. And I don't—I don't have any idea why she would love me. She was—she was in my care when she was kidnapped. I was responsible for her."

"We don't blame you for what happened. Tom says he didn't warn you properly."

"But I was responsible," Adam said. "And I failed. This is why—"

"Why what, Adam?"

Adam looked down and spoke in a low voice. "Why I didn't obey you when you told me not to open the door. Sir. I am very confused."

Dr. O'Keefe put his hand on the boy's shoulder. "All right, Adam. I think you'll do."

"Do for what, sir?"

"Let's just say that I don't think you'll ever betray Poly."

"Dr. O'Keefe, if you ever needed to trust me with her again—if you ever would—I wouldn't fail again."

Dr. O'Keefe nodded. "Yes. I believe you. But you know that I can't trust you with her now, don't you?"

"Why, sir?"

"You must know why, Adam."

"Sir," Adam said, "just let me have a few days to sort things out. If I can just work here quietly in the lab for a while—if nothing here is really secret then I can't hurt Poly or you or anybody else, can I? If I can just get a few things straightened out in my own mind . . ."

"All right. We'll have to let it go at that."

Again the boy looked directly at the older man. "This Carolyn Cutter—"

"What about her?"

"She wants me to have dinner with her at the hotel tomorrow, since I said I couldn't tonight. She's going to have her father call you or Mrs. O'Keefe about it. But if you'd rather I didn't I'd be glad not to."

Dr. O'Keefe shook his head. "No, Adam. If you want to make up your own mind, you'll have to make it up, won't you?"

12

Adam stayed in the laboratory the rest of the afternoon. He worked with happy concentration on tank and file: here was work he knew; here was safety. He was loath to leave when Dennys, changed to clean shorts and shirt, came to call him.

After dinner the two babies were put to bed. The rest gathered in the living room, Sandy, Dennys, and Peggy in their night things. Poly and Charles were staying up to see Joshua off.

"May we sing until time for Josh to go?" Poly asked.

"It's a must," Joshua said, his arm lightly about Poly's waist. "What first?"

"The Tallis Canon, of course, so Father'll know we're thinking of him. You start, Mother."

Mrs. O'Keefe leading, they sang it in canon, one voice coming in after another.

> All praise to thee, my God, this night
> For all the blessings of the light.
> Keep me, O keep me, king of kings
> Beneath thine own almighty wings.

Poly's voice finished alone, light and clear, and full of trust. Adam remembered, unwillingly, the empty washroom on the plane, and thought of Poly drugged, gagged, dumped roughly onto a pile of luggage. He was grateful when Mrs. O'Keefe started the gay "Arkansas Traveller." From this they went into a conglomeration of familiar hymns, madrigals, folk songs, even Bach chorales. Adam had played the guitar at school parties and he knew the bass to much of the music. Joshua and Dr. O'Keefe were both tenors, so he was a welcome addition.

"You're absolutely wonderful, Adam," Mrs. O'Keefe said. "I'm sick and tired of singing bass an octive high. If Old Doc had only told us you could sing it wouldn't have mattered whether you could work in the lab or not. How about 'Come Unto These Yellow Sands'?"

During the singing Peggy, nightgown trailing, came and sat in Adam's lap, at first a little rigid, as though not quite certain of her welcome, then relaxing softly against him, her head on his chest, her breath coming more and more slowly until Adam realized she was sound asleep. He put his arm around the small, warm body, almost afraid to sing lest he disturb her, then relaxing and singing fully. Across the room Joshua, sitting with Poly, smiled at him.

Just as Adam began to feel that he must shift his position, and knew that he didn't want to move, despite his discomfort, for fear of waking Peggy, Mrs. O'Keefe rose and came over to him, saying, "Will you carry her to bed for me, please, Adam? Come on, boys, time for bed."

Adam stood up with the sleeping child. He realized that all evening he had been happy, he had forgotten about Kali, he had felt only pleasure in the children and in the music. He did not want the peace of the evening to end. He did not want Joshua to fly back to Lisbon.

But when the boy returned to the living room Joshua said, "You're coming to see me off, aren't you, Adam?"

"Well, sure."

"I put some riding clothes in your room. Same source as the bathing suits."

Dr. O'Keefe laughed. "It's really not as bad as it sounds. We do make every effort to get the things back to their rightful owners. We'll be waiting for you outside."

Mrs. O'Keefe stayed home with the younger children. Adam set off with the doctor and Joshua, who were both riding stocky, golden-brown horses which Joshua told Adam were an island breed. Poly was on an elderly bay who seemed enormous for her, but was obviously gentle and reliable; Charles rode a shaggy pony, and Adam himself was given a large, white, matronly looking beast, apparently first cousin in disposition to Poly's bay.

The night was bright with a three-quarter moon, and the horses moved softly along the damp sand at the edge of the water, their hoofbeats almost silenced by the slow, steady sound of the sea. Against the dunes fireflies glittered. Poly rode beside Adam. In the moonlight the brilliance of her hair was turned to silver. She sat, tall and erect, her height making her seem more than her twelve years. Ahead of them rode the doctor and Joshua; Charles led the procession, a solitary, small figure. The two men were talking and their voices, though not their words, were blown back on the wind.

"Daddy wants to talk to Josh," Poly said, "and I can see he'd rather I didn't listen. And Charles is in one of his hermit moods. I want to talk to you anyhow. Josh and I went for a long walk this afternoon while you were in the lab working, and he didn't tell me one single thing."

"About what?"

"About anything. Adam, I know children are not supposed to be curious, but life isn't as simple as that any more, and I *am* twelve, and after all, I *was* kidnapped."

Adam's sense of relaxation vanished; he felt himself stiffen in the saddle. "Yes, Poly, you were."

"Well, then, don't I have a right to ask a few questions? I don't think Joshua thought I did. Had the right. I mean, it was okay for me to ask *him* questions, even if he wouldn't answer any of them, but I got the idea that he didn't think it was all right for me to ask *you* questions. Why?"

Adam looked not at Poly but at the moonlight dazzling the surface of the ocean. "I'm not quite sure," he said at last.

"Then is it all right if I *do* ask you some questions?"

"You can ask me anything you want to," Adam said, "though

I may be like Josh and not be very good at answering. But how about letting me start off by asking you a few things first?"

"Of course." She was so willing, the face she turned to him in the moonlight was so open, that Adam winced.

"Poly, on the plane, when you went into the washroom, you were afraid, weren't you?"

"Yes."

"Why?"

"Father Tom had told me it wasn't safe for him to keep me with him."

"Why?"

"Because of the pa——" she stopped herself. "Because they'd know I was daddy's daughter. And they know I know about what daddy's doing."

"About starfish regenerating their arms?"

"Yes."

"But that's not a secret, Poly. Your father said himself that he was sure other scientists were doing the same experiments."

Poly leaned over her horse with a caressing gesture, putting her head down on its neck. After a moment she sat up straight in the saddle again. "But it's more than that."

"What is it, then?"

"Didn't daddy tell you?"

"He doesn't trust me," Adam said starkly.

"But Adam—"

Adam's voice was savage. "He has every right not to trust me."

"I trust you," Poly said.

It was all Adam could do not to kick his heels into his horse's ribs, to gallop away. He growled, "You're much too trusting for your own good."

"Oh, I don't go around trusting everybody, the way Peggy does. I'm not that much of a child. I know there are people in the world you *can* trust, and people you can't."

"How do you decide which is which?"

"You know with people, or you don't. I don't trust that Kali. I wish you weren't going out to dinner with her."

"So do I."

"Do you have to?"

"Yes, I think I do."

Back in the brush an owl screeched, a shrill, terrifying cry. Poly shuddered. "And I didn't trust the steward on that plane. He was weasely."

"When you went to the washroom—were you afraid of being kidnapped?"

"Not exactly. I didn't really know what I was afraid of. After all, I'd never been kidnapped before. But I guess it was really sort of in the back of my mind."

"You're sure it was the steward who put you in the canvas bag?"

"Adam, if you're kidnapped you don't forget the person who kidnaps you."

"But did you really see him?"

"Yes. I was washing my hands, and I heard the knob of the door turn, but I'd locked it, so I didn't expect it to open. But when it did I saw him in the mirror. He put his hand over my mouth before I could scream. He was so much stronger than I am, in spite of being weasely, that I couldn't even make a noise fighting. And then he put that stuff over my nose and got the gag on me and got me in the sack." She began to tremble.

"I'm sorry," Adam said. "I'm truly sorry to have to remind you of it. Will you let me ask you just a couple more questions?"

"If you need to."

"I do need to. I wouldn't do it to you otherwise, I promise."

Poly gave an oddly grown-up laugh. "Don't sound so agonized, Adam. It's all right."

"Well, what about the steward," Adam asked, almost savagely. "Is he just floating around loose? I mean, he might try to come here or something."

"Really, Adam." Poly sounded impatient. "You must think daddy's very careless or something. Interpol went right after him."

"Have they got him?"

"Yes. Last night. Father Tom called from Madrid."

"But—"

"I don't want to talk about it. I don't want to think about it. It's all over." Tension tightened her voice again.

Adam sighed. "I'm sorry. Just one more thing. When you got to the house, they took you right out of the sack?"

"Yes."

"Who took you out?"

"I don't know, Adam. Don't think Josh and daddy haven't asked me this one over and over again, too. I was still groggy and it was so dark in the room all I could tell was that it was a man, and I couldn't really tell about him, because at first I thought he was terribly fat, and then I felt one of his arms, and it was skinny."

It was Adam's turn to shiver. The moon rode placidly in a cloudless sky, the stars dimmed by the brightness. The sea, too, was calm, the waves rolling in gently, rhythmically. Up on the dunes the grasses and the great wings of the palms were almost still, though the fronds made their incessant scratchy whispering. The air was warm and they rode without sweaters or jackets. But Adam shivered.

Poly looked over at him. "He gave me something to drink. I told you that. And it put me back to sleep. And then, later on, whenever it was, when I was awake and it was all dark and horrible and I was frightened and the door was locked and I started to cry, that man came in—"

"Which man?"

"You know, Adam, I told you at the Ritz, the man who drove us, that beast. And then he blindfolded and gagged me and put me in the car and I knew he'd hurt me if I tried to cry or do anything. And then there I was in front of the Ritz, and you were there, too, and you held me, and I knew it was all going to be all right."

In front of them Adam could see Dr. O'Keefe and Joshua talking quietly, their horses close. Charles was still in the lead, sitting up very straight, a stocky shadow on his little pony. A firefly flew across the beach from the dunes, lit for a moment on Charles's shoulder, then disappeared into the moonlight.

"Adam," Poly said, "why haven't daddy or Josh told me anything about you?"

"I don't know."

"How did you happen to be there on the sidewalk? Were you in the car, too?"

"Yes."

"Were you kidnapped, too?"

Suddenly, almost without his volition, Adam's heels kicked and his horse broke into a trot. He kicked again. The horse started to canter.

As he came up beside Joshua he called out, half choking, "It was Carolyn Cutter I opened the door to!"

He pulled the horse up. Joshua dropped behind, then came up on Adam's other side, so that the boy was riding between the two men. Dr. O'Keefe, at the water's edge, was looking straight ahead, not at Adam, not even at the small figure of Charles placidly riding along a few yards in front. Adam turned toward Joshua who smiled at him brilliantly but did not speak.

Behind them there was a thudding, and Poly's bay came ambling along with what was obviously all the speed it considered suitable. "*Hey!*" Poly called.

"I'm sorry," Adam said. "I have to talk to your father."

"Poly," Dr. O'Keefe said, "go ride with Charles, please."

"But Charles wants to—"

"You don't need to talk to him. Just go ride beside him."

In the moonlight Adam could see Poly glower. But she responded obediently, "Yes, daddy," and trotted the large, disapproving bay so close to the water's edge that an incoming wave rippled against its protesting hooves. Charles turned to her and spoke, at which Poly flung her arms up in the air in an abused fashion and trotted the bay around the pony so that the little boy could be next to the water.

"All right, Adam," Dr. O'Keefe said quietly. "And then she took you to her father."

"You know?"

"Yes. But you had to tell us yourself."

Joshua turned to Adam. "Had you ever seen Carolyn Cutter before you met her in the airport in New York?"

"No."

"How did you happen to speak to her there?"

"I suppose," Adam said slowly, "you might say she picked me up. But it all seemed perfectly natural. What with the fog and everything and planes being canceled and flights deferred, all kinds of people were talking who wouldn't have if everything had been perfectly ordinary."

Dr. O'Keefe asked, "Was it just casual chitchat between you?"

"No. She warned me about—about Canon Tallis. And about you, sir."

"Warned you about what?"

"Well—not anything particular. Just a warning in a vacuum. I don't think I really took it very seriously at first. It all just seemed kind of exciting and an adventure."

"And you thought she was attractive?"

"Yes, sir."

Joshua reached over and patted the neck of Adam's horse, as though in this way he could communicate comfort directly to Adam. "And so she is. So when she knocked on the door . . ."

"She told me she'd help me find Poly."

"You believed her?"

"Well, Josh, I *did* find Poly. She was there, at the Cutters' house."

The older men exchanged glances, and Dr. O'Keefe said, "Yes, Poly's description of the man in the dark room could hardly have been of anyone but Typhon Cutter. But we had to be sure. Now, Adam, will you go back to the moment you opened the door and tell us in as much detail as you can everything that happened until you and Poly were put out of the car in front of the Ritz?"

"Yes, sir. I'll try. But I *was* terribly tired, so I may not get it exactly right. I'll do my best." He looked out over the ocean.

The moon made a wide, shining path from water's edge to horizon. Carefully he tried to tell the two men the events of that night that seemed far more than three nights behind him. In spite of the fatigue that had kept him from thinking clearly or acting reasonably his accurate memory again helped him, bringing the events and words of that night up from his subconscious. He looked at the bright swathe of moonlight on water and recalled small details he hadn't even known he remembered, or that, up to this moment, he hadn't remembered. He saw again with his mind's eye the black-and-white room, saw the obesity of Typhon Cutter's body in such repellent contrast to the thinness of arms and legs; he saw again the extraordinary beauty of the young man in the portrait, the young man who had grown into a middle-aged spider.

"If you didn't know it was the same person—how *could* anyone change so completely?"

"The odd distribution of weight is glandular," Dr. O'Keefe said, "but I don't think it's as simple as all that. He also reflects all the choices he has made all his life long."

"Why," Adam asked, with the abruptness with which he had asked it of Typhon Cutter, "why did Canon Tallis lose his eyebrows?"

For a moment the strained look tightened Dr. O'Keefe's face again. "It was in Korea. He not only withstood torture himself, but he helped the men with him to stand up against it. This was what left the greatest mark on him, not his own suffering, but the pain of others."

"Adam," Joshua said, "when we didn't know where Poly was, and then when we didn't know where you were—if he'd had any hair left it would have turned white."

"Stop, Joshua," the doctor said quietly. "Don't make this any harder for Adam than it is already. Go on, boy."

"Yes, sir." He sighed deeply, unconsciously, talking in a voice so low that several times he was asked to repeat himself. Finally he said, "I think that's about it. I'm glad I've told you. But I think I have to tell you that I'm still confused. I'm still not certain or secure about anything."

Again Joshua patted Adam's horse, saying softly, "That's all right, Adam. Who is?"

"So of course I won't have dinner with Kali tomorrow night. I don't ever want to see her again."

Dr. O'Keefe spoke quietly but firmly. "But I'm afraid you'll have to. When you opened that door to her you started a chain of events for yourself that you can't end quite this easily."

Ahead of them Poly called out, "There's the plane!"

Charles's clear voice came, "Race you!" and his little pony tore across the sand. Poly's bay broke into a resigned trot.

The plane lay on the beach ahead of them like a strange, prehistoric bird in the shadows. Again Adam felt a sense of irrational panic at the idea that Joshua was going to leave. Charles reached the plane the pony's length ahead of Poly. They dismounted and walked their horses over to the softer sand where there was an old barnacled pile that could be used as a hitching post. Dr. O'Keefe turned to the children, leaving Joshua and Adam side by side.

"Adam—"

"Yes, Josh?"

"Feel better?"

"I don't really know."

"You will."

"Okay, if you say so."

"Not if *I* say so. But you will. Even though it's not going to be easy."

Adam set his jaw stubbornly. "I will not have dinner with Kali tomorrow night. I will not have anything more to do with the Cutters."

Joshua spoke tranquilly. "Oh, yes, you will."

"I will *not*."

"Listen," Joshua said, "I'll bet you anything you like that you will."

"I wouldn't put money on it if I were you."

"I'd put more than that on it. When I whistled the Tallis canon you said you'd sung it in choir."

"Till my voice changed."

"I was going to say something, but I'm not. Instead—did you ever hear Tom Tallis use a kind of password phrase?"

"Yes. In Madrid. Twice."

"Recognize it?"

"No. It was poetry, that's all I could tell."

"Yes. Robert Frost. *Two Tramps in Mud Time*. A simple sort of little poem it starts out to be, with the poet out chopping wood and two tramps coming along and resenting it because he's doing for fun what they figure they ought to be paid for. Then comes the last stanza, whammo, a lower cut right to the solar plexus.

> *But yield who will to their separation,*
> *My object in living is to unite*
> *My avocation and my vocation*
> *As my two eyes make one in sight.*
> *Only where love and need are one,*
> *And the work is play for mortal stakes,*
> *Is the deed ever really done*
> *For Heaven and the future's sakes.*

I'm not sure about heaven, but I do feel I have to do my best for the future, and if you're any kind of scientist you will, too. And if that means going out with Kali tomorrow you'll do it."

Adam still sounded stubborn. "As far as I'm concerned, Carolyn Cutter is the past."

"Listen, you told us tonight because of Poly, didn't you?"

Adam sighed again. "I really don't know why I told you. I don't know why anything any more."

"It was Poly," Joshua said with certainty. "At least it would have been for me, and I'm willing to bet it was for you. Adam, I don't know about you, but I can't do anything except because I care about people, because I love people. I can't do it for love of God, like Tom Tallis, or for heaven's sake, as Mr. Frost said. But because I love people I have to act according to it—to the fact that I love them. Maybe this doesn't make any sense. But it's the way I am, and you'll just have to accept it."

Adam said softly, "The way you accepted me?"

"I failed you on that this morning, didn't I? I wanted to push you too far, too fast."

"Don't push me now, then," Adam said.

"Touché. But I have the feeling that there isn't much time. That I don't have the time to give you time. Okay, kid, come on, it's time I shoved off."

13

Adam, Poly, and Charles stood at the hitching post while Joshua and Dr. O'Keefe checked the plane. When all was in readiness Joshua climbed into the cockpit; as the motor coughed and the propeller began to spin, making the little plane vibrate as though it must fall apart, the doctor came and stood beside the horses, a little away from Adam and the children. The plane wheeled and moved slowly across the sand, gathered speed, bounced once or twice, and then began to climb.

"Sir," Adam asked, "is that plane really safe?"

The doctor laughed. "Doesn't look it, does it? But yes, as safe as the latest jet. Particularly with Joshua piloting it."

They watched the plane as it gained altitude, flying, it seemed from where they stood, directly along the path of moonlight on water, flying further, higher, smaller, until it lost the reality of being an elderly, battered Hawker Hurricane piloted by a young man, and became a silver bird in the night flying to the moon.

Standing beside Adam Poly let out a low, startled cry. "Charles! Don't!"

Adam turned and saw in the moonlight that Charles's face was contorted in a vain effort at control, that tears were silently squeezing out of the tightly closed eyes and down the little boy's cheeks.

Dr. O'Keefe knelt on the sand in order to bring himself to the child's level. "Charles."

Without opening his eyes, Charles moved into his father's arms.

Poly stamped. "I *hate* it when Charles cries."

"Charles," Dr. O'Keefe said again.

Poly whispered fiercely, "He *never* cries unless . . ."

Adam asked, "Unless what?"

"Unless something is awfully . . . wrong."

Charles stood, leaning against his father, still crying silently. Finally he said in so low a voice that Adam could hardly catch the words, "I wish Josh hadn't gone."

Dr. O'Keefe's voice was quiet. "He'll be back in Lisbon almost as soon as we've had time to ride home. He has a good tail wind and the weather is clear all the way."

"Will he call when he gets back?"

"He always does. And I will come in to you and tell you. I promise. He has no important papers on him this time. I have to correlate and code everything he brought me. Come, now, Charles, it's late and you're tired and we must go. You'll ride with me."

Obediently Charles mounted his pony.

Dr. O'Keefe and the little boy led the way, Joshua's horse ambling along just behind them, with Poly and Adam in the rear. They did little talking. Poly was frowning, seeming unduly disturbed, Adam thought, by her brother's behavior. After a while she began to droop in the saddle, saying, "I'm half asleep. Pick me up if I fall off."

Ahead of them both Dr. O'Keefe and Charles sat straight and still and somehow stern. The moon moved across the sky.

As they neared the bungalows Adam saw that someone was standing on the sea wall, waiting, and for a moment fear leaped into his throat, but Dr. O'Keefe raised his arm in greeting.

"It's José, María's husband," Poly said. "He takes care of the horses."

They went directly to bed. As Adam drifted into sleep he heard the phone ring, and then he heard Dr. O'Keefe pause outside Charles's door. "That was Josh, Charles. All's well. Go to sleep now."

In the morning Adam was wakened by Poly coming in with a breakfast tray. His room was flooded with light and warmth and he felt a sense of pure well-being he had been afraid would never return.

"Sit up, lazy," Poly said. "I let you sleep as long as possible. I'm not spoiling you. Breakfast in bed is one thing we always do. I'm going to take Charles his tray and then I'm coming back to talk to you."

Adam grinned at her. "Okay. Forewarned is, I hope, fore-armed, though I have only two."

Poly turned at the door. "And the starfish has five. You will have exactly time to wash your face and stuff. *If* you hurry." She made a quick exit, and Adam heard her say, "Move, Sandy."

"Does Mother know you're bothering Adam?"

"She said I could ask him, and *he* said it was okay." Their voices continued in friendly argument as they went into the living room.

Poly returned, saying, "Daddy's out in the lab. You're to go on out as soon as you're ready. Then I'll come for you a little before lunch and we'll go for a swim."

Adam poured hot milk, hot coffee. "Will we see—what's her name?"

"Macrina? Yes. If she comes."

"Doesn't she always?"

"Usually. But not always. Then, after lunch, we'll take you to the village."

"What village?"

Poly sat, crosslegged, on the foot of Adam's bed. "The native village. Where María and José come from."

Adam said, rather uncomfortably, his mouth full of croissant, "I don't have to be taken sightseeing, Poly. I've caused enough trouble for all of you already. I'd really rather stay in the lab and work."

Poly frowned, then gave him a stern and piercing look. "It's not sightseeing, Adam. I assure you that's not our purpose in taking you there."

"Are you going too?"

"If daddy'll let me. He usually does." She got down off the bed. "Okay. I'll come over to the lab and yell for you when it's time for our swim."

When Adam went out to the lab Dr. O'Keefe was sitting at the rolltop desk, writing, but he looked up at the boy's step, saying without preamble, "I want to show you something." He took Adam into the small side lab and to the first of the tanks. In it was a starfish in the process of regeneration. It was not a starfish with part of its own central disc; it was an isolated fragment of arm into which Dr. O'Keefe told Adam he had transplanted nerve rings as he had done with the starfish the boy had already seen. The difference between the starfish in this tank and those in the main lab was that this starfish was not developing normally. This particular combination of arm and nerve ring seemed to be generating into a strange, lumpy, three-armed creature.

Without speaking Dr. O'Keefe moved to the second tank. Here was a lizard who had lost a leg. Something was growing where the leg had been; it was not a lizard leg, but a deformed stump. In the third tank was a frog who had lost a forearm; this, too, was growing back abnormally.

Dr. O'Keefe went into the main lab, sitting down at his desk. Adam stood, waiting. For some time Dr. O'Keefe appeared to study a pencil. Finally he said, "Back in the early sixties scientists were able to start babies, actual human foetuses, in a test tube. For a while they developed normally. Then, and no one knew why, their development went awry. They became deformed; monstrosities. You've probably heard about this."

"Yes, sir."

"Why did this happen?"

"I don't know, sir. I don't think anybody does."

"Why is regeneration a normal thing for starfish? Why, if we transplant nerve rings from the central disc can an isolated arm fragment then organize itself? Why is this also true of frogs and lizards?"

"Well, it's because the augmented nerve supply provides the stimulation."

"Why were the animals in the little lab developing abnormally?"

"I don't know, sir. Mutations?"

"In a very small percentage, yes. But usually, no. Where do you think I get my experimental animals from, Adam?"

"Well, from the beach, from around here . . . I used to collect specimens for Old Doc."

"Yes. The children find a good many for me. They bring me any animal they see, marine or land, that has been injured. The villagers bring me some, too, for which I pay them one escudo for twenty-five specimens. I made it absolutely clear that they were to bring me only the animals that had been accidentally hurt. Then, after the first abnormalities began to develop, I learned that two of the men who work at the resort hotel had been deliberately mutilating the creatures. I had thought that the smallness of the payment would avoid this, an escudo being three and a half cents, you will remember. But it didn't. There always have been and there always will be people who have been corrupted into enjoying any excuse for cruelty."

For some reason Adam thought of the Cutters' chauffeur. He could quite easily imagine Molèc tearing the arm off a lizard.

Dr. O'Keefe continued. "It is from these deliberately mutilated animals that the deformities have come. But it isn't even that simple. I had, for a brief while, a lab assistant who was a brilliant man. He was also one of the most evil human beings I have ever encountered. Every animal he tended, every starfish arm into which he transplanted nerve rings, every frog or lizard into whose wounds he injected augmented nerve supply, developed malformations that were malignant and that devoured the creature on which they grew."

"Why—" Adam asked, "why was he evil?"

"You remember the story of the Third Man?"

"Yes. Josh mentioned it."

130

"Antibiotics diluted and sold on the black market, and innocent children suffering and dying through this incomprehensible greed. This kind of thing doesn't happen only in fiction. You don't have to read the book or see the movie to come across it. This man, with a brilliant and utterly warped mind, grew fat on underworld black-market corruption."

"Then why did you employ him, sir?"

"I was asked to. In order to convict him."

"Did you?"

"With Joshua's help."

"What happened?"

"He's in Leavenworth."

Adam said, slowly, "So I guess this kind of thing makes enemies?"

Dr. O'Keefe looked at him. "They *are* enemies, Adam. You don't have to *make* enemies of them."

Adam got his stubborn look. "But what about Poly?" Dr. O'Keefe did not answer, and Adam continued. "If you didn't— if you didn't *make* enemies, I mean, even if they *are* enemies anyhow, then would anybody have wanted to hurt Poly?"

The older man's face tightened. "Nothing is easy, Adam. Nothing. And we're all of us in danger from the moment we're born. You've grown up in New York. You know that if you cross a street a truck can run you down. If you ride in the subway and there's a spot of trouble a bullet meant for someone else can find its way into your heart. And if my research, which I had anticipated as a quiet and hermit-like life, so that I could bring my children up in a peaceful and natural way in the midst of an unpeaceful and unnatural world, has, instead, led them into added dangers, then I must accept this for them, as well as for myself, if I believe in what I am doing."

"I'm sorry, sir. I didn't mean . . ."

"That's all right. I just want you to understand clearly why it is so important that what I am doing does not get into the wrong hands. Remember the deformed babies that came of thalidomide being used before enough was known about it?

We're just at the very beginning of this, and it cannot be taken out of our hands and misused."

"It's like what you said about the atom?"

"Yes. Like splitting the atom. We're just beginning to learn why the regeneration is sometimes abnormal and malignant. We're just beginning to understand that you cannot change stones into bread. This is not the way miracles are worked, but it's always been a temptation. If what we are doing is taken over by the unscrupulous it can cause unimaginable horror and suffering. Here is power to give life to people, or to devour them. What I am trying to do is to go back about two thousand years in my thinking. Somewhere in the last two thousand years we've gone off. When we began to depend on and to develop *things* in the western world we lost something of inestimable value in our understanding. There's something wrong about trying to heal with a surgeon's knife. There's got to be an alternative to cutting and mutilating and I'm trying to learn it from the starfish. But I'm just at the beginning. And I'm afraid, Adam. If it gets out of my hands—I'm afraid." Dr. O'Keefe clenched his fist and pounded it softly against the papers on his desk. Then he smiled. "All right, Adam. I have work to do here at my desk. You get along with your job until Poly comes to take you for a swim."

It was several minutes before Adam could concentrate on his care of the tanks, but, as he began to put the day's observations down in the files, the discipline of the work took hold of him, and he was able to keep his mind on the job at hand. This was a task that fascinated him, that engrossed him utterly, and he was surprised when he heard Poly's voice and realized that the morning had passed.

Poly stood in the lab, wearing a black two-piece bathing suit that did nothing for her still undeveloped figure.

"Daddy," she asked, "what are the specifications for a fashion model?"

"Oh—thirty-four, twenty-two, thirty-four," Dr. O'Keefe replied absently.

Poly signed. "Oh, dear. I'm twenty, twenty, twenty."

Her father laughed. "I really think you look better in the red wool, even if it does fight with your hair."

Poly sighed again. "Yes. Okay. I'll change, while Adam's getting into his trunks. Mother says time will take care of this particular problem, and I suppose it will. Was mother gorgeous when she was my age?"

"Frightful," Dr. O'Keefe said. "Much worse than you."

"That's encouraging, at any rate. And I suppose it's a good thing about time, because right now I'd have an awful time choosing between Adam and Joshua, even if Josh *is* too old for me."

Her father laughed again. It was a good laugh, warm and open and loving. "Time seems to be making its inroads already. A few weeks ago you were announcing that you were never going to grow up."

"Oh, I'm over being Peter Pan. Maybe it's jealousy. Knowing that that Kali has her hooks into Adam. Come on, Adam, let's go. I told María I'd be back in time to help serve lunch."

It was another golden day, the sand was gold; gold shimmered from the sun into the blue of the sky, touched the small crests of waves in a calm ocean. Adam and Poly swam out, side by side, until Poly stopped and began to tread water, making the strange, breathy whistling noise that was her call to the dolphin.

It was longer this time; Poly's calling began to sound tired, and Adam had given up and was just about to suggest swimming back, when silver arched out of water in a swift flash, and Macrina came leaping, diving, flying, to meet them. Again there was the ecstatic greeting, Poly with her arms about the great, slippery beast, Macrina giving her marvelous, contagious dolphin smile, so that Adam felt that he was grinning like a fool. After a while Macrina left Poly, came over to Adam and gave him a gentle, inquisitive nudge. For a moment he was frightened. He knew that dolphins were friendly and gentle, that sailors rejoiced at seeing them because they kept away sharks, but Macrina was so large, so alien, that it was all he could do to make himself keep treading water quietly, and to say, "Hello, Macrina."

Macrina nudged him again, then flashed out of the water, dove, disappeared, and came up on Poly's other side.

"She likes you!" Poly cried joyfully. "Macrina, show Adam your flipper."

As she had done the day before, Macrina obediently rolled over and waved her sleek, wet flipper.

At last Adam realized. "The flipper—" he said. "Did she—"

Stroking Macrina, Poly nodded. "Yes. We don't know how it happened. I found her on the beach, flipper torn off, bleeding to death. I ran and got daddy, and he was able to stop the bleeding. Of course we didn't know her then, but she seemed to know that daddy and I wanted to help. Daddy has some big tanks in the village. They're not in a building; the village is around a cove, and there are some pens in the cove. Luckily Father Tom was here, and he helped, and we managed to get her to the village and into one of the pens. Daddy and Father Tom stayed with her all night. As a matter of fact, we could hardly get daddy away for weeks, he ate there with Virbius, he's their chief, and I guess you'd call him their medicine man, too, he's a hundred and forty-nine years old, and he prayed over Macrina and it all worked, the augmented nerve and stuff, and isn't she marvelous and good and beautiful and virtuous and wonderful?"

Macrina rolled over in the water and smirked.

"Okay, Macrina," Poly said. "We've got to go in to lunch now, I promised María. Give my love to Basil and Gregory."

"Basil and Gregory?"

"Her brothers. They're very intelligent. Of course dolphins are, but we think Macrina's family is more so. It's quite obvious they are, isn't it?"

Macrina waited for no further goodbyes. Down, down she dove, and then, a hundred yards away, Adam saw her flash through the air.

"By the way," Poly said. "While you were in the lab that Kali's father called and talked to mother. They're sending the hotel helicopter for you at seven-thirty. I don't know why daddy wants you to go there for dinner. I think it's just awful. But I suppose if he wants you to go you'll have to go."

"Yes." The pleasure ebbed from Adam's limbs. "If he wants me to I have to."

Poly stopped treading water, rolled over onto her back, blew a jet of water upward like a small whale, and floated. "Promise me one thing."

"What?"

"Don't go without saying goodbye to me. I have something to give you, and you *mustn't* leave without it. Promise."

"Okay," Adam agreed. "I promise. What is it? A charm?"

"No," Poly said. "A weapon."

14

After lunch José brought three horses around to the bungalow, and Dr. O'Keefe, Poly, and Adam set off for the village, riding uphill to the plateau with the monolithic slabs of stone. As Joshua had stopped by the great central table the day before, so did Dr. O'Keefe, although he did not dismount. Poly and Adam reined up beside him. Adam's spirits soared, despite the fierceness of the sun.

The doctor was sitting erect on his horse, as though waiting. He caught Adam's inquiring gaze and said, "Virbius, the chief of the village, wished to meet us here. Visitors aren't encouraged there. The people from the hotel have brought only disease and trouble. But you are under my aegis, and he will escort us."

Adam nodded. Dr. O'Keefe continued to sit straight and tall, and Poly was in one of her rare silent moods. Adam looked around, at the great stone table, above which a large golden butterfly was fluttering. The flash of a bird's scarlet wing led his gaze beyond the encircling stones and through the trees that edged the plateau and into a clearing. In the clearing were a few small, white slabs, with light moving over them, and leaf shadows, green, mauve, and indigo.

Again Dr. O'Keefe followed Adam's gaze. "Yes. It's a cemetery. A small one. The villagers have their own, and if anyone does anything as inconvenient as dying at the resort hotel they're whisked back to the mainland as inconspicuously as possible." He held up his hand for silence, and they could hear a rustling in the brush. A yellow-and-black bird flashed across the clearing, followed by a wizened old man on a horse, a dark and shriveled old man, with a few strands of soft, silvery hair. Adam had no doubt that this was Virbius, the chieftain. Poly had said that he was how old? a hundred and forty-nine? Adam knew that the villagers' way of counting time was probably different from the way he had been taught in school, but if Virbius was not a hundred and forty-nine he was certainly the oldest man Adam had ever seen, far older than Old Doc, who, after all, was ninety.

Dr. O'Keefe raised his arm in greeting; Virbius responded, the gesture full of dignity despite the fact that his hand was tremulous with age. Without a word he turned his horse and headed into the brush again. Dr. O'Keefe followed, with Poly and Adam in single file behind him on the narrow path.

They rode through the low brush along the spine of the plateau; the sun was high and hot, so that their shadows were small dark blobs moving along the scrub. Somehow Adam was grateful for the golden warmth that seeped through him, even though his shirt began to cling damply to his body. The blue, almost cloudless sky was so high that there seemed to be between earth and sky a golden shimmering of sunlight. The red of Dr. O'Keefe's and Poly's hair was touched with gold; gold, gold, everything glinted and glimmered, and light as well as heat penetrated Adam's pores.

He had lost track of time (would time ever seem normal, countable, accountable, to him again?) when the path started to descend. Below them lay the straw roofs of the village, the large central hut, with smaller huts raying out from it, the whole village on a promontory about a perfect, natural bay. In the bay fishing boats were anchored, and Adam thought he could see others, small dark specks out at sea. While they were still a fair distance above the village Virbius stopped his horse, raised his arm, this time in a gesture of command, and let out a strange, penetrating whistle. For a moment all the activity in the village seemed to cease, suspended in time. Then women and children scurried into huts; men, who were working on up-turned fishing boats, on spread-out nets, moved leisurely but definitely away, disappearing either into the thick jungle growth that edged the village, or into the huts.

Poly turned back to Adam. "Don't be hurt; it's just because it's your first time here. They have to make sure. They've been so abused by the hotel people."

"Poly," Dr. O'Keefe said without turning.

"Sorry, daddy," Poly said.

Virbius started forward, his horse moving slowly, carefully, on the last, steep downward grade. As they came into the village Adam saw that each hut was surrounded by a profusion of flowers that seemed to grow wildly; but, remembering his mother's garden on the Cape, he had a suspicion that they were carefully tended. The fishing boats were large, heavy shells, reminding him of pictures he had seen of Phoenician vessels. All were painted with strange emblems. The most startling boats were stark black or white with prows which reared sharply upward and on either side of which were painted two very wide-open eyes.

Virbius led them directly to the waterfront, to the harbor. He raised his hand and two small boys came running to him, appearing, it seemed to Adam, out of nowhere, to take care of the horses.

A long T-shaped wooden dock let out into the water, and Virbius, moving slowly and stiffly, his great age more apparent than it had been while he was mounted, led the way, keeping always a few paces in front of the others. Ahead of them in the water Adam could see what he realized must be the pens Poly had told him about. As they reached the T at the end of the dock Virbius beckoned to Poly, pointed to one of the pens, and began to speak to the child. Adam stood beside Dr. O'Keefe, looking into the pen in which a dead shark floated. It had obviously been wounded, not by another fish, but by some kind of weapon; a long knife, judging by the wounds. A strange odor came from the water which Adam guessed was something to disguise the smell of blood, and the water itself was murky.

Virbius' words sounded like gibberish with a touch of the Portuguese soft *ssh* and *jjh* added. Poly, head cocked, listened, frowning with concentration. "He says that this is the same shark that attacked Temis." To Adam she explained, "Temis is one of Verbius' great great grandchildren, Adam. Last night the shark attacked one of the children right here in the harbor, and one of Virbius' nephews went after him with a knife and drove him into the pen. The child is all right; his wounds are healing cleanly and there will be only a scar on one leg to show that anything happened. They did everything you told them to about the shark, daddy, but the shark has died. Virbius says that he has prayed neither for nor against him, but that it is justice. The shark died this morning and they only kept him for you to see."

From the dock Dr. O'Keefe took a pole with a large hook and pulled the dead beast in. Then he squatted down at the edge of the pen and examined it carefully.

Virbius had moved along the dock and was standing beside the next pen. Adam followed him. Here the water was a brilliant, clear green, with purple shadows. A small school of tiny fish flashed by in a swoosh of silver. At the bottom sea plants moved, their green, white, rose fronds undulating in a sinuous dance. Swimming ponderously in the pen was a large and extremely cross-looking tortoise. His head was stretched out on the leathery neck to its full length, and he glowered and blinked. Adam could see that one of the four legs had been almost, or perhaps entirely, torn off. It was healing neatly. The turtle turned his head toward Adam, put a scornful nose in the air, and then, with an indignant gesture, retired completely into his shell.

Poly shook with laughter. "He's the snootiest animal I've ever come across. Macrina's fond of him, so I suppose he's all right, but he has no manners whatsoever."

Adam was surprised to hear Virbius let out a thin, dry cackle of amusement as he moved on to the next pen. In this was a shark whose dorsal fin had been ripped off in some kind of marine battle. Small, ugly lumps were appearing where the fin had been.

"Of course we don't *get* many sharks," Poly said, "but we've never had one regenerate normally. I can't even be sorry for them and Josh says I'm a fool about all animals. But not sharks. I hate them. I would far prefer to meet a sting ray coming around a corner, and *they* look like bats out of hell if any beast ever did."

Dr. O'Keefe moved up to join them. "I'm very pleased about the turtle, bad manners or no. One of our most exciting successes has been a sea-gull wing. We would never have managed that without Virbius. While the bird couldn't fly it was all right, but he wanted to use his wing too soon, and only Virbius could control him."

Virbius spoke, and again Poly translated. "He says his gods are very powerful, and they gave him some of their power."

Virbius spoke again, spreading out his hands.

"He says it was the way Father Tom's God gave him of His power the night he stayed up with Macrina. Virbius says they must be good friends."

"Who?" Adam asked. "Canon Tallis and Virbius?"

"No, silly," Poly said impatiently. "Their gods."

Virbius nodded. If he spoke nothing but his own native tongue he understood, Adam guessed, almost everything that was said. And if he understood English it was more than likely that he also understood Portuguese. Adam realized that the old man was no one to underestimate. As a matter of fact, he reminded the boy in many of his mannerisms of a combination of Old Doc and Mahatma Gandhi.

There were two other tanks which were presumably empty at the moment, because neither Virbius nor Dr. O'Keefe went to them. Virbius led the way back up the dock to the village and to the green clearing in front of the central hut. Around the hut and climbing up its walls were flowers of every shade of blue, and Adam noticed that none of the other dwellings had blue flowers; there was every color of red, orange, yellow, but no blue. Virbius squatted down, beckoning to Poly to sit on his right side, Adam on his left. Dr. O'Keefe sat crosslegged opposite the old man.

From the central hut came a woman and a child, a girl perhaps Poly's age, perhaps younger. They bore coconut bowls which they set down in front of the visitors. Poly gave a warm, welcoming grin to the child, which was equally warmly returned, but neither of them spoke.

Virbius raised his hand for silence, although no one was speaking, then bowed over his coconut bowl, murmuring in his native tongue and swaying slightly from side to side. He took the bowl, raised it over his head in a gesture of offering, then sipped from it. Dr. O'Keefe raised his bowl in a similar gesture, and Poly and Adam followed suit. Adam did not know what it was they were drinking; something strange and cool and sharp.

Virbius beckoned to the child, who squatted down on the grass in front of the old man. Adam decided that she was definitely younger than Poly, although already more developed physically. She had straight, lustrous black hair, and a dark skin through which a golden glow seemed to shine, as though she had caught and contained the light in which the island was drenched. She smiled at Dr. O'Keefe, who smiled back, a smile of both compassion and joy. Virbius spoke and Poly translated.

"It is all right?"

Dr. O'Keefe nodded. "Tell them that Josh brought back all the lab reports Father Tallis got in Boston. Everything is perfectly normal."

As Poly spoke the child raised one golden-brown hand, looking wonderingly at the five outstretched fingers.

Adam turned to Dr. O'Keefe.

"Yes. This is Temis, the child the shark attacked six months ago. Her body was badly slashed, and one of her fingers was severed."

Beside him Adam heard a strange sound and looked to see that Virbius was crying, tears rolling unchecked down his wrinkled cheeks. Putting one hand on the child's shoulder the old man stood up, then raised both arms heavenward, calling out in a loud voice. With the tears still streaming he turned to Dr. O'Keefe and embraced him. There were tears in Dr. O'Keefe's eyes, too. Temis stood quietly, smiling.

Poly said to Adam, "We were sure it was all right, but it's good to have all the lab work say so, too. When the shark attacked Temis, Virbius called daddy. I've never seen daddy so upset. He said he wasn't ready, that it wasn't time. The body would heal; that wasn't the problem; it was the lost finger. You couldn't say: let's try, there's nothing to lose. There'd been the deformities. And there'd been the—the horrible malignancies. Father Tom came, and he and Virbius and daddy sat up all night, and then daddy said they'd try. Father Tom stayed to help. He never left Temis, he and daddy and Virbius. And then it happened, Adam, it happened, and it's all right, and Temis has five fingers again." Her eyes filled. "But Adam, if it hadn't been all right—if the new growth hadn't been natural—if it had devoured Temis the way it has some of the animals when things haven't gone right—" she choked and stopped.

Her father took her hand. "Hush, Poly. It's all right." He said to Adam, quietly, "Poly's anguish during this time was making her ill. As soon as we were sure that everything was going as we prayed it would, Tom Tallis took her away with him. The trip to Boston was to take slides and X-rays to a zoologist there, but served as a needed change for Poly, too. When you landed in Madrid instead of Lisbon and had to be bailed out of the airport things were complicated, but Tom managed to get the reports to one of our friends, who in turn got them to Josh. So, in spite of a little unexpected confusion, we have all the final lab reports and clearances."

"And it's all right!" Poly cried, joy driving the tension from her face. "It's all right!"

Dr. O'Keefe said heavily, "Through the grace of God it's all right. I know now that I know nothing, and many men think that I know everything, and this is where the danger lies. If only we had more time—"

Virbius said something, and Poly translated for her father,

"He says that time is a dream, but that his gods and Father Tom's are awake."

Dr. O'Keefe put his hand for a moment on the old man's shoulder. Then he and Virbius bowed in silent farewell, and the doctor moved quickly away. Adam and Poly followed him, and as they walked away from the harbor and the village the two little boys came up with the horses, which had been watered and rubbed down.

They rode in silence. The sun was beginning to move toward the horizon. The long fronds of the palms rattled in the evening breeze, their shadows like great, dark birds. Adam's white horse blew gently through her nostrils and her flanks lifted in a patient sigh. But to Adam it was as though everything were bathed in light, as though the golden sun of the island had at last penetrated the darkest reaches of his mind.

He understood now. All the pieces had fallen together to make a clear and unmistakable picture. He knew why he was important to Mr. Cutter, why anybody even remotely connected with Dr. O'Keefe would be important to all the Mr. Cutters. And he knew why the Mr. Cutters of the world must never be allowed to see Dr. O'Keefe's papers, particularly Dr. O'Keefe's papers on Temis. Unconsciously he heaved a sigh less patient than the old white horse's.

" 'Smatter?" Poly asked.

"Nothing. I just wish I didn't have to have dinner with the Cutters this evening."

But it seemed there was no evading the dinner. When they got back his good suit had been pressed and was laid out on the bed with a clean shirt and his most colorful tie, a rather splotchy blue-and-red affair that Adam called his 'Jackson Pollock.'

Mrs. O'Keefe told him, "María chose the tie, so if you don't mind wearing it, Adam, it would make her very happy."

"As long as you think it's okay. I'm kind of fond of it."

He dressed carefully, but more to please María and the O'Keefes than Kali. He would have liked to go to Kali in his lab clothes, already slightly stained, and a symbol of his work, and somehow also a symbol of where he stood. But this, he realized, would be a rather Don Quixote sort of gesture, and not very effective.

Shortly before time for the hotel helicopter to come for him Dr. O'Keefe summoned him to the laboratory.

"Adam, you are probably wondering why I want you to have dinner with the Cutters tonight."

"Well, sir, I suppose maybe it would be wisest if they didn't know I'd made up my mind. I mean, it might be a good idea if they think I'm still willing to work for them."

The doctor looked at him with approval. "Exactly. I hate to ask you to do this, Adam. It's going to be difficult for you. One of your most evident qualities is a direct honesty, and prevarication of any kind isn't easy for you. However, there is an urgent and immediate need for this. Once the results of any experiment are in I have to get them off the island as quickly as possible. The papers on Temis are finally complete. I don't have to tell you how important they are. All the lab reports from Boston are in code, and I will now double code them. This will take me about a week. There is only one man—and he's in Lisbon—who can break the code so that they can get from the Embassy to Washington. During this week I'll keep the real papers on me and leave others, indicating another experiment, in the lab. Josh took a set of these phony papers with him and will be careful to see that the right—or wrong—people get hold of them. Now we come to the problem of getting the Temis papers to Lisbon. Joshua, of course, has been courier many times, but now it's safe neither for him nor the papers. I've used María once, José twice, but it's not fair to ask them again. The Ambassador himself has been errand boy on occasion. Next week it will have to be you. If you can make Cutter think you're willing to play along with him because you think he's right, then you'll be under less suspicion than anybody else. I don't think anything has been discovered about Temis, and it must not be." He stopped, repeated slowly, "It must not."

"I know, sir."

"So I want you to make a date with Kali in Lisbon. I'll give you some papers to give her. They'll look legitimate, and they'll follow the ones I'll appear to be working on this week and that Josh took back to Lisbon with him. We'll talk later about getting the real papers away. The point is that tonight you must appear to be still confused about me: you are *not* confused any longer, are you?"

"No, sir." Adam's voice was firm and confident.

"Let Typhon Cutter do his emotional patriotic act for you. It's very effective."

"Yes, sir. He's already done it. It—it *did* confuse me."

"All clear now?"

"Yes, sir."

"You understand what I am asking you to do?"

"Yes, sir." Adam swallowed. "It will kind of make up for—"

"Not to make up for anything. That's over and done with, and no real harm, thank God. You're doing this for the future."

"*For Heaven and the future's sakes?*" Adam asked softly.

Dr. O'Keefe nodded. "This is where Joshua has been so remarkable. His love and need *are* entirely one. And while the work has been play for him he has been well aware of the mortal stakes. *Only where love and need are one, and the work is play for mortal stakes, is the deed ever really done for Heaven and the future's sakes.* Think of Joshua tonight if you like. You couldn't have anybody better to follow." Above them they heard a loud droning; Dr. O'Keefe remarked, "They're very prompt," and stood up.

The helicopter dropped clumsily to the beach in front of the bungalows. Poly, running with the other children to say goodbye, called, "You'll get sand in your shoes."

"It'll shake out," Adam answered.

Barefooted, she caught up with him, gently shoving Peggy ahead and saying, "Run look at the helly, Pegs." She whispered to Adam, "I have what I told you I'd give you. Here. Just pretend you're holding my hand."

Charles asked, "What're you whispering about?"

Poly stamped her bare foot against the sand impatiently.

"Charles. Please. Oh, do run get Johnny for me, quickly, and let me say goodbye."

"Adam's just going out for dinner," Charles said, but he went after Johnny who, fully dressed, was heading for the water.

Adam put his hand around Poly's firm, thin one. "What is it?"

"Adam, have you ever seen a switchblade?"

"Yes," Adam said, smiling. "Is that what you're giving me?"

Poly scowled darkly. "You're condescending to me."

"I'm sorry; but if it's a switchblade I don't want one and I don't like the idea of your having one."

Poly shook her head impatiently so that her red hair flew about her face. "Okay, I know you coped with gangs on the streets of New York and all that jazz. This isn't an ordinary switchblade."

"What's extraordinary about it?"

"It looks like a switchblade and it works like a switchblade—I'm taking this on hearsay because I've never actually used one. But it's really a kind of hypodermic needle."

"Poly, for heaven's sake—"

"There's a channel in the blade filled with MS-222."

"—what do you expect me to do with it, use it on Kali?"

Again Poly pawed the sand. "She'll probably ask you to go for a moonlight swim, and there have been sharks at the hotel beach this summer, though they won't admit it. I wouldn't put it past that Kali to send you straight into a shark's jaws, and daddy says MS-222 is still the best thing; it knocks them out right away. When the blade is released the capsule of MS-222 is punctured and it goes right in, so you don't have to aim for a vital spot or anything. It's on a belt, and it looks just like an ordinary knife. It's quite flat, so you can wear it under your bathing trunks. You've got them with you, haven't you?"

"Yes. Your mother told me to bring them along."

"Which ones?"

"Just the plain navy ones, Pol. I guess I'm not uninhibited enough to wear the wild ones the way Josh does."

"You promise me you'll wear the belt with the knife?"

Adam knew that he could not hurt Poly by laughing at her intensity. "Well, I don't really think Kali wants to dispose of me. But thanks anyhow, Pol."

Poly pulled at his jacket sleeve. "Promise me you'll never go swimming without it."

"Even when I go with you?"

"Not with me, goosey. Macrina keeps the sharks away. But anywhere else. Promise."

"But, Poly—"

"*Promise.*"

"All right."

Poly heaved a great sigh of relief. "Okay. I know I can trust your word. Goodbye. I suppose I'll be in bed when you get home. I don't really want you to have a good time but I'm going to be polite and tell you to have one. But it's just courtesy. So have a good time." She turned and ran back to the bungalows, not standing on the sea wall to wave and watch him off as he had expected her to. The other children called and waved, and Adam waved back, but he found himself looking beyond them for Poly.

The pilot was Portuguese, and if he spoke English he kept it a closely guarded secret. Adam was glad for the minutes of silence: no, silence was certainly not the word, for a helicopter is a noisy bird, but for a time of not having to listen to new ideas, of not having to respond.

As they landed on the flat roof of the hotel Kali was waiting and came running to meet him. She flung her arms around him, whispering, "Adam, help me, help me. I've been all wrong about everything. I know now that daddy's doing things that aren't—that aren't right. Adam, what am I going to do?"

15

Before Adam could make any response to this outburst Kali whispered, "Here comes daddy. Hush."

Typhon Cutter looked even more like a spider than Adam remembered. It seemed incredible that this obese mass with the stringy appendages could possibly be father to the beautiful girl at his side. Then the boy remembered the portrait of the angelic young man and wondered if Kali could ever be anything but young and radiant and lovely.

She pressed her fingers quickly against his, a gesture that was both intimate and warning. Adam did not return the pressure and her look flickered quickly over him like a flame.

"Of course," Typhon Cutter was saying, "all the rooms have balconies overlooking the ocean, and our guests, in a primitive setting, nevertheless have every modern convenience."

Kali explained, "Daddy's part owner of the hotel."

They walked through a rooftop bar and lounge, Typhon Cutter gesturing expansively with one thin arm. "I think our service can compare with any of the great hotels in the world. We'll stay up here and cool off before going down to dinner."

In the lounge, long windows opened to the terrace, and there were groups of comfortable chairs and couches around low tables. The walls were painted with lush murals of the native village, so glamorized that it was a moment before Adam recognized it. The mud and straw huts, the fishing vessels, the natural harbor, were all enlarged and garishly ornamented, and the natives themselves wore elaborate leis and looked more as though they came from a tourist's dream of Hawaii than a primitive island off the south coast of Portugal. In one corner of the room was a huge television set around which a group of young people was clustered. The volume was on high. Without looking around Typhon Cutter raised his hand and snapped his fingers, and a uniformed page went running over to the set and adjusted the dials.

At one of the low marble tables sat a solitary man in a dark suit. Adam could see only his back, but it looked somehow familiar.

Mr. Cutter turned toward him, saying, "Dr. Ball hopped over with us. His busy schedule doesn't permit him to get away often, but he's badly in need of the rest. We're flying him back tonight since of course he can't be away over Sunday."

Adam said nothing. Silence, as a matter of fact, was his plan of campaign: to look naïve and innocent and gullible (not too difficult, he realized ruefully); to be swift to hear, and slow to speak. He caught Kali looking at him anxiously, then glancing away as her father turned toward her. Adam felt a hot surge of resentment. He had enough on his hands without coping with a confused Kali. If she'd tumbled to the fact that her father was a stinker she'd have to work it out her own way.

Dr. Ball rose as they reached him, shook hands effusively with Adam, and kissed Kali. Adam found that he enjoyed this latter even less than the handshake.

"Dear boy," Dr. Ball murmured, lowering himself into his comfortable chair. "How delightful to see you again, and in less hectic circumstances than our first meeting. What will you have to drink?" He indicated his own glass.

—Get the prospective victim drunk or drugged, Adam thought. Aloud he said, "I'm not thirsty, thanks."

Kali put a hand lightly and briefly against his knee. "The bartender has Cokes. I'm going to have one."

149

Dr. Ball urged, "Do join us in our libation."

"Okay, a Coke, then, thank you." Adam realized that a uniformed boy was hovering by Typhon Cutter waiting to take their order. Mr. Cutter nodded at the boy, who went to the bar.

"Now, Adam," Mr. Cutter said, "when last I saw you we had reached a certain understanding, had we not?" Adam said nothing. "You did agree to help me, did you not?" Adam tried to look blank and made a slight gesture of his head that could have been interpreted either as affirmation or negation. An edge of impatience came to Mr. Cutter's voice. "I believe that I made it reasonably clear to you that I am in a position to be useful to the Embassy, and that I feel that it is my duty to my country to help out when I am called upon."

"Yes, sir," Adam said.

"You were understandably tired, but you did agree to help."

"Yes, sir. I would consider it my privilege to help them at the Embassy." This seemed to be a nice, double-barreled response, the Embassy, being in his mind, Joshua.

"Good." Mr. Cutter's voice spun upward, a high, thin, plausible web. "At that time—I am referring to the time of our first meeting—my men, in order to inspire your confidence and insure your cooperation, went to a great deal of trouble and not a little danger to rescue the O'Keefe child from the very organization to which her own father belongs! A great man, but you know how stupid scientists can be. I may say that I personally underwent danger: our enemies are ruthless, so ruthless, indeed, that they do not hesitate to use an innocent child, the child of one of their own members, for their purposes." He paused, waiting.

Adam knew that a further response was indicated here. "I've only been with Dr. O'Keefe a couple of days and everything's all secret and hush-hush around me. Just what *are* their purposes, sir?"

Now Dr. Ball leaned forward, his well-manicured hands spread out on the table. "You have spent these two days in working for O'Keefe, have you not, lad?"

"Well, yes, sir, but . . ."

"Are you aware of the nature of his experiments?"

"Well, to some extent, sir. I mean, I knew before I ever came."

Mr. Cutter asked sharply, "You have actually been working *with* the starfish?"

"Well . . . just cleaning tanks and simple jobs like that, so far."

Dr. Ball put his hand on Adam's knee. It felt heavy, and very unlike Kali's leaf-like gesture. Adam felt his skin crawling. He raised his eyes from the hand to the immaculate white dog collar to Dr. Ball's handsome, smiling face.

"Adam, dear boy," the doctor said, lifting his hand and passing it over dark, well-pomaded hair, "you do realize what O'Keefe is doing, don't you?"

"Well, yes, sir, working on the regenerative process of the arm of the starfish."

"In the starfish—" (—Dr. Ball sounded as though he were in the pulpit, Adam thought) "—and in certain other specified beasts, this is a perfectly natural thing. O'Keefe is taking it beyond the point of nature. But not only is he usurping the prerogatives of the Almighty, he is then allowing his work to get into the wrong hands, hands soiled with the taint of sin."

Adam tried to imagine Canon Tallis saying these words. It didn't work. He mumbled, "I'm afraid I don't understand."

"Un-American hands," Mr. Cutter said. "Hands that do not have their country or its economy at heart."

All Adam could think of at this point was that hands do not have a heart. He shook his head slightly to try to pull his thoughts together. This time he did not have lack of sleep as an excuse for not being alert.

The young waiter put two Cokes down on the marble table, a fresh drink for Dr. Ball, and a drink for Mr. Cutter. The bartender evidently knew, without being told, exactly what Mr. Cutter wanted. "Adam," Typhon Cutter said in his soft, tenor voice, "I am a very wealthy man. I admit to you perfectly openly that I enjoy my money."

Dr. Ball broke in, "But you are a generous man, a very generous man."

"That's not the point. I try to do what I can, of course, and if I have been able to be of some small service to you it gives me great gratification. Eliphaz—Dr. Ball—is on the boards of several hospitals and orphanages and old people's homes as well as attending meticulously to his regular parish duties."

—It's catching, Adam thought. —Even Mr. Cutter's beginning to talk in Dr. Ball's pompous pattern.

Perhaps Typhon Cutter realized this, for he cleared his throat before saying, "All I'm trying to tell you is that although I enjoy my money and the things it can buy, my country comes first. In fact, I love my native land so well that I am willing to live outside it, in voluntary exile, because in this way I am better able to serve. I've been asked by people who must remain nameless to find the results of Dr. O'Keefe's work and to get them into the hands of our own government before unscrupulous agents grab them."

"But, sir," Adam said, trying to sound innocent and reasonable, "Dr. O'Keefe is an American."

"Pink," Dr. Ball murmured, "tinged, alas, with scarlet."

Standard tactics, Adam realized. Accuse those who might well accuse you before they have a chance to get in a word edgewise.

"Adam," Mr. Cutter asked, "how much do you care about your country?"

"Very much," Adam answered with complete honesty.

"Would you make a sacrifice for it if necessary?"

"Yes, sir." Here again he could speak with the ring of truth.

Dr. Ball asked, "Do we have your word of honor that you are willing to work for your native land, no matter how difficult it may be for you personally?"

"Yes, sir." Adam added mentally, —and I'm quite sure that this doesn't mean working for you. It's Dr. O'Keefe who cares about the things you're talking about, not you. You're—you're nothing but a whited sepulcher.

Mr. Cutter put his glass down with a click. "When do you think you can get back to Lisbon?"

"Well—I—I think I could manage it next weekend." Dr. O'Keefe would have the Temis papers ready by then; it would be time for him to go.

"Make a date with Kali."

"Well, yes, sir, that would be my pleasure anyhow." Kali smiled at him and he managed to smile in return.

"Arrange to meet her on Friday. The hotel taxi service schedules a routine Friday morning flight. By then you should know more about O'Keefe's work. And, so that you have more than my word to go on that I have my country's rather than my own interests at heart, you may bring your information directly to the Embassy."

"Oh, good," Adam said with deliberate innocence. "I have a friend there. I could go right to him. Joshua Archer." He turned and smiled at Dr. Ball. "He's a good friend of yours too, isn't he?"

Dr. Ball forced a toothy smile. "Yes, indeed. Indeed, yes. But O'Keefe's work is too important to—if the Ambassador himself is busy we'll see to it that you talk to someone very close to him. This is nothing for mere underlings, no matter how delightful they may be. This is more than a patriotic duty, my son. It is also a very big opportunity for you. It may make all the difference in the world to your entire life."

"Yes," Adam said. "I know."

"Come to me at the rectory as soon as you reach Lisbon," Dr. Ball said. "Perhaps that would be easier for you than braving all those formidable secretaries at the Embassy."

Mr. Cutter rose. "I'll have instructions waiting for you at the rectory. We'll go downstairs for dinner. The air conditioner works passably well in the Coral Room. I don't know what they do with the air conditioners; must get an investigation going. I'll order some good American food; I imagine you're tired of these Portuguese messes. Drink up, Kali girl, Adam must be hungry."

The Coral Room, too, went in for murals. These, Adam gathered, were meant to be of Manhattan, though it was only a faintly recognizable Empire State Building that told him this.

The artist, if he had ever been to New York at all, had seen it last in the days of elevateds; one enormous wobbly structure ran right by what appeared to be the main branch of the Public Library, since there were two lions in front of a pillared building approached by an enormous flight of steps.

The fourth wall was French windows leading out to the tennis courts, the pool, and finally the ocean. Adam sat between Kali and Mr. Cutter at dinner, and across from Dr. Ball. Mr. Cutter ordered steak and French fried potatoes, and salad with Thousand Island dressing. "That all right with you, Adam?"

"Oh. Well. Yes, sir. Fine." Anything he could agree with legitimately was fine with him. There was no longer the slightest question in Adam's mind as to who was serving his country, Mr. Cutter or Dr. O'Keefe, and there had never been any question as to who was serving God, Dr. Ball or Canon Tallis. The critical moment Joshua had predicted had definitely been passed. There could be no more holding back. He had chosen sides, whether he liked it or not. At the moment he found to his immense surprise that he was liking it. A new kind of excitement surged through his veins. He felt tingly and alert from toes to fingertips, and ready to go.

There was only one hitch, and it was an unexpected one. Kali's anguished greeting had doubled all the complications. He knew that if Kali needed him he could not reject her plea for help. Joshua had said that his side cared about the fall of the sparrow; Kali, in her frantic cry as Adam climbed out of the helicopter, had become a sparrow.

But how to help her, he pondered, as he chewed his rather tough steak and kept one ear on the conversation. He tried to think what Joshua would do. Joshua would not turn away from anyone who needed him. That was the first thing. After that he would probably play it by ear. Adam only hoped that his ear would come close to being half as true as Joshua's.

What he must do now, he decided, was to manage to sound suspicious about Dr. O'Keefe when Kali was out of the room. He felt a surge of anger. This whole business about Kali was off the schedule entirely. He had written her out of his life except as the daughter of the spider, and here she was, a new and unwanted responsibility, and a sparrow instead of a spideress. Canon Tallis had put Polyhymnia in Adam's charge, and he'd muffed that one. Here, out of the blue again, he was being handed another problem, and this time he must not goof. He wondered if Dr. O'Keefe would have sent him off to dinner at the hotel if he'd known what was going to happen. Joshua, in playing by ear, seemed to have perfect pitch. Adam wasn't at all sure that he himself wasn't tone deaf.

After dessert he had the chance he was looking for. Typhon Cutter said, "Adam, we adhere to the rather old-fashioned custom of the gentlemen's lingering over the port for a brief respite after dinner. We'd be delighted if you'd care to stay with us. You can join Kali in a short while. I believe she has some idea of a moonlight swim."

"Thank you, sir," Adam said. "I don't think I'll have any port but I'd love to stay and talk if I may." Kali sent him a stricken look, and he added, "We'll have time for a swim, too, won't we?"

Typhon Cutter moved his ponderous head so that the folds of pink flesh rolled over his immaculate shirt collar. "Certainly. I've arranged for the helicopter to stand by to take you back whenever you're ready. There isn't any hurry, at this end, at any rate."

When Kali, reluctant and pouting, had left, and the port had been brought, "Sir," Adam asked, looking from one man to the other, "this Dr. O'Keefe—"

"Yes?" Typhon Cutter asked.

"Well, sir, Dr. Didymus, the man I worked for before, you know, he's no slouch, but he didn't—well—"

"Well, what, lad?" Dr. Ball asked in his gentlest voice.

"Well, sir, I know it's only been a couple of days, but all I've done is scrub the lab floors and clean tanks. I mean, junk *any*body could do. I haven't been doing things like that since I was in seventh grade. I mean, it's not Oliver Twist kind of stuff exactly, but it certainly doesn't challenge my *mind*, and he keeps the files locked, and I have a feeling . . ."

"A feeling?" Dr. Ball prompted.

"Well, that he doesn't trust me."

Dr. Ball said smoothly, "It's probably not personal, son. I don't think O'Keefe trusts anybody. And if a man trusts no man, then he cannot trust God."

"I've been very careful," Adam said. "I mean, I've been very discreet. I've just done my job, whatever he's asked me to do, no matter how silly. And I've kept my eyes open, so that I'm getting *some* idea of what's going on, whether he wants me to or not . . ." He paused, frowning slightly.

Dr. Ball raised one pale hand. "Under these circumstances, my son, do you think you *will* be able to get to Lisbon next Friday?"

"Well, yes, sir. Mrs. O'Keefe wants me to do some errands. I mean, shopping, knitting wool and stuff that absolutely anybody could do. And they did say something about the hotel plane. After all, I could have used my mind more if I'd stayed with Dr. Didymus in Woods Hole, no matter how old he is."

Typhon Cutter shifted position in his chair, the topheavy body swinging cumbersomely. "Don't worry. We'll give you a chance to use your mind."

"Yes, Mr. Cutter. I hope so."

"You know what your instructions are?"

"Yes, sir. I'll fly over to Lisbon on Friday, ostensibly to do some shopping for Mrs. O'Keefe. I'll manage to wangle permission to have a date with Kali to give me the extra time I'll need. I'm to go right to the rectory to Dr. Ball."

"How," Typhon Cutter asked slowly, "will the idea of a date with Kali be received?"

"Well, they *know* I like her, sir. After all, she *is* very attractive. I mean, any red-blooded American male . . . And after all, they gave me permission to come here tonight. I mean, it's not as though I were in prison or anything. It's just that the work I've been given seems kind of silly for someone with as much background in marine biology as I have."

Typhon Cutter poured more port. "A reasonable precaution on O'Keefe's part, isn't it?"

"Well, yes, Mr. Cutter, I guess it is."

"All right, Adam. You're a bright lad. Now's your opportunity to use that mind of yours. Keep your eyes and your ears open. You *will* be able to bring us some information, won't you?"

"Yes. I think so."

"Be careful not to arouse suspicions. What you don't accomplish this time can be done next, though we don't have all the time in the world. Remember that."

"I'll remember."

"If you want your swim with Kali we'll excuse you now. She'll be waiting in the lounge. Make your arrangements to meet her on Friday."

"Yes, Mr. Cutter."

Dr. Ball smiled again, rubbing his hands. "Be gentle and understanding with her, dear boy. She's a particular pet of mine."

"Yes, sir. It's been very nice to see you again." He turned with equal courtesy to Typhon Cutter. "It was a wonderful dinner, thank you, sir. Just the ticket." He shook hands with both men, first the steel grip, then the hail-fellow-well-met one.

"Until Friday," Dr. Ball said softly as the boy left.

Outside the dining room Adam breathed deeply.

So far so good.

16

Kali, already changed to a scanty black bathing suit and a white terrycloth beach robe, was waiting for him in the lounge. "Come on and I'll show you where to dress," she said. "We'll swim in the ocean, not the pool. I want to be sure we aren't overheard. Hurry up." She spoke quietly, quickly, nervously.

As Adam changed to the plain navy blue trunks he remembered Poly's gift. He took it out of the box and looked at it, a canvas belt with a holder for what looked like an ordinary knife. He took the knife carefully out of the sheath and inspected the mechanism for triggering the blade. He couldn't check the blade for the vein filled with MS-222 without releasing both blade and chemical, but it looked as though it would be perfectly simple to manage. Although Adam had never owned a switchblade he had seen several, and he knew how they worked.

He shrugged and put the knife and belt back in the box. If he wore the belt Kali's keen eyes might spot it, and the evening was complicated enough already. He did not worry about needing the knife; Poly was an imaginative kid, still frightened from the kidnapping experience, and Typhon Cutter would hardly allow Kali to swim in dangerous waters.

Then, with his hand already on the doorknob, Adam swung around and went back for the knife. At the corners of his mind he felt that something was wrong with the evening. It seemed as though he had done exactly what he had set out to do, but he had an uncomfortable, nagging feeling that somewhere, somehow, he was being stupid. And a promise is a promise. He had promised Polyhymnia that he would not go swimming without the MS-222, and even if it were not for that small worry at the edge of his consciousness he would have to honor that promise.

He strapped the belt around his waist. The sheath was tapered and made very little bulge under the trunks, which were slightly loose for him in any case. Then he went to join Kali.

She was waiting at the edge of the big pool, herself in a pool of golden floodlight which made her tan glisten. Her black bathing suit was sleek against her supple curves, and cut more deeply in the back than Adam would have thought possible. As she saw him walking down the path toward her she picked up her robe and ran to him, taking his hand. "See why we can't swim here? The pool is full, and I don't dare trust *any*body. Daddy has an enormous organization and I don't know half the people involved in it, though I thought I did."

Across from the pool the tennis courts, too, were floodlit, and a game of singles and a game of doubles sounded in the night, the ping of ball against gut, against the clay of the court. There was calling and laughter from the pool. Ahead of them the ocean lay dark and its murmur was almost lost in the light and sound about the hotel.

As they got to the long ramp leading to the beach, and out of the glare of the floodlights, Kali seemed to relax. She held Adam's hand lightly, instead of clutching. But her voice was still wound with tension. "Oh, Adam, everything's so *awful!*" She moved closer to him, seeking, it seemed, the strength and comfort of his body. "Adam, oh, darling, darling Adam, can I trust you?"

"Trust me how?" he asked cautiously.

They had reached the end of the ramp and stood on the night beach. Kali let her robe drop onto the sand, and turned to

Adam, putting her arms tightly around him, leaning her head on his shoulder. "I need your help so terribly."

The light fragrance of her hair brushed against his nostrils. Kali, despite her sophistication, was just as vulnerable as Poly. She might be a few years older, but she was just as helpless against the powers of evil that surrounded them. "How do you need me?" he asked gently.

Kali lifted her head and looked at him. The moonlight fell full on her, so that her skin was milkwhite and her lovely features seemed chiseled out of marble. Her eyes were imploring. "Adam, I know you have no reason to trust me. I wouldn't blame you a bit if you—if you just rejected me now. But please don't."

"I'm not rejecting you, Kali."

"Let's just sit down for a few minutes before we swim and I'll tell you as quickly as I can. All the awful things I've done because daddy told me to and everything." She led the way along the beach, back through the soft sand to the foot of a high dune. Here she sat down, pulling him after her, and lay back. "We can wash the sand off when we go in for our dip. Adam, what would you do if you discovered that your father was doing things—things that were wrong?"

This was something Adam could not possibly imagine. If he had to choose one word to describe his father it would be *integrity*. So he answered, "I don't know." He did not add, "Because it would never happen."

But Kali must have caught the unspoken thought. "I used to think daddy was perfect. I thought that no matter what he did, as long as it was daddy who was doing it, it must be right. But now I know—" she stopped with a sudden intake of breath. "I can't tell you anything more unless you promise me something. I shouldn't have said this much."

For a moment caution returned to Adam. "What do you want me to promise?"

"Oh, nothing difficult. I don't want you to *do* anything or anything. Just promise that you'll never, never, never say anything to anybody in the world about what I'm telling you."

"Why would I want to say anything?"

Kali sat up, looking down at him broodingly. "Adam, I know now that O'Keefe and Tallis and their people are right and daddy's wrong. I'm sure you know it, too. You might want to tell them. O'Keefe and Tallis. But I'm not going to tell you anything they don't already know; I wouldn't put you in a position where it would be your duty to tell them. I promise you. But I couldn't bear—please, Adam, promise me you won't tell them. It's—maybe it's just a matter of pride. I still love daddy, you see. He's still my father. So please just promise me you'll never tell. I can't work for O'Keefe and Tallis or anything. I can't work *against* daddy, even—so please, please promise you'll never tell them any of what I've told you or what I'm going to tell you now." She flung herself at him, pressing her face against his shoulder, so that he could feel her tears hot against his flesh.

"All right, I promise," he said, stroking her back gently as though she were Poly.

She heaved a great sigh of relief. "Oh, thank you. *Thank* you. Adam, daddy only returned Poly to you to get you to work for him. But I guess you know that, anyhow."

"Yes," Adam said.

"And I know daddy's asking you to work for him again." Adam didn't say anything, and Kali continued, "I'm not going to ask you about that. That's your problem, and you have to handle it whatever way you think is right. I know it'll be the right way. Maybe you don't trust me, yet. But I trust you. Implicitly."

She paused, so Adam mumbled, "Thank you."

"You're supposed to go into Lisbon this week, aren't you?"

"Yes."

"And you're supposed to meet me?"

"Well, yes, you know that."

"On Friday, isn't it?"

"Yes."

"I know about the plans, of course, because daddy doesn't know I know about him, and I couldn't ever let him know. He might—Adam, he might hurt *me*. I know now that all he wants is more money and more power, and he doesn't care who's hurt as long as he gets them. There are people in China, for instance, who are willing to give daddy almost anything he wants if they can get hold of O'Keefe's findings. They think people are—what's the word—expendable—and so does daddy. It isn't anything as simple as communism versus democracy. It's power pitting itself against power. So I'm—I'm trapped in the middle. By Friday I ought to know more what I have to do. So if we can just pretend to play along with daddy—and it will just be be pretending—we can meet in Lisbon and things ought to be clearer by then. The main thing is that you *have* to keep your promise, Adam. You must *not* tell anybody, not *any*body anything I've told you."

"I'm not in the habit of breaking promises," Adam said.

"I know you're not. But you see, a promise simply doesn't mean a thing in the world to daddy. He'll promise anything in order to get what he wants and break it the next minute without a thought. So I'm—so I just have to make extra sure. It isn't that I doubt you. You're the only person in the world I trust."

"I'm sorry, Kali," Adam said, helplessly. Kali was lying back against the dune, her fair hair spread out on the sand. The moonlight fell full upon her beautiful face and body. He felt a profound longing to protect her, to rescue her from the evil that held her in thrall.

She whispered, so that he could hardly catch the words, "Thank you."

"For what?"

"For being you. It was the best day of my life when our planes got held up by fog and I met you in the airport." She turned her face toward him, then reached out and touched him gently on the cheek, moving so that she was closer to him. Very lightly she put her lips against his, then, abruptly cutting his response, she jumped up, saying, "That isn't fair to you. Come on, Adam darling, let's have a quick dip and then you'd better get on back to the O'Keefes."

Like a naiad she ran swiftly across the sand and into the water, and he followed her, splashing through the waves.

The moon was high and the ocean quiet. It was not long before they were beyond the breakers and into the rhythmic swells. Kali rolled over onto her back and floated, staring up at the moon. "You see, Adam, I think I can help you now. I can't work against daddy, you do understand that, but I think I can help you not to work against O'Keefe. It won't be safe for you to call the apartment when you come in to Lisbon on Friday, so we'll have to arrange to meet somewhere. We could meet for lunch, couldn't we? That would be perfectly natural, wouldn't it?"

Adam, too, was floating, letting the water ripple gently against his body, slap lightly at his cheeks. "That's pretty much what's expected, I think."

"Someplace large and obvious would be our best bet. There's a good seafood restaurant, the Salâo da Chá. Anybody can tell you where it is. Meet me there at one."

"Fine." Adam looked up at the moon. He thought of Joshua in the little plane flying straight along the path of moonlight as though he were heading toward the clear, cold light of the moon itself.

"Adam, I'm so jittery about everything I could jump out of my skin. Let's have a race." She flipped over and faced out to sea.

"What about undertow and stuff?" Adam asked.

"Oh, *Adam*."

"Sorry, but I've learned to treat the ocean with a good deal of respect."

"For goodness sakes, Adam, I'm as used to this beach as I am to my own bathtub."

Adam asked, doggedly, "What about sharks?"

"That's nonsense. Daddy says it's just a malicious story made up by people who'd like to see the hotel lose business. Come on. I'm going. If you're scared you can go in to shore and wait for me." She thrust her body forward in the water. After a moment's hesitation Adam followed.

163

Kali swam easily and well and she had a head start. Adam was stronger, his arms and legs longer, but he had to work to catch up with her.

Just as he drew even and began to forge ahead he heard Kali scream.

They were in the path of moonlight, now, and in the water beside them he could see a large, dark body. He felt a moment of cold blankness. Then, almost without thinking, he reached for the knife Poly had given him.

17

As Adam's hand touched the sheath he felt himself being butted.

Kali shrieked. "It's a shark! Swim for your life!"

He was butted again.

His next reaction was not on the thinking level. He simply knew that a shark does not butt. A shark turns over on its back, white belly exposed, and attacks. The dark body bumping against him in the night water was not a shark.

"Macrina!" he shouted.

The moment of recognition was not conscious, it was pure and joyful instinct.

Macrina kept butting at him. She was deliberately turning him around and heading him toward land. Kali was already swimming in, cleaving swiftly through the water, not looking back for Adam.

"Thank you, Macrina," Adam said, loudly, hoping that Macrina would understand the intonation if not the words, since he could not, as Poly seemed able to, talk in dolphin language. He turned and headed in to shore, looking back to see Macrina's body, bright with moonlight, flash through the air and disappear into the sea.

Kali stood, knee deep in water, waiting for him. She flung

herself into his arms, sobbing and gibbering. "I was going to run for help—and then I saw you swimming in—it was a shark—oh, Adam, I'm terrified of them—oh, Adam, it was so horrible—oh, Adam, oh, oh, oh—"

He held her, patting her gently. As her torrent of sobbing ceased he said, as calmly as he could, for his own legs were quivering and his heart thumping madly against his ribs, "It wasn't a shark. It was a dolphin."

"You're crazy," Kali said. "Look." She pointed to the water and he could see the swift black triangle of a shark's fin moving across the path of moonlight. "That's a shark. A porpoise leaps out of the water. Adam, I don't know why it didn't kill us. You saved me."

"I didn't do anything," Adam said. "We both swam in as fast as we could." But it *had* been Macrina who had butted him. That was it! he realized. Macrina had been warning him of the shark.

"Sharks swim much faster than people. I just don't understand." Kali still clutched at him in a terrified manner.

Adam tried to sound matter-of-fact. Instinctively he knew that he could not tell Kali about Macrina. "Let's just be grateful that we're here and that we're okay. You're shivering, Kali. Get your robe and let's go in and get dressed." He was still acting on an automatic level, his brain arrested, frozen by the icy bath of terror and moonlight.

Kali leaned against him as they walked across the sand to where her robe lay in a small white pool by the ramp. Adam picked it up and held it for her as she got into it, shivering. Strangely enough he felt no desire to take her into his arms now, to hold her, to comfort her, to brush his lips against the fair hair, the delicate mouth. His mind was still suspended; his emotions, too, seemed caught and frozen in the moonlight. Everything about him was calm and cold, but somewhere inside was a small, still voice telling him what to do. His earlier anger at having Kali added to his responsibilities was gone; the moment of joy that had come when he recognized Macrina was gone. He knew that all that was required of him at the moment was to take Kali back to the hotel; then he would be free to go home to the O'Keefes.

Typhon Cutter and Dr. Ball were drinking coffee and brandy in the lounge.

"Dear children," Dr. Ball cooed, "did you have a pleasant swim?"

Kali walked up to her father. "Daddy, there *are* sharks. Adam and I saw one."

Typhon Cutter's voice was unperturbed. "I think that highly unlikely, Kali. Were you in the ocean?"

"Yes."

"I thought you were going in the pool."

"It was too crowded."

Mr. Cutter pulled out a platinum case, extracted a cigarette, and lit it unhurriedly. "I would suggest that, if you think you saw a shark, you follow the hotel rules in future. They are, if you will remember, *my* rules, and I've asked you before to swim in the ocean only during the day time when there is a lifeguard."

"All right, daddy. Sorry. I just thought you'd want to know."

Typhon Cutter swung his cumbersome body toward Adam. "Did you see a shark?"

"Yes, sir. I think so."

"You're not positive?"

"Not a hundred percent, Mr. Cutter. But as far as swimming at the hotel beach is concerned I'd certainly go on the assumption that there *are* sharks."

Dr. Ball stretched and crossed his legs. "A proper scientific attitude, my boy."

"I think I'd better go now," Adam said. "I don't expect anybody'll be waiting up for me, but it's getting late, and I do have to get up early."

He said goodbye to the two men and Kali took him to the roof. Before he climbed into the helicopter she moved close to him. The moonlight shone down on her face and he could not avoid or evade her imploring look. He took her gently into his arms. "See you Friday, Kali. Everything will be all right." She nodded, rubbing her face against his shoulder, then lifted her lips to be kissed.

He was surprised at his reaction, for he seemed to be two separate Adams; one responded fully to the physical excitement of the kiss and to her body pressed against his; the other, and the Adam who seemed at the moment to be in control, was thinking only of Friday, of the dangers and problems involved, and that he must not let himself be blinded by emotion no matter how badly Kali needed him. Indeed, if he was to be able to help Kali at all, he must keep his mind clear and disengaged. After Friday was over would be time enough to think of other things.

He turned away from her firmly and got into the helicopter. As it rose clumsily straight up into the air and then headed east he could see her watching and waving after him.

Again during the homeward journey the pilot did not speak. Adam, jumping down onto the sand, called "Obrigado," which he had picked up as meaning "thank you," and hurried toward the lab where he could see a light still burning in the big room.

Dr. O'Keefe was working at one of the tanks, but went to his desk and sat down, rather wearily, as Adam knocked and entered. "I'm making some hot chocolate over one of the Bunsen burners," the doctor said. "I find if I drink coffee this late at night I'm apt not to go to bed at all. Want to get yourself a cup from the cupboard over there?"

"Thank you." Adam got a cup and set it down beside the doctor's on the counter top. "I'll finish making this, sir."

Dr. O'Keefe looked at him probingly. "How did the evening go?"

Adam stirred the fragrant chocolate. "All right, I think. There's something that bothers me, and I can't put my finger on it." As he said 'finger' he almost dipped his own into the saucepan to see if the chocolate was hot enough, then decided that Dr. O'Keefe might not approve of this distinctly unsterile procedure. There *was* something wrong with the evening, and it was something quite unconnected with Kali. It had been bothering him off and on all during the flight home, although it had been Kali who had been in the forefront of his mind. He wanted very much to tell Dr. O'Keefe about Kali, but he had promised. However, at the moment Kali seemed to be on the periphery of the central problem which was to get the phony papers to Dr. Ball and the real papers to Josh or the Ambassador. On Friday when he met Kali at the restaurant he would make her see that he must tell Dr. O'Keefe. He could understand her feelings about this: Typhon Cutter was her father and she must still love him very much no matter what she had learned about his actions. You cannot suddenly stop loving where it has been the central emotion of your entire life.

"Want to tell me about it now?" Dr. O'Keefe asked, "or would you rather wait until morning?"

Adam decided, from the bubbles at the edge of the saucepan, that the cocoa was hot. "I don't think it'll take too long," he said as he poured. "I can tell you while we have our chocolate."

Dr. O'Keefe reached into a desk drawer and brought out a tin of biscuits. He handed it to Adam, and accepted the steaming cupful.

"I'm not quite sure how to start . . ." Adam took a biscuit.

"Begin at the beginning, go on to the end, and then stop."

That, of course, was the trouble. He could not begin at the beginning, which was Kali's cry for help. So he began with going into the terraced lounge.

"So Ball was there," Dr. O'Keefe murmured.

"He's a whited sepulcher!" Adam said vehemently.

The doctor laughed. "He may be beautiful without, but yes, he's full within of dead men's bones and all uncleanness."

"Then how can he possibly have a church and everything?" Adam asked.

"The scribes and pharisees were respected by a great many people, and a great many of them did a respectable job. I suppose most people see only the outside—he's a great one for rather showy good works—and have no idea of what's within. Go on."

Adam's memory again served him well. He was able to give a

detailed account of the conversations in both the lounge and the dining room.

When he had finished Dr. O'Keefe sat twirling a pencil. "It seems to me you did very well. What's bothering you?"

"I wish I knew."

Dr. O'Keefe continued to twirl the pencil, staring at it with concentration. At last he said, "Do you think maybe you feel that it was all too easy?"

Adam looked up, his face alight. "That's it! They believed me too easily. That I'd work for them, and that I didn't trust you."

"It sounds to me as though you'd been pretty persuasive. Why do you think it was too easy?"

Adam said, slowly, "I don't think I'm *that* good an actor. I don't mean that I was bad or anything, I really think I did all right, but—"

"You think there may be a trap somewhere?"

"Yes. But I don't know *why* I think it. It's just a feeling, and I may be all wrong."

Dr. O'Keefe swirled the dregs of hot chocolate in his cup. "No. I think I know why you feel the way you do. Cutter and Ball aren't to be underestimated, and they aren't easily sold a bill of goods, and that's just what you were trying to do, and what you seem to have succeeded in doing, isn't it?"

"Yes, sir."

Again there was a pause, during which Adam wished even more strongly that he hadn't made his promise to Kali. Dr. O'Keefe took both cups to the sink and rinsed them out. "Tom Tallis will be in Lisbon on Friday. That's one good thing. I think you ought to go directly to Tom, rather than to Joshua or the Embassy."

"But what about Dr. Ball—"

"Yes, you'll have to go there first, though I hate to have you with the papers on you when you see him. I'll try to work out a plan between now and Friday. You've blundered into enough danger since you left New York without my sending you into more."

Adam said, "I want to do anything I can."

"I know, Adam, and I'm grateful. But you *are* in my care. If there were anyone else to send to Lisbon—"

"There isn't, and anyhow they expect me, and it would make them suspicious if I didn't come."

Dr. O'Keefe stretched and yawned. "Let's go to bed, boy. We'll sleep on it."

They had turned out the lab lights and shut and locked the door behind them, when Adam said, "Dr. O'Keefe, I forgot to tell you one of the most important things of all."

"What's that?"

"It's Macrina."

Dr. O'Keefe listened, standing quiet and unmoving, as the moon dropped slowly behind the hills. "If Macrina did that for you—"

"But I could be wrong again, sir. Maybe I just thought—"

"No. I don't think there's any doubting what happened. And each separate event added up makes me realize—" He paused, sighing.

"Realize what, sir?"

"That you *are* the one to go to Lisbon on Friday, no matter how much it goes against the grain for me to send you into what we both know will be danger." The older man's hand dropped onto Adam's shoulder, but it was a touch completely unlike that of Dr. Ball. Whereas Adam had wanted to pull away from Dr. Ball and had had to will himself not to move, Dr. O'Keefe's hand felt like his father's; it seemed to be giving him strength, and determination, and the courage to do whatever it was that he had to do.

"Good night, Adam," the doctor said. "See you in the morning."

18

The next day was, in a quiet and unexciting way, everything Adam had hoped the entire summer would be. Poly brought him his breakfast but was surprisingly reticent and the only question she asked about the evening before was what he had had to eat. Adam wondered if her father or mother had told her to leave him alone. He did his chores in the laboratory, drank coffee with Mrs. O'Keefe while the doctor was busy at his desk; Mrs. O'Keefe knew a great deal about her husband's work and had often assisted him.

Before lunch Poly called for Adam and he went swimming with all the children; they did not see Macrina, which was only partly a disappointment. Macrina would have made him think about the night before and all its implications, and he wanted a day of simple, straightforward work.

In the afternoon Dr. O'Keefe rode over to the village. Adam was left in charge of the laboratory, happy and uninterrupted. Mrs. O'Keefe brought him tea, but left him alone, and he spent the time deep in concentration on the files.

After dinner they sang again, and, as Adam's mind had been held during the day by his concentration on his work, so now the music held him and he relaxed into the singing. When the younger children were in bed he walked with Poly at the edge of the ocean. Poly had slipped off her sandals on the sea wall, and walked silently, teasing her bare toes against the incoming waves, her white cotton dress blown tight against her twenty-twenty-twenty body. Not quite twenty-twenty-twenty any more, Adam realized. It wasn't going to be long before Poly would be bursting out of childhood as she was already beginning to do out of her dress.

As it grew darker there was a glittering against the dunes and Poly ran, colt-like, across the sand crying, "Fireflies!" and tried to catch the small sparkles between her hands. "Sometimes I catch them in a jar, just to look at for a little while, just to make a small lantern. But I never hold them for very long. I used to think they were tiny stars, but then I found out how cruel they are, and I don't think stars should be cruel."

"Fireflies cruel?" Adam asked with tolerant good humor.

"Oh, *you* know," Poly said impatiently.

"Fireflies have been pretty much left out of my education. All I know is that they're the only source of light that provides illumination without incandescence."

"So far so good." Poly held her cupped hands out to him, and a small startled spark flew out and up. She put her hand in Adam's and pulled him down onto the dune. "Let's sit for a while."

Adam leaned back against the soft, warm sand. How different this was from the night before with Kali. He sighed with relief at the release from tension. Ahead of them the moon was rising. Above, fireflies glittered. "It's really fantastic," he said lazily, looking at one small, moving spark. "Every light man can make is mostly heat. I forget the proportion it is in an electric bulb, but something like ninety-five percent of the energy needed to make an ordinary light bulb for an ordinary lamp in an ordinary house is used up in heat. If we could find out how the fireflies do it, cold light, electricity would cost only a fraction of what it does now. It would be so cheap it would hardly cost anything."

Poly lay back, looking out to sea. "The light and power companies wouldn't like that."

"I think Old Doc was working on it for a while. He used to

pay me a penny, way back when I was a little kid, for every ten fireflies I caught for him in a jelly jar. I spent all evening chasing them. Didn't make much money but I had an awful lot of fun."

Poly rolled over, leaning on one elbow and looking at Adam intensely. "Do me a favor and leave fireflies alone."

"Hunh?" Adam turned to look at her.

"Listen," Poly said, still up on her elbow so that she could stare down at him. "Did you know they're divided into different levels or classes?"

"I've told you all I know about fireflies. They don't seem much of a menace to me."

Poly did not laugh. She continued to stare at him with a serious, probing expression, so that she looked much older than her twelve years. "Well, they are. And they mate by their flashes. A male firefly will give his flash—maybe four flashes, say. And if the female is in the same class or category that he is, she'll answer back with four flashes. But if she's in the class that has three flashes, or two, or five, she won't answer. Unless she's hungry. Then she'll give him back four flashes and when he comes down to her, instead of making love with him she'll eat him."

"What a bloodthirsty fiendess," Adam said lightly.

"That's exactly what I mean. Leave fireflies alone, Adam." She stood up, calling, "Race you back to the house!" and went streaking across the sand.

Sunday morning the whole family went up to the monolithic stones and sat around the large table while Dr. O'Keefe read morning prayer. Then they rode to the native village, Mrs. O'Keefe carrying Rosy in a canvas sling on her back, Dr. O'Keefe carrying Johnny, and Adam riding with Peggy in front of him on the saddle. He had one arm around the little girl and she leaned back against him contentedly and slept.

Virbius entertained them with a lavish and exotic meal, and Poly and Temis rounded up all the O'Keefe children and the village children for a series of dancing and singing games. Adam, sitting next to the doctor, felt lapped in peace and joy.

Friday seemed a long way off. It seemed a long way off all during the week of working in the lab with the doctor, of swimming with the children, of singing in the living room in the evening, of coming to feel that this island and this family was his home. He knew that in actuality Friday was moving closer and looming larger with every passing minute, but he kept it out of his mind until Thursday night when all the children, including Poly, were in bed, and he was sitting in the living room with Dr. and Mrs. O'Keefe. Mrs. O'Keefe was mending a pair of Dennys' shorts, but her face had a watchful, waiting look, and she raised her head as the doctor said, "I've arranged to have the helicopter pick you up in the morning, Adam. You have a hard day ahead of you, and it's a tiring ride by horse over to the hotel."

"Whatever you say, sir." Adam's heart began to beat so that he could feel its thumping.

"You should get to Lisbon around ten in the morning. The plane leaves for Gaea again at six, but you can arrange to miss it. Joshua will fly you back."

Adam smiled with pleasure. "Oh, great. Something really good to look forward to."

"Now, Adam, there hasn't been time for you to learn any Portuguese, has there?"

"Just a few isolated words and idioms."

"Here's a small phrase book you may find useful, then. This is a good street map of Lisbon which will help you to find your way about. In the morning I'll give you the Temis papers. María and José report that the laboratory has been watched all week. One small paper I carefully dropped 'inadvertently' has disappeared. I hope we are leading them away from any thoughts of Temis into thinking I have been experimenting on one of the horses. José has dropped hints of this to the stable boys, and one of the horses has a badly cut hoof. This non-existent experiment is important enough to excite much interest, but what is more, in the long run it would not work. As for the papers on Temis, we'll try to have them on you for as short a time as possible. María has made a concealed pocket for you to carry them in. She has also made a slightly less clever pocket for the phony horse papers. If you are searched this pocket will be discovered first. You are of course aware that you will be followed wherever you go."

"Yes, sir, I figured I would be."

"Know too that someone from the Embassy will have an eye on you. I don't think you yourself will be in any danger, although the papers may be."

"I won't let anything happen to the papers," Adam said fiercely.

"I know, Adam. If I had not come to trust you implicitly I could not allow you to go."

Adam, remembering that until the promise was lifted he could not tell Dr. O'Keefe about Kali, bowed his head.

"Adam will be all right," Mrs. O'Keefe said softly.

Adam looked over at her with gratitude. Dr. O'Keefe continued, his voice quiet, calm, but containing absolute authority. "The first thing you must do when you get to Lisbon is to call Father Tallis. You will be most private in a public phone booth. Now, Adam, you have already learned that it is the unexpected that usually happens."

Adam controlled a shiver that threatened to ripple through his body. "Yes, Dr. O'Keefe. I have."

"We've tried to prepare, as much as possible, for the unexpected, to foresee the unforeseen. I think you're right in your suspicions about Dr. Ball and Typhon Cutter the other night: they're hot on the trail and you're being used as a decoy. I wish I knew what move they're going to make, but I don't. I can only guess that they'll try to keep you from getting in touch with either Joshua or Father and certainly they'd prevent you from getting through to the Ambassador. And the Temis papers are too important to go to anybody else. So, to try to prepare for the unpreparable, we have worked out alternate times and places for you to call Tom Tallis. I'm only grateful that he is able to be in Lisbon instead of Gibraltar or heaven and the bishop know where else."

"Sir," Adam asked, "how did Canon Tallis get involved in this—in this kind of business?"

"Inadvertently and unwillingly. Like most of us."

Adam nodded. "Yes. How am I to get in touch with him?"

"He will be moving all day Friday. I cannot give you a list of where he would be, because it would be too dangerous for you to carry. You'll have to memorize the places where he'll be available at each particular hour. The phone numbers will be no trouble since they'll be, in each case, numbers you can look up in the public phone book. Ready?"

"Yes, sir."

"Until ten-thirty the Russian Embassy." Adam looked startled, but Mrs. O'Keefe smiled serenely, and Dr. O'Keefe continued. "You must try to get him there, because we want the papers off you as soon as possible. Ask for Dr. Fedotov. Don't speak to anybody else."

"How will I be sure—"

"He will identify himself to you through the Frost poem, since it's the only one of the pass codes you know."

"What about the Tallis canon?"

"That's more a trademark than a code. Dr. Fedotov will put you through to Canon Tallis. If all goes well, and there's no reason it shouldn't, you'll be able to give him the papers before you go to the rectory to Dr. Ball. But if anything should happen to prevent your calling or getting to him, after ten-thirty you'll be out of touch until eleven—it does take time to get from one place to another—but between eleven and twelve you can call the Monastery of Saô Juan Chrysostom. Ask for the *senhor paroco*, Father Henriques."

"The *senhor paroco*, Father Henriques," Adam murmured, memorizing.

"If by noon you still haven't been able to talk to Tom you'll have time at the restaurant when you go to meet Kali. Between one and two-thirty call Rabbi Pinhas. Look in the phone book under the name of Senhora Leonora Afonso. Got it?"

"Yes. In my passport."

"If you haven't been able to phone by two-thirty—and you

177

should be able, Adam, these are just emergency procedures like the life belts on a plane that you never really expect to use—then from three-thirty to five call Joshua. You have his numbers, don't you?"

"Yes."

"Whatever happens don't let anybody get hold of them. I hope long before afternoon you'll be all through with your job. If, by any mischance you're not, in the evening Joshua and Father Tallis are going to the opera. If you have to call them, ask for Dr. Magalhâes and say it is an emergency. Tom Tallis will have left that name, and say that he may get a call. I repeat, Adam, this should be an unnecessary precaution. Now I'll go over the list again."

Adam listened carefully. Mrs. O'Keefe finished patching Dennys' shorts and reached for a sweater of Peggy's. "Poly's growing out of everything," she murmured. "I'll have to go into Lisbon myself soon."

"Got it?" Dr. O'Keefe asked Adam.

"I think so," Adam said. "Until ten-thirty Dr. Fedotov at the Russian Embassy. Between eleven and twelve Father Henriques at the Saô Juan Chrysostom Monastery. Between one and two-thirty the Rabbi Pinhas, in the phone book under the name of Senhora Leonora Afonso. From three-thirty to five, Joshua. In the evening the opera house, and ask for Dr. Magalhâes."

"Good. A friend of Arcangelo's will have the plane ready for you and Joshua after the opera. We can't use Arcangelo any more since Ball saw him with you at the airport. He's now pinpointed as one of our men, so don't try to get in touch with him whatever happens. He can't help you any more, and it would only be putting him in jeopardy."

Adam gave an involuntary shudder because he understood now just how grave the danger to Arcangelo could be. For some reason he remembered the chauffeur, Molèc, and the brutality of the huge hand as it sliced against his knee.

"Arcangelo's a good man," Dr. O'Keefe said, "and absolutely loyal. We'll miss him badly."

Mrs. O'Keefe looked up. "Is it safe for him to stay in Lisbon?"

"Safer than to try to leave."

"Dr. O'Keefe," Adam asked, "is the Rabbi Pinhas the one who was on the plane—"

"Yes. Now, Adam, you'd better get to bed and get a good night's sleep. We'll be waiting for you and Joshua tomorrow night."

"Yes, sir," Adam said. "Good night. Good night, Mrs. O'Keefe."

He lay in bed in the small airy room that had so quickly come to seem like home. A fresh ocean breeze came in the open window. He pulled the blanket up over him, but he was not sleepy. His body was tense and ready to spring, as though he were already in the plane on the way to Lisbon. He ran over in his mind the list of the places he was to call Canon Tallis. Then he tried to project his imagination beyond the unknown quantity of the day and to the trip back to the island with Joshua. But he could see in his mind's eye only the daytime trip the week before, and Joshua sending the little plane into the great, turbulent clouds, his voice rising above the tumult of the elements.

Back in the hills a night bird hooted. Dr. and Mrs. O'Keefe walked past his door on their way to bed. Adam did not look at his watch because he did not want to know how much time had passed. If ever he needed a good night's sleep it was tonight, so that his mind would be clear for whatever might happen the following day. In the next room Charles made a noise in his sleep. Adam wondered if the children would see Macrina when they went swimming, and if Poly would tell Macrina that he was in Lisbon, and if Macrina would care. There was no questioning Macrina's intelligence, but Adam wondered whether or not things mattered to her. How did a fish, even a mammal, show sadness? A crocodile might be supposed to shed tears, if only crocodile tears, but what could Macrina do to show sorrow?

As he thought about Macrina the thoughts got more complicated and more confused and he was in Gaea and he was in Woods Hole and Macrina was sitting at the concierge's desk at the Avenida Palace and Adam was asleep. . . .

Mrs. O'Keefe brought him breakfast in the morning. "Our thoughts will be with you all day, Adam," she said.

"Thank you. I'm glad."

Poly knocked and came in. "Take care of yourself for heaven's sake."

"For heaven's and the future's sake," Adam quoted.

"For my sake," Poly said.

Charles slipped into the room. "Just take care of yourself."

Peggy came running along the corridor, calling for her mother, plummeted into Adam's room, and was barely stopped from leaping up onto the bed and spilling the breakfast tray. "When will Adam be back?"

"Tonight," Poly said tightly.

"Tonight," Charles said, looking at Adam.

Mrs. O'Keefe pulled Peggy up onto her lap. "But late, Charles. Very late. Long after midnight. They should arrive with the dawn."

Charles looked at his mother, at Adam, nodded without speaking, and left the room as quietly as he had entered it.

Mrs. O'Keefe put Peggy down. "Come along, Pol, Peg. Let's give Adam a few minutes to eat breakfast in peace."

The whole family stood on the sea wall and waved as he left in the helicopter. —It won't be long, Adam thought, —before I'm back here and everything will be all right.

It was the same silent pilot who had taken him to dinner with the Cutters, and they whirred across the island with the pilot scowling out the windshield, seemingly wishing to avoid even looking at Adam. They circled the hotel, then flew over the pool and tennis court, and down the beach to a small cement landing strip. The taxi plane was there, and Adam was allowed to get on and settle in his seat, although he was early. There was room for twelve people in the compact cabin, but not much leg room. A pleasant-looking stewardess offered him coffee, but he was suspicious of all stewardesses and not at all sure of anything offered him to drink. He thought he could handle himself and protect the papers in María's special pocket as long as he was wide awake and alert, but he did not want to risk a Mickey Finn and someone searching him between the island and Lisbon. So he smiled politely and said, "No, thanks, I've just had gallons."

"Would you care for a magazine?" she asked in her charming accent. "We have the latest American magazines, *Esquire, Mad—*"

"No, thanks, I've brought some work." And he did have a sheaf of magazines Dr. O'Keefe had given him, some American, some English, some European, in a number of which Dr. O'Keefe had articles. The first magazine he opened, an Australian one, had a lead article by T. S. Didymus, and Adam felt that this was somehow a propitious omen.

He read the piece by Old Doc, smiling affectionately at the old man's individual quirks of phrasing. Then he managed to lose himself in various other articles that caught his interest, grateful for the discipline of concentration he had learned at school. Dr. O'Keefe's writing style was spare and clear, with unexpected, vivid illustrations, and a quick sense of humor. —How could I ever have thought he wasn't okay? Adam wondered, and then remembered that his doubts were all seeded before he met the scientist, and that if it had not been for the New York fog for which Kali was so grateful, he might not be heading for Lisbon and danger now.

But this was purposeless thinking. He shook himself and returned to the magazine, reading until the passengers from the hotel came aboard. A portly, porcine man with a briefcase settled himself beside Adam. The boy kept his nose in the magazine, determined not to be drawn into conversation, no matter how innocent. But the man appeared as averse to chitchat as Adam, opened his briefcase immediately, and set to work on a sheaf of papers, only grunting in assent as the stewardess offered him coffee.

Adam read, holding his mind at bay. He managed not to think of the hours ahead, but discovered that he was not retaining anything from the articles in which he had thought he was engrossed.

They landed at the small airport from which he and Joshua had taken off, and where he had first met Dr. Ball. A limousine was waiting outside to take the passengers into the center of Lisbon, and Adam found a seat, seeking the portly man as a seat companion so that he would be assured of silence.

But the man did not reopen his briefcase. Instead he turned to Adam, smiled pleasantly, and said, "I'm Donald Green of the Singer Sewing Machine Company. Haven't noticed you around the hotel."

Adam did not in his turn introduce himself. Instead he answered politely, "Well, no, sir, I haven't been staying there."

"*Is* there any other place to stay on Gaea?"

"Oh, yes, sir."

"Where? Except for the hotel it seems a jungle as far as I'm concerned."

Adam did not know how to get out of this one. "Well, I have a summer job with a scientist who has a laboratory there." He tensed his body and mind for further questioning.

But Mr. Green of the Singer Sewing Machine seemed satisfied. To Adam's surprise he asked no more questions but went into a eulogy on the merits of his machines and how they were changing the entire life of the Iberian peninsula. "I feel that I'm doing a great service to these people. Tried to get those savages over in the Gaean village interested but was most rudely turned away." Adam mumbled politely and Mr. Green of the Singer Sewing Machine continued to talk about his experiences until the limousine stopped.

"Nice to have met you, sir," Adam said, and strode purposefully down the street as though he knew exactly where he was going.

He did not.

He had no idea.

Dr. O'Keefe had given him a street map of Lisbon, and Adam had studied it. But Lisbon is not the simple chequer board that makes up most of Manhattan; Lisbon is unexpected hills, open squares, closed alleys, a city of twisting, turning, revealing, hiding, light, dark, a city of mystery and beauty and fascination.

And Adam realized that he did not know where anything was in Lisbon. If he could find the Ritz then he thought he could find, in one direction, the Avenida Palace hotel, and, in the other, Joshua's apartment. If he could find the Ritz he could go in and look at the map again, phone Canon Tallis, and figure out how to get to the rectory.

No. He shouldn't go into the Ritz because of Arcangelo. But if he could find the Ritz then he would be able to find someplace else to look at his map and make his phone call. He stopped a man, saying, "Ritz, por favor?"

The man went into a torrent of Portuguese, and Adam simply shook his head. The man spoke slowly and at full volume, but this did not help, and Adam grinned foolishly and shook his head again.

Then a voice came from behind him. "I show you where go."

Adam turned and faced the huge body and coarse face of Molèc.

19

"This way," Molèc said, and Adam followed helplessly.

"Não, não," the man who had been trying to direct him called, and pointed in the opposite direction.

Molèc scowled, speaking rapidly and angrily. The man responded shrilly, flung up his hands in exasperation, and strode off.

"Where are you taking me?" Adam demanded.

"Padre Ball."

There was nothing to do but go with him. Molèc led Adam back to where the limousine was just pulling away to return to the airport. Parked nearby was Mr. Cutter's car. Adam would not easily forget this car, and he had no desire to get into it again, but he clenched his teeth and climbed in as Molèc opened the door to the back seat.

—If Mr. Cutter was going to have him meet me why didn't he tell me? Adam thought. —Or is this some kind of test or trick?

He looked out the window, trying to see something he recognized, trying to remember the route, to see street signs, but he realized that as far as finding his way around Lisbon was concerned he was completely helpless. Squares with fountains, sidewalks in mosaic patterns, laundry hanging, fountains splashing, all seemed to flash by him in an unassimilated jumble as Molèc drove.

"Igreja," Molèc said, pulling up abruptly in front of a grey stone cross-topped building on a broad, tree-lined street somewhere on the outskirts of Lisbon, though at which point of the compass Adam did not know. His sense of direction had completely forsaken him. Once he could study the map he would feel a little more secure.

A narrow, cobblestoned street led to a modern villa behind the church, and to this the chauffeur pointed. "Padre Ball."

"Obrigado," Adam said, quitted the Cutters' car and Molèc with a sense of relief, and walked quickly over the cobblestones.

The villa was a handsome one, large, faced with patterned tiles in Venetian red. He rang the bell and the door was opened almost immediately by Dr. Ball himself who grasped Adam's hand in his usual overhearty grip.

"Dear lad, I'm so grateful that you're here safely. So Molèc found you."

Adam retrieved his hand.

Dr. Ball led him along a narrow corridor into a large study. It was a light and cheerful room, filled with books and leather-covered furniture. Although it did not seem to Adam to reflect Dr. Ball's personality at all, it was no doubt the kind of study that the rector thought he ought to have. He sat down at his large, leather-topped desk, indicated a comfortable chair near him, and showed his teeth in a smile. "We should have thought of having Molèc meet you when we talked with you last week, but alas, we did not, and both Mr. Cutter and I felt that a phone call to you would be most unwise under the circumstances, and that we'd just have to trust Molèc to find you. He's a most reliable fellow. Though I'm sure you'd have managed to get to me anyhow, wouldn't you?"

"Well, I think so, sir. As a matter of fact, I didn't see Molèc right away, so I planned to look up your address in the phone book and then figure out how to get to you from the map." —I'll tell the truth whenever possible, he thought, —and when I can't I'll try not to say anything at all.

"Clever boy," Dr. Ball told him. "Are you hungry? Would you like something to eat? What can I get you?"

"Nothing, thank you. I had a good breakfast and I've arranged to meet Kali for lunch."

"Where are you meeting Kali? Perhaps it will simplify things if I show you on the map and tell you how to get there."

"That would be fine. It's a seafood restaurant called the Salão da Chá."

He gave Dr. Ball the map, and the rector spread it out on the desk. "Ah. Ah, yes. Here we are." He indicated a central point. "Here is the Salão da Chá. Here is the rectory. If you will walk three blocks east from here—thus—you will be able to get a number 198 bus which will take you to the Saláo da Chá in about ten minutes. Or perhaps it would be simpler just to take a taxi. Yes. Yes, of course. That would be better."

"Well, no, thank you, sir, I think I'd rather take the bus."

"Why, boy? Do you not have enough money?"

Dr. O'Keefe had given Adam a sizable roll. He answered promptly, "Oh, yes, sir, I have the money for Mrs. O'Keefe's shopping, and I have my first week's salary, so I'm fine."

Dr. Ball sniffed. "O'Keefe is not known for overpaying his assistants." He took a wad of bills from his wallet and handed it to Adam. "We took that into consideration, of course, so let it be no problem to you."

"I really don't want the money, sir. I don't care about taxis."

"Kali is not accustomed to ordering inexpensive lunches."

"I can manage."

"My dear lad, I think you should feel free to accept a little payment for what you are doing for us."

"I'd really rather not take any money."

"I appreciate your sentiments, dear boy, but accept it as a loan. If you don't need it you can return it. But you may run into expenses you haven't anticipated."

Further arguing would be suspicious, so Adam took the money, putting it gingerly into his pocket. "About the taxi. I'd really rather take the bus so that I can learn my way around Lisbon a bit; it'll help give me the lay of the land."

"All very well and good if there's time. We shall see. Now for instructions. You have something for us?"

"Yes. Some papers I managed to get from the file when it was unlocked. Shall I give them to you?"

"Oh, no, sonny, no, no, no. It wouldn't do at all for me to have the papers, nor would it be right for me to act as courier. You must understand that. I do what I can to help, of course, but my position naturally limits what it is fitting for me to do."

"Well, then—" Adam let his voice trail off. He had a feeling that Dr. Ball was leading him around in circles with his questions, his bus numbers. The rector was like a well-fed cat who nevertheless enjoys playing with a mouse.

Now Dr. Ball looked at his watch. "Ten forty-five. What time are you meeting Kali?"

"One."

"Very well." An edge came into the voice that made Adam feel that now they were getting down to business; they were through playing games. "Professor Embuste of Coimbra is upstairs. I will take you to him." He rose, looked at his watch, checked it against a clock on the mantlepiece, then led Adam through the quiet house and up a flight of back stairs. "Professor Embuste does not speak English but his French is fluent. Yours?"

"Pretty good."

"Splendid, splendid. Cutter and I were betting on it, though we have an interpreter in readiness. We prefer not to use an intermediary if we can avoid it." He paused on the landing. "If Dr. Embuste is satisfied with what you have for us, you will be free to meet Kali at the Salâo da Chá, where you will receive further instructions."

"Further instructions?" Adam asked blankly.

"Surely you didn't think your job would be over when you had delivered the papers? You are not that naïve nor that young."

—And it will give this Professor Embuste more time to go over the papers, Adam thought. Aloud he said, "I really don't think it's a question of naïveté, Dr. Ball. It seems to me that once I've delivered the papers my use is over."

"You may be wanted for questioning." Dr. Ball started up a second, narrower flight of stairs. "Remember that you work closely with O'Keefe. We may need to know more than his progress in the regeneration experiments."

"But what—there's nothing I know—"

"You know his habits. What time he gets up. When he is out of the laboratory. Where he goes. When the files are unlocked."

"I see," Adam said slowly. "It seems to me Joshua would be lots more use to you than I, sir, since he's such a good friend of yours and he's known Dr. O'Keefe so much longer." Perhaps this was a dangerous gambit, but it seemed to go along with the rôle Adam was trying to play.

Dr. Ball cleared his throat, went up two more stairs, paused. "Although our young friend Joshua is not a churchgoer, alas, I consider that he is still within my parish and therefore my responsibility spiritually. He is lost now, and so, despite my disapproval of his way of life—he is really no fit companion for you—I must never abandon him. I would really prefer it if you did not see him." He hurried up the last few steps, walked down a short hall, knocked briskly at a door and opened it to reveal a small, almost bare room. At a desk sat a man with a sallow, intelligent face. An unshaded light bulb hung over the desk. It reminded Adam of the room in the airport in Madrid.

Without making any introductions Dr. Ball closed the door on Adam and disappeared. Adam could hear his footsteps descending.

The sallow man looked up. "Embuste."

"Adam Eddington," Adam said, looking at the professor.

Professor Embuste glared back, the corners of his mouth turned down in a bitter and unwelcoming expression. Adam was becoming accustomed to being examined, so he stood his ground.

Professor Embuste did not ask him to sit down. Without moving in his chair he said, "The papers, please."

Adam handed them across the desk.

"You will wait," the professor said sourly, "while I look at them."

Adam stood, watching the professor go through the papers, eyes flicking quickly over the formulas. Those eyes, small, close-set, dark in themselves and darkly shadowed, seemed to Adam to be sharp, cruel, and frighteningly intelligent. Minutes moved and Adam did not dare check his watch. He shifted uncomfortably from one foot to the other. But Dr. O'Keefe had prepared the papers well, for Professor Embuste put them down on the desk, looked at Adam, and said, "Very well. You may go. You will receive further instructions at the Salâo da Chá."

Adam felt that he could not get out of this small trap of a room quickly enough. He opened the door and came face to face with Dr. Ball. If the rector had descended audibly, he had come back up the stairs in his stocking feet. Putting a finger to lips that were curved in a peculiar smile he led Adam to the front door, then took his hand in the too-strong grip. "My dear good lad, I am immeasurably relieved that all is well. You still wish to take the bus?"

"Yes, please."

"You remember the number?"

"198."

"Bright boy. We will be in touch." Adam's hand was pumped, blessings were rained upon his unwilling head, and he fled down the street.

At the bus stop a lonely young man waited. He wore heavy, horn-rimmed spectacles and carried a pile of books under his arm. He beamed at Adam and said in studied English, "A million pardons, but are you an American?"

"Yes."

"I am a student at the University of Lisbon and am taking courses in the English language and the literature of England and America. It is always my deepest pleasure to talk to students from either of these great countries." The light glinted against his spectacles so that Adam could not see his eyes.

"I'd like to talk to you," Adam said, trying to sound courteous, "but I'm in a terrible hurry. I'm off to meet a girl and the last time we met—well, we had a misunderstanding—so you see—" his voice trailed off.

The bespectacled student waved his books gleefully. "A lover's quarrel! How delightful! So of course I understand that you are not interested in my idle chatter."

Adam was spared a reply by the arrival of a bus, 198, —what luck, he thought gratefully. He smiled, waved courteously, jumped on and ran up the stairs to sit in one of the front seats on the upper deck, then looked down the street. The student was no longer at the bus stop, so presumably had boarded the bus, too, but he did not come upstairs. Adam alternately checked his watch and the map. It was already eleven-thirty, but with luck he would be able to manage a phone call to the Saô Juan Chrysostom Monastery. He felt a terrible need to be in touch with Canon Tallis. Something about Professor Embuste had frightened him, and although the false papers had for the moment been accepted, the boy knew that the Professor must now be going over them more carefully.

He left the bus, the Temis papers seeming to burn in María's pocket, bumped by several young people who pushed out ahead of him and stood clustered on the sidewalk. He knew the papers had not been touched but he still felt panic. The young people stood talking together animatedly and he was not sure whether or not he was imagining sidelong glances. Some of the glances came from girls, and to this he was moderately accustomed, but was the boy with his back turned the young man with glasses? Was Adam being watched as he walked quickly down the street?

It was not yet twelve. He knew, from the map, where the restaurant was, but to walk there before calling would be cutting the time too close for comfort. He went into a small hotel and found a phone. It was not in a closed booth, but no one, as far as he could tell, had followed him in. He struggled with the phone book and managed with considerable difficulty to find the number for the Saô Juan Chrysostom Monastery. With the help of the phrase book he was able to give the operator the number, and after a good deal of clicking and clacking he heard a distant ring. Then came a rough voice, and Adam said, "Senhor Paroco, Padre Henriques, por favor."

There was a long pause, during which Adam felt that everyone in the hotel lobby was staring at him. This, he knew, was not likely, and he would not be alert to the people who might really be following him if he was suspicious of everybody else. A gentle voice, an old voice, sounded in his ear: "Padre Henriques."

"Adam Eddington," Adam said. "Canon Tallis, por favor."

"Momento."

A shorter pause. Then the familiar, brusque voice. "Adam?"

"Yes."

"Where are you?"

"Lobby of the Hotel Sâo Mamede."

"How much time do you have?"

"Until one."

"Lunch with Kali then?"

"Yes."

"Are you being followed?"

"I'm not sure. Maybe I'm being too suspicious."

"I doubt it. Leave the hotel and turn right down Rua Sâo Mamede. Go into the coffee shop at number 28, over the oculist. I'll be there as quickly as I can."

A wave of relief broke over Adam as he hung up. He found the coffee shop without trouble, climbing a steep flight of stairs to a long, narrow room filled with small tables. The table by the window was empty and he sat there, looking out over the enormous gold spectacles that signified the oculist's office and shop below. Across the narrow street were more shops, a tobacconist, a music store, a shoe store. Down the street, which seemed purely commercial, he saw the ubiquitous laundry hanging out.

He ordered coffee and tried to appear relaxed and casual, but he could not keep from looking out on the street. He did not know from which direction Canon Tallis would approach, so he would take a sip of coffee and look up the street, another sip and look down the street. He was looking down the street, leaning forward, thinking he saw the canon in the distance, when somebody sat down opposite him, and he turned, thinking he must have been mistaken, to be met by the beaming face of the student from the bus stop.

"But what good fortune to come across you here!" the student cried. "Perhaps I can be of assistance to you. It would be my unutterable delight. Where is your—what do you call it—girl friend?"

"I'm meeting her in a few minutes." Words came quickly, almost without thought, to Adam's lips. "The bus was faster than I'd expected and I don't want to be *too* early. Bad for them to think you're too eager, if you know what I mean."

The student giggled convulsively. "You Americans! You steal our girls right out from under our envious noses. We are all so poor that it is difficult for us on the surface to compete with you."

"And below the surface?"

The student shrugged apologetically. "America is a rich country and life is easy for you. But the ability to love a woman and to please her to the ultimate fullest comes only through centuries of experience and suffering. I think that in the inner matters of the heart you have much to learn." He beamed at Adam as though he had paid him a great compliment.

A dark figure moved deliberately by Adam, and the Canon seated himself at the next table, so that Adam faced him and the student had his back to him. Adam felt a moment of frantic frustration. He had a wild impulse simply to take the Temis papers from María's pocket and give them to the canon then and there. Canon Tallis looked at him, raising what, if he had had hair, would have been eyebrows.

Adam stood up, saying rather loudly to the student, "Well, it was very pleasant meeting you. It's time for me to go to my girl, now." He could not resist adding, "And I assure you that I, too, have more charm than money."

The student burst into roars of laughter, slapping his knee in enormous appreciation. He, too rose. "Perhaps it would amuse you if I walk along with you and show you some of the particular points of interest."

"But you haven't had your coffee."

The student shrugged and waved his arms in a windmill gesture. "Coffee I can have any time. The chance to exercise my English and simultaneously talk with an American is rare. Where are you meeting this lovely her?"

"At the Salão da Chá."

The student made a face. "The Salão da Chá prefers money to charm."

"Oh, well, you know," Adam said, "girls. I won't eat for a month."

Behind the student's back Canon Tallis' lips moved silently. "Phone." Adam's eyes met his for a brief moment of acquiescence. Then he paid for the coffee and left.

20

The student chattered gaily about Portuguese architecture, history, wine, cheese, until they reached the restaurant. Adam listened enough to respond intelligently and, he hoped, innocently, but he was busy learning streets, memorizing landmarks. At the entrance to the Salâo da Chá they said goodbye, the student pumping Adam's hand with affection, as though they were old friends, Adam trying to sound cordial. He did not know whether the bespectacled young man was one of Cutter's boys or not, but he was inclined to think so. The innocence was too calculated to ring true. And what about Adam's own?

The Salâo da Chá was a large restaurant with a fountain in the center, and a balcony. The maître d'hôtel came bustling up to him, saying in English, "May I help you, sir?" Was he that obviously an American?

"I'm meeting a young lady for lunch," Adam said, "but I'm afraid I'm rather early." There was no use in trying to telephone now. He would have to give Canon Tallis time to get to the Rabbi Pinhas, since that was the next place Dr. O'Keefe had told him to call.

The maître d'hôtel was looking through a small black book. "Would you perhaps be Mr. Eddington?"

"Yes."

"Miss Cutter called. She has reserved a table on the balcony. It is more private, there. Would you like to go up and wait?"

"Fine. Thanks." He wouldn't like to go up and wait at all. He wanted to dash back out onto the street and find Canon Tallis; but Canon Tallis was probably on his way to the rabbi's. Adam decided that he would call in ten minutes, so he asked, "Is there a telephone I could use?"

"Yes, indeed, sir. There is one in the gentlemen's lounge upstairs."

Adam thanked him and was escorted up the stairs to the balcony. He sat at the table and tried not to keep checking his watch. A waiter brought him a carafe of water and asked if he wanted to wait for the young lady before ordering. It seemed that everybody in Lisbon knew more about Adam's plans than Adam himself. He drank a glass of water thirstily and went to the men's room.

He was relieved to find it empty. The phone was on a table, the phone book beside it. He looked up Senhora Leonora Afonso. With the aid of the phrase book again he gave the operator the number, having to repeat it several times, wasting time in giving the numbers in French, German, English, and finally going back to Portuguese. At last he could hear the phone ringing. Ringing. Ringing. Then a man's voice: "Sim?" Adam knew that this meant *yes*, but the voice was formidable, unwelcoming.

"Rabbi Pinhas, por favor."

The voice replied, switching into English (was Adam's accent as apparent as all that?), "Speaking."

"Canon Tallis, please."

"Who?"

"Canon Tallis. Canon Thomas—I mean John Tallis."

The Rabbi Pinhas—if it was he—said, "I think you must have the wrong number."

"This *is* the Rabbi Pinhas?"

"Yes, and I am extremely busy. Please check your number with the operator."

"Sir, this is Adam."

"Young man, look up your numbers more carefully in the future."

"But sir, I know *you*. You were on the plane when—"

A cross voice cut him off. "Young man, this is most definitely not a restaurant. We serve no meals. I do not wish to be discourteous to a foreigner, but you must go to someone else with your problem."

At this apparent non sequitur Adam realized that the rabbi might not be alone, or able to speak freely. "Sir," he said, "if you think you'll be seeing Canon Tallis could you pretend I'm asking you for money?"

"Of course I can't lend you any money, young man. I suggest you go to the American consul. He is supposed to take care of his nationals."

"Do you expect him soon?"

"Young man, you are taking too much of my time. I am expecting a colleague in a few minutes."

"I'm at the Salão da Chá waiting for Kali. I'll try to call again. I'll be here for at least another hour."

"My dear young man, I lead an extremely busy life and several things have come up. Of course you can't come to see me. I'm going out in half an hour."

"I'll try to call back within half an hour, then," Adam said.

He went back to the balcony, to his table. There, at the next table, was Mr. Green of the Singer Sewing Machine. He saw Adam and smiled pleasantly.

"My young friend! And what are you doing here?"

"Meeting a friend for lunch."

"A young lady, I presume?"

"Well—yes."

"Lucky boy. You may wish me luck, too. I'm hoping to bring off a sizable deal." Mr. Green turned from Adam as two men with dark hair and rather flashy suits came up to the balcony, spoke to them in easy, if heavily accented Portuguese, and settled down to what seemed to be business, paying no further attention to Adam. The boy was inclined to think that Mr. Green's appearance was only an accident. Kali had said that the restaurant was well known, and it seemed a likely place to bring someone if you wanted to clinch a business deal.

He looked at his watch. After one. He felt twitchy. Where was Kali? There was no point in trying to call the rabbi's number again yet. He looked over the balcony to the tables below, to the fountain in the center. The restaurant was filling rapidly now, and when Kali came in it was with a group of other people, so that Adam did not see her at once. Then he caught sight of the familiar shining hair, the slender, expensively dressed body, the self-assured walk. The maître d'hôtel hurried to the girl, ignoring other guests who had come in first, and bent gallantly over her hand. Kali smiled and spoke to him, then moved swiftly through the crowded room and up the stairs.

"Adam, darling, I'm sorry I'm a few minutes late. Oh, how lovely to see you." She kissed his cheek exuberantly. At the next table Mr. Green winked at Adam.

Kali stiffened and leaned over the table, saying in a low voice, "Do you know those men?"

"One of them was on the plane this morning."

"There is absolutely *no* privacy in the world any more. Let's eat something quick and get out. They have a kind of prawn here that's just marvelous. I'll order those and we can pick up some tea later. We'll do some sightseeing first."

"While you're ordering," Adam said, slowly and deliberately, "I have a phone call to make."

"To whom?"

"Just a call. I'll be right back."

He went into the men's room. An elderly gentleman with a white goatee was washing his hands, but left without even looking at Adam. This time the boy managed to get the number over to the operator without trouble, and the phone was answered almost immediately. He recognized the rabbi's voice. "It's Adam."

"Hold on."

A short pause, then Canon Tallis. "Adam?"

"Yes."

"Are you alone?"

"At the moment. I'm in the men's room."

"How long are you going to be with Kali?"

"I don't know. She wants to take me sightseeing."

"Fine. Make one of your stops the Saô Juan Chrysostom Monastery. I'll have Father Henriques on the lookout for you. He'll ask if he can be of any assistance to you—he speaks excellent French, so you won't have any language problem—and you are to ask him who was the pagan orator who taught law to Saô Juan. If he simply answers *Libanius* you are to call me at the theater tonight. It's not safe for you to go to the Embassy or to call Joshua this afternoon. Cutter's men are all over the place."

The door to the men's room opened and Mr. Green came in. Adam said, "All right, Susie honey, I understand, but what else do you want me to do?" If the rabbi could play this game so could Adam.

There was a snort at the other end of the line. "Company?"

"Absolutely."

"If he goes on to tell you that John studied theology under Diodore of Tarsus you must manage to get back to the monastery before six, when the doors are locked. I will be there at five-thirty, and will be by the sarcophagus of Princess María Fernanda."

"Anything you say, darling."

Canon Tallis gave another snort and hung up.

Mr. Green grinned conspiratorially. "Quite the young Don Juan, aren't you?"

"Well, you know how it is . . ." Adam replied modestly.

Mr. Green sighed. "Not any more. Those days are gone forever. All I can say is make the most of your hay while the sun shines."

Adam went back to Kali. He still thought that Mr. Green was all right, but he was taking no avoidable risks. Kali was dabbing butter on a bread stick. "I thought you were never coming back," she said crossly. "Who on earth were you talking to?"

"A girl friend."

She glowered as the waiter put a dish of shellfish in front of them. She took her fork and a pick, "Watch," and ripped the meat out of the shell. "I bet it was that Joshua," she said, as Adam tried clumsily to open his shell.

"Joshua who?"

"Don't play innocent. I may not approve of what daddy's doing, but I know what's going on. And I know Joshua. I've seen him dozens of times at Embassy things and he's always been very rude to me. I can't stand him." She spoke in a low and rapid voice, so that Adam had a hard time catching her words.

He leaned across the table and took her hands in his, so that to an observer it would seem like a love scene.

"Adam, I'm scared out of my wits. Daddy's utterly ruthless. He doesn't care how many bodies he tramples over to get what he wants. I'm sorry I sounded all snarly about Joshua. I know he's working with O'Keefe. I guess I'm just jealous of anybody who takes you away from me."

Adam released her hands. "We'd better eat."

"Yes. Let's get out of here. Adam, darling, if it hadn't been for you I'd probably never have questioned daddy. I'd have gone on thinking that anything he did was perfect just because he did it. But after I saw Molèc drive off with you and the O'Keefe child I was—I began to think. There's never been anybody I cared about enough to think about before. I mean, if Molèc drove off with somebody else I wouldn't have given a second thought whether they'd end up dumped in the Tagus or not. But I found myself thinking about you. And then I had to go on and think about all the rest of it." She dropped her eyes as though afraid of having said too much, leaned back in her chair, and began to pick the meat out of the shell with precision. She ate with rapid concentration, and long before Adam had finished she pushed back her chair, saying, "Let's go."

Adam picked up the check and stood up. "How much tip should I leave?"

Kali took the check from him, reached into her own pocketbook and put money down. "Quicker this way. You can pay me back. Come on."

At the next table Mr. Green gave another conspiratorial wink and Adam, giving a foolish grin in return, followed Kali down the stairs. The student spy had been right. The Salâo da Chá was interested in money. One of Adam's favorite restaurants in New York was The Lobster on 45th Street, and it was a good deal more reasonable.

"We have to talk," Kali said intensely as they emerged into the crowded street.

"Well, let's do our sightseeing and we'll be able to talk then."

"Where do you want to go?"

"Just the usuals. The Bélem Tower and the Jeronymos Monastery and the Saô Juan Chrysostom, and maybe the Madre do Dios church."

"We can do the Bélem Tower and the monasteries without any trouble; they're all fairly close together along the waterfront. What about Mr. Eiffel's tower?"

"I'd like to see that, too. Let's do the things along the Tagus, and then we can do the Madre do Dios and the Eiffel if there's time."

They were standing on the street corner, Kali's hand resting lightly on Adam's arm. Several taxis slowed down suggestively, but she waved them on. "As soon as I see a driver I'm sure of," she said. "It has to be someone who doesn't speak English, so we can talk. How are you for time?"

Adam replied cautiously. "I have until five, maybe. See, there's this shopping I have to do for Mrs. O'Keefe." This he and the O'Keefes had decided to make legitimate for the benefit of anyone following his movements; easy enough, Mrs. O'Keefe had said, since the children always needed socks and underwear.

Kali flagged a taxi and Adam opened the door for her. As she climbed in she spoke in swift and charming Portuguese to the driver, giving him what appeared to be complicated directions. Adam thought he heard her mention the tower and the monasteries. She settled back in the seat. "Only till five? What about dinner? Can we have dinner together?"

"I'm afraid not."

"Why not?"

"I just can't, Kali."

"There has to be a *reason*. Are you having dinner with somebody else?"

"I'm not sure."

Kali gave a little cry and turned toward him. "You still don't trust me!"

"I don't know," Adam said with painful honesty, "whether I trust you or not."

Suddenly, unexpectedly, Kali's eyes filled and she butted her face childishly against Adam's shoulder. Through sobs she choked out, "If you don't trust me . . . if you don't love me . . . I can't bear it. . . . I'll want to die. . . ."

At this weakness, so strange in Kali, Adam was flooded with a wave of protective tenderness. He held her closely, saying, "It's all right, Kali; it's all right."

Her sobs dwindled and she raised her head, asking like a child, "Is it really all right?"

"Of course."

"And you *will* help me?"

"In every way that I can. But I don't really see how."

Kali's voice rose. "By keeping me with you. By not sending me away." She began the sharp, frantic sobbing again.

"How can I possibly keep you with me? What about your father, anyhow?"

Kali's eyes darkened. "Oh, Adam, it's so awful. I do love him, but I don't want to see him, and I can't help him any more. All he wants O'Keefe's stuff for is money and more money, he doesn't care how it's used. He says there are too many people in the world anyhow and of course he's right but . . . Did you see Ball this morning?"

"Yes."

"Daddy said you were going to have papers from O'Keefe."

"That's right."

"You mean you *did*?"

"Did what?"

"You gave Ball O'Keefe's stuff?"

"No, Kali. I gave it to Professor Embuste."

"That repulsive little shrimp. Adam, you didn't, you couldn't!"

"Couldn't what?"

"Give him—you know—the things you've found out from O'Keefe." Adam was silent, and Kali cried, "The only way I can think of to make you trust me is to stay with you, so you'll know I'm not going to anybody with information. And it's safest for me, too. If daddy finds out I've told you anything he'll kill me."

"But you haven't told me anything."

"I've told you that I know what he's doing."

"But I already know that, Kali."

The taxi stopped. Kali jerked around and looked out of the window. Adam realized that he had been looking at the girl and not at where they had been driving. She said, "It's the Bélem Tower. Come on." She spoke again to the driver, saying over her shoulder to Adam as she climbed out of the cab, "He'll wait for us."

They walked down a rough path. "Manueline architecture," Kali said absently. "Let's not go in."

Adam tried to look like an innocent tourist as he faced the great white building jutting out into the water. The tower was something out of Africa, and he could imagine a white-robed man standing at one of the corners (which one would face Mecca?) calling the faithful to prayer.

He could not keep Kali with him, but if she were telling the truth he could not let her go.

Kali turned away from the tower and the water. "All right. I'll tell you something else. I said I couldn't work against daddy, but I can't let you be hurt, either. Because I love you, too, Adam. That's what makes it so awful. If you double-crossed daddy this morning, I mean, if what you gave Embuste wasn't right, he'll be out for blood. He has plenty of people who'd be glad to shoot you down for a small sum—or for past favors. But everybody knows me, and as long as you're with me you'll be safe. Look." Adam could see a dark figure slip into the shadows of the tower. "That's one of daddy's men. I don't know if they've found out anything about you—I don't know what you've done—so I don't know if he's really after you or just keeping tabs. Let's go back to the taxi."

They walked over the gritty pavement. Adam held the cab door open, saying, "Let me think."

"All right, darling, darling." She sat close beside him, so that her thigh touched his, but she did not put her hands on him, and she did not speak. At the Mosteiro dos Jeronymos she led the way silently, walking rapidly around groups of tourists. When she spoke it was quietly, unemotionally, in the polite way of someone showing the sights to a distant acquaintance or the friend of a friend.

"It's a rather austere entrance, but I guess that's all right for a monastery. One of daddy's men is over there, stay close to me. The reddish color of the stone is lovely, don't you think? Daddy says that the proportions are more harmonized than in any other building in Lisbon except the Saô Juan Chrysostom. He's looking at us. This is Vasco da Gama's tomb, but they had the wrong man in it for a while or something. Come on, this way. The cloister is famous because it's two-tiered, like the Chrysostom, and they both have these open cells leading off them. I don't know what the monks used them for. Let's go, Adam." The control of her voice slipped. "I want some tea."

Adam took her hand. It was warm and dry, while his, he discovered, was becoming cold with nervousness. "We'll have tea after we've been to the Saô Juan Chrysostom Monastery."

"Let's skip it. It's very much like the Jeronymos, only smaller, and less ornate."

"I'd still like to see it."

"Adam, you can't be interested in sightseeing *now*."

A sightseeing bus pulled up in front of the monastery, and a group of chattering young people got off. Was that the student with the spectacles again? "If we're being followed," he said, "we'd better act as natural as possible, and it would be natural for me to see the Saô Ju——"

Kali cut him off. "All right. Maybe you have a point. Let's go."

In the taxi Adam felt his hands getting colder by the moment, beginning to ooze icy moisture. He must not hold Kali's hand and give away his tension.

The Saô Juan Chrysostom Monastery had fewer tourists than the more famous Jeronymos. It was smaller, less ornate, but there was a purity to it that reached Adam even through his whirling mind. The double cloister soared heavenward, forming a narrow rectangle about a garden with a fountain in the center. In the church itself the light had an underwater-green quality, reminding Adam that the Tagus was just outside. This time Kali gave no tourist's spiel; her face was brooding as they walked slowly, footsteps echoing on the stone floor. They turned into an octagonal bay with a low font in the center, surrounded by seven columns. As they entered by one arch a tiny, elderly priest in a shabby cassock came in by another, bowed, and smiled at them. "May I help you?" he asked, first in Portuguese, then French. Adam answered in French.

"Well, Father, I was studying St. John Chrysostom for a school project once, and I can't remember—what was the name of the pagan orator who taught him law?"

"Show off," Kali whispered.

"Now let me see," the priest said. "That would be Libanius, wouldn't it? It was Diodore of Tarsus who instructed him in theology. I'm delighted at your interest, young man. May I inquire where you're from?"

"New York," Adam said.

"And the young lady? Is she interested, too?"

"No," Kali was impatient. "I'm afraid not. Please, Adam."

The priest smiled at Adam, his faded blue eyes twinkling. "Perhaps you will come another time and let me show you around? I am Father Henriques."

"Thank you, Father. My name is Adam Eddington, and I'll be back as soon as possible, I promise you."

"*Adam*," Kali said. "Sorry, Father, but we have to go."

When they were back in the taxi Adam said, "You weren't very polite."

"If you're not keeeping track of time, I am. Adam, I have to know. Are you going to let me stay with you or not?"

Adam sighed.

"Is it such a horrible prospect?" Kali asked in a low voice. "I did think that you might—that you might care about me a little. I'm not used to telling people I'm in love with them. I'm used to it being the other way around. It's either you or the Tagus as far as I'm concerned."

Looking at her strained face and rather wild eyes, Adam was torn between belief and doubt.

She continued, "I'm not trying to threaten you or say it'll be all your fault if I throw myself into the river. But there isn't any alternative for me. Everything I've ever cared about is all smashed. If you turn me away I don't want to live." Slow tears trickled down her cheeks.

Adam thumped a tight fist into a cold palm. "All right. Look. Tell the taxi driver to take us to Eiffel's Tower."

21

Kali leaned toward the driver obediently and the cab headed back into the city. Adam, straining to look out the window, tried to keep landmarks, street names in his mind, but the problem of Kali kept whirling about, driving away all other thoughts. He could not abandon her either to the Tagus or to the web of steel threads being woven so mercilessly by her father. But he had to go back to the Saô Juan Chrysostom Monastery, and he had to go there alone.

Why? If he believed that Kali was telling him the truth why wasn't taking her with him to Canon Tallis the best possible thing to do?

He believed her and yet he was not quite sure. A week ago the confiding way she was holding on to his arm would have undone him utterly. Now all he felt was cold, cold inside and out.

"Why are we going to Eiffel's Tower?"

"To give me time to think."

"But you're going to keep me with you?"

"I'm going to try to."

"You're going to take care of me?"

"Yes."

The tower loomed up grotesquely in the street, the observation platform balanced precariously on top of the spindly elevator shaft. It was built, it seemed, out of a small boy's erector set. Adam had never seen the Eiffel Tower in Paris, but he had seen pictures of it, and both were obviously the result of the same rackety imagination. The Lisbon Tower, however, also served a purely practical purpose. Lisbon, like Rome, was a city of steep hills, and the foot of the tower was on one street level, the observation platform on another, and riding the elevator was for many people simply a useful short cut. At any other time Adam would have been immensely pleased with it. Now he gave the wild construction the scantiest attention. As they waited for the elevator to take them to the upper level he said, "Okay, I think I've got things straight."

"Tell me."

"If you'll do the shopping for Mrs. O'Keefe—it's just socks and underthings for the kids, and I have all the sizes and every-thing written down—then I can do one other errand at the same time, and then we can meet for dinner."

"What's your errand?"

"Something for Dr. O'Keefe."

Kali frowned as though this was something she needed to ponder about. Finally she said, "I'm sorry, Adam, but how will I know you'll ever come back to me? You could send me shop-ping and just disappear."

"I give you my word."

"People's words don't mean much to me any more. I need something more tangible than that."

"I don't have anything more tangible. I'll do my errand and then I promise you I'll meet you wherever you say."

Kali thought again. "Have you got your passport with you?"

"Of course."

"Give it to me as a hostage. Then I'll know you can't go off and leave me."

"I thought you trusted me."

"I do. More than anybody else I know. But you see the people I know have been daddy and his people, and I always trusted daddy. So how can I trust anybody? Please, Adam, if you *are* coming back to me there isn't any reason not to give me your passport."

Slowly Adam took the passport out of his breast pocket. Still holding it, he asked, "Where will we meet?"

"At the Folclore, as soon after six as possible. The food's good and you ought to hear some Fado and see some of the folk dancing." She held out her hand. Adam put the passport in it. She began leafing through it. "Oh, Adam, what an awful picture, I'd never recognize you!" Between the next two pages was the slip of paper with Joshua's phone numbers. "What's this?"

"Just some phone numbers. Give it to me."

Kali shut the passport. "Oh, no, I'm going to keep the whole thing."

To make an issue over the numbers would be to give them importance in Kali's mind.

Adam swallowed. His hands felt colder and colder. His feet, too, seemed to be lumps of ice. He was doing what he had promised not to do. He said, "The numbers are just for the errand for Dr. O'Keefe. I'd appreciate it if you'd let me have them."

"Look them up in the phone book." Kali put the passport into her bag. "You don't trust me, Adam. I can't bear it."

Adam felt physically sick. His stomach clenched with fury at his ineptness, with frustration at his inability to do anything right. He did not dare press the issue of the phone numbers further. If he could convince Kali that they were unimportant and if he could get back to the Saô Juan Chrysostom in time to deliver the Temis papers to Canon Tallis, then he could meet Kali for dinner, get the passport and Joshua's numbers back, and no real harm would be done.

Mr. Eiffel's elevator creaked down and groaned to a stop, disgorging a chattering group of Lisbonese on their way home, and tourists gawking at and commenting on the tower in all languages.

"Come *on*," Kali said, pushing through the crowd into the elevator, pulling Adam after her.

People continued to jam in long after Adam felt capacity had been reached. He could not see the usual comforting sign to tell how many the elevator could safely hold. The air was thick with sweat, smoke, perfume. With each passing second he felt more of a sense of pressure and more as though he were going to be sick. He was pressed close against Kali and she managed to slide one arm confidingly around his waist. He was glad she had not taken the clammy hand that would have given away his intense nervousness that was bordering on fear.

They were standing near the elevator operator and Kali spoke to him in Portuguese, explaining in Adam's ear, "He's an old friend."

"One of 'daddy's men'?"

"*Really*, Adam," Kali said as the door clanged shut. "I thought I'd made myself clear." Her voice choked up and Adam was afraid his stupidity was going to make her burst into tears there in the crowded elevator.

"I'm sorry." His voice was gruff. He clenched his fists. He *must* keep in control of himself and the situation while he carried the Temis papers and while Kali had the passport with Joshua's phone numbers.

The elevator started to creak upward. People going home from work continued their conversations or stood in stolid fatigue. The tourists exclaimed in excitement, one fat woman giving small shrieks of nervousness at the reluctant jerking of the elevator.

Just as they neared the observation platform there was a groan, a shudder, and they stopped. The operator fiddled with the controls. He said something in Portuguese, then loudly in English, "STUCK."

There was a burst of excited, multilingual talk. Kali said in a clear voice as the fat woman's shrieks grew louder, "It's all right, don't worry, this happens all the time, he'll get it going in a moment. It's perfectly all right, don't get panicky."

The operator broke through her words to call up through the roof. From both the upper and lower levels came shouts of excitement and, evidently, directions, because the operator began jerking at the controls. The elevator dropped a foot and stopped. The fat woman let out a piercing scream.

Adam could feel, particularly among the tourists, a sense of terror compounded by his own. Kali, strangely, seemed less nervous than she had all day. She said something in a very low voice to the operator, but a Frenchman, standing close to them, had evidently heard, because he said, "What was that?"

"I beg your pardon?" Kali asked icily in French.

The Frenchman accused, "*You* told him to stop the elevator."

"Why under the sun would I do that? I'm in just as much of a rush as you are."

"I heard you say *parar*. That means *stop*."

Kali burst into shrill laughter. "Your Portuguese isn't very good, is it? *Para* means *in order to*. I told him to call someone in order to get us out."

The Frenchman looked sourly at Kali. "I don't believe you. I think we are being forcibly detained." He shouted above the babel, "Start this car at once!"

The operator shrugged. "Stuck."

The fat woman cried shrilly, "Somebody *do* something! *Help!*"

"Madame," the operator said, "I 'ave already press ze alarm button."

From the streets above and below the shouts were louder, as though larger groups were gathering.

Adam felt suffocated. Seconds were passing and the Temis papers still on him. He had to get to Canon Tallis. Above him he could see the floor of the observation platform. If the doors of the elevator were opened he would be able to climb up and out onto the platform.

But when he suggested this to Kali and she spoke again in her fluent, rapid Portuguese, the operator shook his head. "Not safe."

Kali's arm tightened around Adam's waist. "Are you in that much of a hurry? Nobody here eats dinner before nine."

Adam's head reeled, but through his dizziness a high English voice cut, "I was stuck in the lift at Harrod's once, but not for nearly as long as this."

It was stiflingly hot in the elevator with all the jammed-in bodies, and the laughter was beginning to have a hysterical edge that was ready to slip over into panic, and he, in his own panic, was being no help. He could feel his heart pounding. Kali's arm was tight about his waist. The fat lady gave a thin, bubbly scream, but before her hysteria got over the edges of control the elevator gave a groan and a jerk, and the operator, as though he were piloting a plane, brought it to a stop at the upper platform.

Adam, forgetting all courtesy, pushed out, dragging Kali after him. He looked at his watch. Almost six. He swung on Kali, shouting, "You do the shopping. Here's the list. Here's some money." He thrust Dr. Ball's bills into her hand. There. "I'll meet you at the Folclore as soon as I can." Without stopping for any kind of response from her, without giving her a chance to hold him back, he rushed off up the street. An empty cab was passing. He hailed it, and got in, panting. "São Juan Chrysostom Monastery, por favor." He saw that Kali had run up the street after him, but he slammed the taxi door, giving her a vague nod and wave. If she had heard where he was going it was too late now.

He looked from the window of the taxi to his watch and back to the window. The streets were full of people going home, streaming out of stores, hotels, subway stops, their shadows long as the sun began to drop.

The driver wove skillfully around pedestrians, buses, cars. Adam looked at him through the dividing glass, a rough-appearing man in a fisherman's sweater and cap and an unkempt beard. He looked at Adam in the rearview mirror and winked. Adam froze. One of Cutter's men? Had he walked into a trap?

Still with his foot on the accelerator the driver turned to face Adam, gave a jerk to the beard, which came off, revealing Arcangelo. A swift movement and the beard was back in place.

"Arcangelo!" Adam gasped. "What—"

"I've been following you all day," Arcangelo said in his careful English. "So have others."

"But it's not safe for you!"

"You did not recognize me, did you?"

"But it's still not safe. Dr. O'Keefe said—"

"You think I would let those snakes drive me under cover?" Arcangelo swerved scornfully around a bus and turned down a side street. "If anything happened to you Polyhymnia would be unhappy."

Ahead of them a large black car swung out of a side street so that Arcangelo had to jam on his brakes. "*Duck!*" he said suddenly, and in a quick reflex Adam dropped to the floor.

"Molèc," Arcangelo growled between closed teeth. "We are in for what you would call the showdown. Where is the Cutter girl?" He spoke with as little lip motion as possible, then puckered his lips up in a whistle, so that anyone looking back from the dark car ahead would not know he was talking to the passenger. The whistling resolved itself into a melody. The Tallis Canon.

Adam felt a surge of excitement despite his cold hands and feet. "She's safe. She's shopping. I have to get to the Saô Juan Chrysostom Monastery before six. Canon Tallis is waiting for me."

"Six now," Arcangelo said. "They are trying to slow us down and I cannot let them know I know who they are or they will know who I am."

"It closes at six."

"I know a side door but we will have to get rid of Molèc." Arcangelo swung around and down a side street, then turned back into the city. Adam raised his head, but Arcangelo said sharply, "Stay down." The boy could not see where they were going, but he could feel that it was a rapid and devious way. The taxi stopped with an abruptness that threw him against the seat in front, and Arcangelo said, "Get out."

Cold though Adam's hands might be, his reflexes were functioning satisfactorily. He grasped the handle of the door and pitched himself into the street. They had stopped at a rank of taxis. Arcangelo was leaning out the window, talking to one of the drivers, and indicated with a gesture of his thumb that Adam was to get into the other cab. As the boy slammed the door Arcangelo said, "He will take you to the Saô Juan Chrysostom. I will continue to drive so that Molèc will be put off the trail. Go now, quickly."

The taxi shot off. Adam called back, "Arcangelo, take care of yourself."

The taxi driver, a thin young Negro, looked at Adam in the rearview mirror and smiled. Then he began to whistle, softly. The Tallis Canon. Adam joined him. They smiled at each other. Adam knew that he must not make the mistake of thinking that either he or the papers were safe because Arcangelo was taking charge, because he liked the young man who was driving him, but the terror had left the pit of his stomach, and he sat, coiled like a wire, ready at any moment and whenever necessary, to spring.

"Saô Juan," the driver said, and ahead of them was the beautiful, austere building. They drove past the entrance, the great doors closed, only darkness showing behind the stained-glass windows which were drained of color as light was slowly draining from the sky. They turned the corner and went past the Chapter House. Beyond this was an iron gate that opened to a long, narrow, hedged-in path to the cloister. The driver looked quickly around, stopped, and jumped out. Adam followed him, and together they ran to the gate. The driver pulled at the bell, once, twice, three times. In the distance they could hear it clanging.

Bong. Bong. Bong.

Through the sound of the bell came the sputter of an engine. The driver grabbed Adam and together they pressed into the shadows. A diesel-powered taxi drove up and someone sprang out.

22

It was Joshua.

"Muito obrigado," he said to Adam's driver, "apresse se," clapped him in a swift, comradely gesture on the shoulder, and turned to Adam. The young driver ran back to his cab. They heard him gun the engine and roar down the street.

Joshua pulled a key out of his pocket and bent to unlock the gate.

"How did you know—" Adam started.

"Kali phoned me. How did she get my numbers?" The gate creaked open. Joshua pulled Adam through, clanged it shut, locked it. When Adam did not answer his question he did not repeat it. They hurried down the path, brushed by early evening shadows cast by the tall hedges. Behind them they could hear the squeal of tires, screech of brakes, slamming of car doors.

"Run." Joshua sprinted ahead, Adam close on his heels. The path turned, leading them to an arched side entrance. Again Joshua bent to the lock. As the door swung open they could hear footsteps pounding down the path. Joshua slammed the door and leaned against it for a moment, panting. "Are the papers still on you?"

"Yes."

Behind them there was a pounding at the door. Joshua pulled

214

Adam away as shots rang out, splintering the heavy wood. "Quick."

The room they were in was so deep in shadows that Adam could see nothing after the light outside. Joshua grabbed his hand and they ran, Adam stumbling, slowing them down, ran through the room, through a corridor illuminated by high, dusty windows, and then out and into the light of the cloister. In the center of the garden the fountain rose high, catching the long rays of sun in a shower of silver. They ran pounding down the echoing stones; their footsteps echoed, and the echo was lost in the crash of heavy feet seeming to close in from all sides.

Ahead of them a hulking form loomed up: Molèc.

"God," Joshua said. He swung Adam around and shoved him into one of the monks' niches as a shot rang out.

Still running, Joshua fell.

Out of the niche beside Adam came Typhon Cutter, and Kali ran swiftly along the cloister and plummeted into his arms. "Well done," Typhon Cutter said, and Adam saw, with a feeling of nausea, the look of adoration she gave her father, the spider weaving his inexorable web in which they were all trapped. How, now, was there any escaping the tightening threads?

Despair burned in the pit of Adam's stomach, then burst into a fierce and controlled anger such as he had never felt before. He stood, crouched like a panther ready to spring.

Another shot.

The gun dropped from Molèc's hand and he gave a scream of rage and pain. Another shot dropped him, writhing, to his knees. Typhon Cutter pulled Kali back into the monk's cell.

Joshua lay, without moving, on the stones a few feet from Adam.

"Stay back!" A voice catapulted across the cloister as Adam started to leap out of the niche into which Joshua had shoved him.

He had no weapon. No gun. He could not help, only hinder. There was, at the moment, nothing to do but obey.

Across the cloister he saw the dark form of Canon Tallis,

smoking gun in hand. He thought he saw Arcangelo. A shot rang across the cloister from Typhon Cutter's cell and ricocheted from a stone column.

Adam looked at Joshua's still form, only a shadow as light began to withdraw from the cloister, and let out a cry of anguish and rage.

His cry was echoed in the high shriek of a siren. Turning, he saw Typhon Cutter and Kali slip out of their cell. As they disappeared into the darkening corridor he was after them, and with one leap he flung himself on Mr. Cutter, throwing him to the ground.

"Daddy, don't kill him!" Kali screamed.

Adam's fingers clamped around the wrist that held the gun, his knee was on the bloated stomach.

"No," Kali said. "No." She grabbed the gun from her father and pointed it quaveringly at Adam. He could barely see the gun because the passage was almost entirely locked in darkness. The light filtering dustily through the high windows was above their heads and they were enclosed in shadows. "Let him up," Kali ordered.

Adam looked toward her. In the dim light her face was contorted in a horrible mixture of emotion. If ever she had been beautiful for him she was not beautiful now.

"Let him up," she said again, her voice steadier, "or I'll shoot. I mean it."

Adam lifted his knee from the belly, released his hold on the wrist. Typhon Cutter struggled to his feet as a searchlight swept across the cloister, penetrating the dark reaches of the corridor where the three of them stood, panting.

"The papers," Typhon Cutter said.

"I gave you the papers."

"Not those. You have others. Give them to me." The treble voice soared.

"No," Adam said. "I don't have any papers."

"The gun, Kali."

"No, daddy. No."

If he shouted, Adam thought, they might hear him in the

cloister and come. But no sound emerged from his constricted throat.

"The gun."

The muzzle pressed against Adam's chest.

"The papers."

"Go ahead and shoot," Adam croaked, "for all the good it will do you." He expected to hear the explosion of the bullet if, indeed, he heard anything.

But Cutter said, "Kali," and the boy felt, instead of a deadly burst of lead, her long fingers moving over him, coming closer, as she searched, to María's pocket.

Without conscious volition his hand flashed out and slapped across the girl's face, the sound sharp and unexpected and immediately followed by a shot and the crash of the gun dropping from Typhon Cutter's hand.

The shot had not come from Cutter's gun. From where?

Cutter began to back down the passage, holding Kali in front of him as a shield.

Through the darkness came the voice of Arcangelo. "Let them go. My men outside."

Adam reached down in the shadows to look for the dropped gun, but he could not find it. His breath came in painful gasps as his heart thudded against the rib cage.

"Come," Arcangelo said. "It's over. Everything is over. Come."

The searchlight swung around again, and Adam moved toward it and to the cloister that still contained the last rays of the sun, the fountain glistening as it rose toward the sky, Joshua, lying sprawled on cold stone.

With an absolute carelessness and indifference to what was going on around him Adam ran across the pavement to Joshua and knelt by him. Joshua's eyes were open, but he did not see.

"Joshua!" Adam cried. "Joshua!" He put his head against Joshua's chest, listening, listening, and thought he felt the faint thread of a heartbeat. He noticed two uniformed men going by with Molèc bellowing on a stretcher, noticed it only because the sound kept him from listening for Joshua's heart. He pressed his cheek to Joshua's lips to try to feel the faintest breath.

"Adam." It was Canon Tallis' voice.

Adam looked up.

The priest stood there, gun still in hand, with two uniformed policemen beside him. Adam could tell that the canon was thanking them, that he was giving them instructions. When they turned toward Joshua he spoke to them brusquely, and they bowed and moved away.

"Get up," Canon Tallis said to Adam, and the boy stood. The canon knelt beside Joshua. A faint sound came from his lips, the single word, "God." It was also the last word Joshua had said.

Out of the shadows Arcangelo and Father Henriques emerged, Arcangelo looming enormous beside the tiny priest. Canon Tallis looked at them. "Morto," he said.

"No," Adam babbled, "no, he's not dead, he can't be."

"He is dead. Be still," Canon Tallis said. He leaned over Joshua again and it was as though the two of them had gone two thousand miles away, that they were not in the cloister with Adam and Father Henriques and Arcangelo. The canon took Joshua into his arms, holding him close in a gesture of infinite tenderness and love.

Father Henriques touched Adam's arm and drew him away. The three of them, Father Henriques, Arcangelo, Adam, walked slowly along the cold stones of the cloister, their feet muffled in darkness and grief, leaving Canon Tallis with Joshua.

23

Was it only that the light bulb in Father Henriques' tiny office was dim, like the light bulb in the Avenida Palace, or was the darkness in Adam's mind?

He sat on a straight chair across from Father Henriques and Arcangelo. Their faces were closed and emotionless, as though turned to stone. Adam did not know when Father Henriques and Arcangelo started to talk in low voices, nor when he realized that they were speaking French, until he heard Father Henriques ask, "Arcangelo, how did you know—"

"You think you could keep me away," Arcangelo asked, "when I am needed? You think I will hide in safety when you are in danger?" His voice deepened with emotion. "You think I cannot find out when you try to protect me?"

Father Henriques held up a thin white hand, and Arcangelo rumbled into silence.

A dark shadow moved across the doorway and Canon Tallis came into the office. "The papers," he said without preamble and, as Adam handed them to him, he demanded, "Why was Joshua here? He was to be at the Bélem Tower."

Adam stood up, but his knees were trembling so that he sat down again immediately. "He was here because of me."

Then came the questions, Canon Tallis clear, precise, ice

cold, Father Henriques gentle but nevertheless touching every raw and open nerve.

It had been again (again and again: would it never end?) the unexpected, the unforeseen that had happened. The papers Adam had delivered to Professor Embuste at Dr. Ball's rectory had indicated a meeting at the Bélem Tower. Joshua, working with Interpol and the Lisbon police, was to have been there. Typhon Cutter was to have been led into his own spider web.

"As indeed he was," Father Henriques said. "But not in the way we thought."

And not before Molèc's bullet had found Joshua.

Adam cried in anguish, "I killed Joshua. I believed Kali and I didn't tell Dr. O'Keefe." He began to gasp through sobs that racked his body. "I let Kali get Joshua's phone numbers and he came to save me—"

Canon Tallis cut him short. "Stop."

"But he would still be alive—"

The canon's voice was quiet, firm as a rock. "You cannot see the past that did not happen any more than you can foresee the future. Come, Adam. We must go."

In the back seat of a police car Adam rode beside Canon Tallis. Two policemen sat in front, talking casually. The last late light of evening had left the sky, so time must have passed, and light from street lamps, shop windows, neon signs, streamed across the mosaic sidewalks. A mule-drawn wagon turned into the street in front of them, a lumbering, cumbersome wagon bearing great red clay jars of wine. The mule ambled along, paying no attention to the honking of the police car. The driver shouted threats at the mule driver, and finally managed to swerve around wagon and mule, almost knocking down an elderly man in a tam-o'shanter who was riding along on a bicycle. The man wobbled precariously, shrieking at the police car and shaking his fist. The policeman leaned out the window and yelled back, zigzagging toward the curb to more shouting from excited pedestrians.

Beside Adam the canon sat still and stern, paying no attention. The driver regained control of the car and himself, and turned down a side street, then down another and darker street where laundry flapped, ghost-like, in the breeze from the Tagus.

The car stopped and the canon got out, beckoning to Adam, crossed to a narrow house faced with blue-and-white tile, and banged a brass knocker against a blue door. Above them a window was flung open and a man with a long white beard and a nightcap stuck his head out.

"A.H. 173-176," the canon said.

"E.H. 269," the man in the nightcap replied.

"ΦΩΣ ἱλαρὸν ἁγίας δόξης ἀθανάτου Πατρὸς, οὐρανίου, ἁγίου, μάκαρος, Ἰησοῦ Χριστὲ, ἐλθόντες ἐπὶ τοῦ ἡλίου δύσιν, ἰδόντες φῶς ἑσπερινὸν, ὑμνοῦμεν Πατέρα, καὶ Υἱὸν, καὶ ἅγιον Πνεῦμα Θεοῖ," the canon said.

" "Ἄξιος εἶ ἐν πᾶσι καιροῖς ὑμνεῖσθαι φωναῖς ὁσίαις, Υἱὲ Θεοῦ, ζωὴν ὁ διδούς. Διὸ ὁ κόσμος σε δοξάζει," the man with the beard replied, and disappeared, pulling the window closed behind him.

It had sounded like Greek to Adam. As a matter of fact, it probably *was* Greek.

The door creaked open and the man in the beard led them into a small side room containing only a high desk and a stool. The canon explained curtly, "Father Metousis is the only one who can break Dr. O'Keefe's code."

The patriarch sat on the stool, steel-rimmed glasses slipping down his nose. He wrote with a scratchy, sputtering nib which he had continually to dip into ink. Adam did not know how long Canon Tallis and he stood there while the old man wrote, thought, wrote, scratched out and wrote again. It must have been more than a few minutes. It was probably less than hours. Time had no meaning: it was not.

Finally Father Metousis handed the papers over.

"Joshua?" he asked.

Canon Tallis nodded. "Tomorrow afternoon."

"Gaea?"

"Yes."

Adam no longer attempted to understand. He swayed. Canon Tallis gestured to him and they left, climbing back into the police car which was waiting outside. "The American Embassy," the canon said, then, dryly, to Adam, "We don't usually have this kind of escort."

At the Embassy a party was in progress. Lights and music filled the night. Uniformed servants were passing trays of champagne, platters of canapés. The canon walked by the open archways that led into the rooms in which the party was being held. At one end of the large room to the right an orchestra was playing, banked by palms. That they could play on the night of Joshua's death, that the world could still turn, the Tagus flow, seemed to Adam incredible.

"Come," Canon Tallis said.

They went up a flight of wide marble stairs. Adam could feel himself climbing, but he could not see: he was blind with rage, and even the brilliant lighting of the room into which he was led could not clear his vision. The kaleidoscopic events of the past hours crackled around him. He stood obediently by Canon Tallis while the echoing shots in the Saô Juan Chrysostom Monastery sounded in his ears.

He knew that he was being introduced to the Ambassador, and that he was being questioned kindly. He answered, but he did not hear what he said. In the bright room the Ambassador had to repeat a question.

Adam replied, the question slowly filtering through. "Oh. He was with the Singer Sewing Machine Company. I don't think he was one of Cutter's men."

"No," the Ambassador said. "One of ours."

"Poly—" Adam said to the Ambassador, but heard no answer to the name that was now a question. "Charles cried," he said, but when the ambassador, with gentle patience, asked, "What was that, Adam?" the boy only shook his head as though to try to clear it. Then he was able to answer the questions he had already answered once for Canon Tallis and Father Henriques.

Through the open windows of the Ambassador's bright room the singing of summer insects came clearly, and it was as though their buzzing was in Adam's head. The Ambassador was looking through the decoded papers. Later Adam would remember that there had been a transatlantic call to Washington. There were other calls.

Later it would all sort itself out in Adam's memory, questions and answers finally settling like sediment in a test tube. Next to Canon Tallis' steel control the Ambassador seemed excitable, harried, but Adam realized later that although he was undoubtedly the second he was not the first.

"But why did Arcangelo let Cutter and Kali *go?*" Adam exploded once. "Why did he let them leave the Saô Juan Chrysostom?"

"The police and Interpol were both there. If you remember, they were already at the Bélem Tower."

"But how—"

The canon silenced Adam with a stern glance. "When your young taxi driver friend left you and Joshua at the Saô Juan he went, as Arcangelo had directed him, to Bélem."

"But what about Cutter and Kali *now?* Where are they?"

"Free," Canon Tallis said, "in a manner of speaking."

"But—"

The Ambassador sighed. "You are not at home, Adam. Trying someone like Typhon Cutter in a Portuguese court is difficult if not impossible—"

"You mean he can buy his way out?"

Now the Ambassador's voice was hard. "You think *our* courts are entirely free from corruption? Of course Cutter would be able to buy and subvert at least part of the testimony against him. But this is nearsighted oversimplification. Even in America it's difficult to arrest someone on suspicion of intent to commit murder. You have to have real and absolute evidence."

"But Molèc—"

"—is being tried for murder. And will be found guilty. The beast caught in his master's trap. One can't help being sorry for him."

"I can."

"That's evading the issue. He is, in a way, our scapegoat, too. Remember that the Portuguese are not interested in the moral and ethical qualities of expatriates, especially people whose extremely lucrative businesses bring employment and money where it is rather desperately needed. This is worth thinking about."

But Adam was not capable of thought.

The Ambassador continued—or was it before? when? words floated to Adam's mind with no consecutivity: "Has it occurred to you, Adam, that we don't want to air Dr. O'Keefe's experiments in court? The need for silence has not been removed. Has it occurred to you that both the Portuguese and the United States governments would wish to avoid the appearance of an international incident which Cutter would not hesitate to exploit? Something like this, allowed to snowball, could start a holocaust. Is this what Joshua would have wanted?"

"But—"

The Ambassador banged down onto the desk a coffee cup Adam hadn't even realized he was holding so that the dark liquid slopped into the saucer. "We are not going to try to do more than we know we can do. If this seems to you inadequate expediency, try to remember that one battle won today permits us to embark on the next, and then a next, and all the long ones that are to follow." He rose. Was it then, or later? In any case the blinded time in the bright office was finally over and Adam followed the dark, erect form of the canon down the stairs. They left the light and music of the Embassy and climbed into the police car.

"I'll take you back to Gaea," Canon Tallis said.

Adam nodded.

"We'll take Joshua's plane. I'm not the pilot he was, but I'll get us there."

"And Cutter?" Adam repeated, thickly.

"How much were you able to listen to?" There was no censure in the question. "He's been given a week to leave Portugal. He'll lose his property here, and all the money he has tied up in it. His Portuguese operation is over."

Adam clenched his fists. "That's not—" he started savagely.

"No revenge is, Adam."

At the little airport Arcangelo was waiting. He held out the heavy jackets, the goggles, helped strap them in. Then he looked in silent questioning at Canon Tallis, who said, "Father Henriques is bringing Joshua tomorrow. Come with him." He leaned out of the pilot's seat and reached for Arcangelo's hand. "Thank you, Arcangelo. Thank God for you."

Arcangelo shrugged, smiled briefly, went to the propeller. The plane shuddered into life, moved slowly along the runway, jerked, and left the ground.

Once again time was outside Adam, or perhaps it was Adam who was outside time. He sat in the cockpit of the same small plane where Joshua, in the pilot's seat, had sung the "Ode to Joy" as they bucked wildly through the boisterous clouds. Now Canon Tallis sat darkly at the controls, closed in, stern. Above them and around them the stars were thick. Below was a sea of white clouds.

—He's flying this crate much too high, Adam thought fleetingly.

It didn't matter. They would or they would not get to the island, and whichever one it was didn't matter, either.

The plane jerked and dropped. Canon Tallis grimly pulled on the stick and the plane steadied and nosed upward again.

"Why didn't you kill Molèc?" Adam shouted suddenly. He strained for the answer.

"Would that have brought Joshua back?"

With the taste of ashes in his mouth Adam realized that his grief was nothing beside the canon's. He slouched down in his seat as though to avoid the piercing light of the stars. Behind them the moon, just beyond fullness, sailed lopsided and serene. Through a rift in the clouds it made a path upon the water below.

And all Adam wanted to do was to swear, to split the pure and silver air with every blasphemy he had ever heard on the streets. He shuddered, controlled himself, shuddered again. He bellowed, the words coming out like oaths, "She has my passport!"

"Kali?"

"Yes."

"All right. We'll get it."

"I don't want it," Adam cried. "I don't want anything."

To this the canon did not reply. He seemed to be concentrating only on the plane, the stars above, the clouds below.

They moved through space; they must also have moved through time. The clouds were gone and below them lay the vast, slowly breathing surface of the sea. Ahead was the dark shadow of the island. The plane nosed downward, and suddenly along the beach flares were lit, one after another, outlining a runway for the landing.

Dr. O'Keefe was there, with José, María's husband. Four horses were hitched to the barnacled pile.

Canon Tallis climbed stiffly from the plane. Adam unstrapped himself and followed. Beyond the barest greeting there was no talking. Dr. O'Keefe and Canon Tallis rode ahead, Adam and José behind. José spoke no English, but once he looked over at Adam and said softly, "Jhoshuajh . . ." and Adam could see that tears were trickling quietly down his cheeks. Looking at José's tears Adam fought down a reaction to shout, "*Shut up!*" He bowed his head and let the horse carry him along the water's edge, the drumming of the hoofbeats muffled in the sand.

The horses moved with unhurried pace, taking them inexorably through time, through space.

In the bungalows lights were on in the living quarters.

—Make Poly be in bed, Adam thought savagely. —I cannot see her. I cannot see Charles.

They dismounted. The horses followed José, and Adam followed Dr. O'Keefe and Canon Tallis. Only Mrs. O'Keefe was in the living room and she drew Adam to her in a quick, maternal embrace. Adam felt an enormous sob rising within him and pulled from the circle of her arms. She held him not with her arms but with her eyes. "You must not blame yourself."

"It started with the door at the Avenida Palace," Adam said. "If I hadn't opened the door—"

The canon cut brusquely across his words. "Or the fog in New

York. Or if I had not asked you to take Poly back to Lisbon. This is foolish talk and must be stopped."

"But he died for me," Adam choked. "I gave Kali his phone numbers and he pushed me into one of the monk's cells and Molèc's bullet hit him."

"He died for us all," the canon said, "and if you love him you will have to stop talking and thinking like this, because what you have to do now is to live. For him, and for us all."

Mrs. O'Keefe moved to the arch that led to the living quarters. "And what you have to do at this particular moment is to go to bed. There will be work tomorrow."

—Work? What work? Adam thought numbly, but he bowed a clumsy good night and went to bed.

24

In the morning Poly brought Adam his breakfast. She put the tray down on the bed and then stood looking at him steadily and, it seemed to him, accusingly. He had been weighed again and found wanting.

But when she spoke she said only "Adam—" and then, "Adam, I do love you and I'm terribly sorry." At the door she said in a muffled voice, "Daddy and Father expect you in the lab as soon as you're ready."

"The lab?" Adam asked stupidly.

Poly ran her fingers with impatience through her hair. "The starfish have to be tended to. Daddy's work doesn't stop because—" she broke off. A tremor moved across her face like the wind moving upon water. She stamped angrily to regain control. "Why do you think Joshua went rushing off to you when Kali called him? You don't think he thought it was fun and games and the good of his health, do you?"

Adam shook his head.

"All right, why, then?"

Adam banged down his cup. "Starfish and sparrows," he said loudly.

Poly stamped again, "*Okay*, then," and hurried out of the room.

Adam finished the cup of now lukewarm coffee, poured another, drinking slowly, unwilling to leave what seemed the comparative safety of his room. Seeing Poly had been bad enough. He wanted to put off seeing anyone else. Slowly, deliberately, he drained the last drops of coffee and milk from the little pots, picked up each crumb of his roll and ate it. Finally there was nothing to do but get dressed, and since his lab clothes were nothing but chino slacks and a tee shirt he could not prolong the process by more than a few minutes. Then he almost ran through the living room, hurried across the breezeway and into the lab.

Dr. O'Keefe and Canon Tallis were standing by one of the tanks. Dr. O'Keefe beckoned to him.

"Look at this, Adam. This is the tiny fragment of starfish arm we planted with nerve rings several weeks ago. Yesterday I'd about given up on it, but look, there's regeneration beginning. Check the other tanks, will you, please? and let me know if there's anything unusual."

Nobody was behaving as though it were an ordinary day, but nevertheless the work in the laboratory was going on, and this was still a shock to Adam. He took care of the starfish, pointed out new growth on a lizard, wrote up his notes in the files. He worked automatically, adequately, but his mind was no longer out of time as it had been the night before. He was thrust back into time, and therefore into pain.

This time the day before Joshua had been alive. In the short space of twenty-four hours more had happened than it would seem time possibly could take care of. And time hadn't taken care of it. Molèc's bullet had sped through space and time and into Joshua's heart.

"Adam," Canon Tallis said, "will you go over these figures, please? These are from Scotland and we want to see if they gibe with Dr. O'Keefe's findings."

"Sit down to it," Dr. O'Keefe suggested as Adam took the sheaf of papers. "It's important that you check them accurately. You'll find the equations perfectly straightforward, but you'll have to concentrate if you don't want to make errors. We'll see you later."

"All right, sir." Adam had not wanted to come in to the lab to see Dr. O'Keefe and Canon Tallis; now he did not want them to leave. But they went on out, without telling him where they were going. Perhaps to the village to see Virbius or to check the pens there. He did not know. He concentrated on the letters and numbers written in black ink on thin paper. He found that if he was to check them properly he could not think about anything else. At first it was an effort to pay attention to what he was doing; then, as always, the discipline of work took hold of him and he bent over the papers, his lips moving, his bruised mind occupied only with the job Canon Tallis had given him.

He was surprised when Peggy came to call him, hugging him, twining her arms around him lovingly, kissing him over and over again, but not speaking, not explaining the sudden passion of affection.

Mrs. O'Keefe stood in the lab doorway. "Have a quick swim before lunch, Adam. The children are looking for you."

Adam changed to the navy blue trunks, trying not to look at the zebra-striped ones. The children were waiting for him on the sea wall. Poly wore the red bathing suit, but the color seemed drained from it, from her hair. There was no running and jumping over the sand, no delighted leaping into the surf. Peggy held Adam's hand. When she was ankle-deep she let go, saying, "I don't think I'll go swimming today if you don't mind, Adam. I want to go back in with Johnny and Rosy."

Sandy and Dennys sat at the water's edge, letting the small waves wash over them, letting the damp yellow sand sift through their fingers, talking only to each other.

Poly said, "If you'll come with me, Adam, I want to swim out a bit."

"I'll come, too." Charles moved to Adam's other side.

The three of them walked out into the water, not jumping through the waves, simply pushing against them, letting the water break, unheeded, over them, until they were out deep enough so that first Charles could drop down and start to swim, then Poly and Adam.

He did not ask about Macrina. After a while he said, "That's far enough out, Poly," and obediently she stopped swimming and began to tread water. She did not make the breathy, whistling noises with which she usually called Macrina. She simply kept treading water and staring out to sea. Charles lay on his back and floated, his eyes closed against the glare of the sun. Adam dog-paddled between them.

He was about to say, "Okay, kids, we'd better go back in," when there was the familiar flash of silver and Macrina was with them. Poly gave a great cry and flung herself at the dolphin. Charles continued to lie on his back in the water, his eyes closed. Poly's sobs were enormous, racking the thin body in the red wool bathing suit. For a moment Macrina thrashed the water with her tail. Then she gave a shudder and swam slowly around Poly, keeping her head with the great smiling mouth constantly toward the child. The mouth was smiling but there was no doubt in Adam's mind that Macrina, now nuzzling Poly's shoulder, was trying to comfort the child, that Macrina cared. Then the dolphin left Poly and swam over to Charles, nudging at him gently until he opened his eyes, rolled over in the water, and flung his arms around the great, slippery body. When Charles let Macrina go she came to Adam, seeming to look at him questioningly. Then, with a flash of silver, she was gone.

The children swam in. "Come on, Sandy, Dennys," Poly said to the two little boys who were building a sand castle. As they walked across the burning beach to the bungalow Poly murmured, "She's not an anthropomorphic dolphin, she's an anagogical dolphin."

"Hunh?" Adam asked.

"I don't know what it means. It's something Father Tom said once and I made him say it over until I remembered it. I think it's something good."

Canon Tallis and Dr. O'Keefe were not at lunch. The younger children chattered desultorily. Adam tried to choke down a few mouthfuls because Charles was looking at him, and when Adam took a bite, Charles took a bite. Once Mrs. O'Keefe turned to Adam, saying in a steady voice, "The Cutters are at the hotel, Adam. They'll be flying to Spain from here, and then to America. My husband and Father Tallis will go over tonight to get your passport."

Adam bowed his head to show that he had heard, and took another bite.

Mrs. O'Keefe rose. "Do whatever María tells you to, children. I won't be very long. Adam, Poly, Charles, come."

It was only then that Adam noticed that Poly and Charles had changed from their bathing suits to their riding breeches. Mrs. O'Keefe said, "María has laid out your riding clothes for you, Adam. We'll wait outside."

The riding breeches Joshua had given Adam the first night on the island were on his bed, together with a clean white shirt. Lying carefully placed on the shirt was the canvas belt with the switchblade knife containing the lethal dose of MS-222. Adam looked at the knife broodingly. Had María put it there? Had Poly? He stripped off his lab clothes and strapped the knife on under the riding clothes.

Poly led the way inland. Since her storm of sobbing in the ocean and the silent comfort of the dolphin she seemed less tightly drawn. As the horses began to climb Adam realized that they were going to the great golden stones where Joshua had taken him the morning he had arrived on the island, the morning he had failed to notice the small cemetery in the clearing.

When they reached the plateau there were several boys from the village waiting to take care of the horses, and Adam saw that there were already other horses there. Around the great table was a large group of people, some seated on the stones, more standing. A few of them Adam recognized: Virbius was there, with Temis. Rabbi Pinhas was there, and Mr. Green, Father Metousis and Arcangelo. Was the inspector from the Madrid airport sitting on one of the stones by the young taxi driver? Their faces were turned away; he could not be sure.

Canon Tallis held the burial service.

Adam had heard the words before. For his grandparents. For a teacher at school. It was the American words which the canon was using for Joshua. Now the words seemed tangible, material; steeled by the English voice they held him erect on the stone bench where he sat between Poly and Charles.

". . . Remember thy servant Joshua, O Lord," Canon Tallis said, "according to the favor which thou bearest unto thy people, and grant that, increasing in knowledge and love of thee, he may go from strength to strength, in the life of perfect service. . . ."

Charles reached over and took Adam's cold hand in his smaller but equally cold one.

"Unto God's gracious mercy and protection we commit you," Canon Tallis said. "The Lord bless you and keep you. The Lord make his face to shine upon you, and be gracious unto you. The Lord lift up his countenance upon you and give you peace both now and evermore."

They moved from the golden stones across the rough grass and into the clearing where the open grave waited. Charles continued to hold Adam's hand. Once he pressed his face against Adam's shirt. Then he turned and looked back at Canon Tallis. On Adam's other side Poly stood, still as death.

Adam closed his eyes.

It was over.

The group dispersed quietly. It was only as Adam went with Charles to the horses where Dr. and Mrs. O'Keefe stood waiting with Canon Tallis that he realized that Poly had gone from his side, that she was nowhere to be seen.

"Stay with Charles," the doctor said. "We'll look for her."

They waited, and Charles said only, "Don't worry, Adam, Poly's all right."

When Dr. O'Keefe and Canon Tallis returned alone, Charles said, without anxiety, "I think she's gone to the village with Temis. She has to be away from us for a little while."

Mrs. O'Keefe looked at her husband. "Will you ride over and see?"

The doctor nodded. "Tom, come with me. She may need you."

Now there were just the three of them on the plateau, Adam, Mrs. O'Keefe and Charles, and to one side two little village boys staying faithfully with the horses. Adam asked Mrs. O'Keefe, "Would you and Charles be all right if I ride over to the hotel? I'd like to get my passport back myself."

She looked at him. "If this is what you think you want to do, Adam. Charles and I will be fine in any case. But please be home in time for dinner."

Adam agreed absently. He was not thinking of dinner. As he rode toward the hotel darkness closed in on him again. He did not see the sun, or even feel its rays, although he frequently raised his arm to wipe off the sweat that streamed down his face. He rode through darkness and through time. The sun was slipping down the sky toward the west when the path opened out between the hotel landing strip and the tennis courts and swimming pool.

He did not know what he was going to do or say when he saw Typhon Cutter and Kali. He was not thinking primarily about his passport. This would be easy enough for Dr. O'Keefe and Canon Tallis to get. He only knew that the anger that burned in him would not abate until he had seen Kali, Kali who had deliberately led him into the killing at the Saô Juan Chrysostom Monastery. Her high, shrill laugh echoed in his ears.

He hitched the tired white horse to a tree at the end of the path, walked past the landing strip, along the beach, up the path between tennis courts and swimming pool, glancing at the courts where two paunchy men were playing. The pool was emptying; only a handful of young people remained splashing in the water, or sitting on the sides of the pool, dangling their legs and sipping Cokes. He almost walked by without seeing a girl in a black bathing suit sitting alone on the diving board. Her head was down on her knees, and her fair hair fell in a graceful sweep across her face.

He went up to her. "Kali."

She raised her head. When she saw him her eyes widened, but she did not move. "What do you want?"

"My passport."

She rose to her feet in a quick, lithe gesture. "Catch me and I'll give it to you," she cried, and gave her high-pitched laugh which rose shrilly almost into hysteria. She dived cleanly into the water, flashed to the end of the pool, climbed up the ladder, ran along the path, down the ramp, and across the beach, Adam following, losing ground, hampered by his riding breeches, his boots.

Kali ran splashing into the water, looking back over her shoulder, laughing. She dove through a wave and started to swim.

Adam pulled off his boots, his trousers, ripped off his shirt and, in underclothes and Poly's canvas belt, he ran into the sea, flinging himself against the waves, thrusting through the breakers, until he could throw himself down and swim. He looked up, panting, to see Kali's arms flashing through the water ahead of him. Each time he looked she was less far ahead.

Then he heard her scream.

His first thought was that it was Macrina.

But the second scream that rang across the water was one of mortal terror.

He saw the shark, the sleek malevolent body, its murky darkness unable to leap to a flash of silver, its only light the sickly white of its belly.

The shark would do for him more than he had dared hope to do.

"Adam!" The scream throbbed against his ears.

He snatched the knife from the sheath, gave a mighty kick that shot him through the water toward the screaming girl, and plunged the knife into the shark.

There was blood in the water, Kali's blood, but the shark was still. Adam took Kali in a one-arm hold and started to swim in to shore. She was limp in his grasp although an occasional scream bubbled from her lips. When he could stand he picked her up. Her arm was ripped and bleeding copiously. He put her down at the water's edge where loose sand would not get into the wounds, and picked up his shirt from the beach, ripping the white material so that he could wrap it around her arm to stanch the blood.

He carried her to the hotel. She was sobbing and beginning to writhe in his arms. He felt neither hate nor love toward her, only an infinite weariness, as though she were a tremendous burden he despaired of ever being able to put down. He tried not to think of the horribly ripped arm.

He endured grimly the clamor of excitement and curiosity that greeted their entrance, pushing blindly through the avid guests toward the elevator, calling, "The doctor, quickly."

The hotel manager rushed after him, wringing pudgy hands. "But what is it? What has happened?"

"A shark," Adam said, grittily. "Get her father. Get a doctor."

In a luxurious room he put her down on the bed. She was white from shock. Her head moved feebly on the pillow. "Adam. Adam. Help."

Typhon Cutter and the doctor arrived together. "What have you done to her?" Typhon Cutter asked, face contorted with accusation.

Adam did not answer.

"He said it was a shark," the manager babbled, "but it couldn't have been a shark, it's not possible that it was a shark."

The doctor undid the bandages Adam had made, looked at Kali's arm. "A shark," he stated categorically. "Get me blankets. Get me hot water bottles." He opened his bag and began to work over the girl.

Typhon Cutter watched sickly. The room was silent except for the movements of the doctor and the sound of the surf outside. The flesh of Typhon Cutter's face had gone greenish and seemed to sag. "In the ocean?"

"Yes," Adam said.

"Why? She knows I have forbidden—"

"I asked her for my passport and she said 'Catch me.' You know how quick she is."

"Yes." The older man's eyes were focused on the girl on the bed, on the doctor's actions. "Then?"

"I hadn't quite caught up with her when I heard her scream."

"The shark had attacked her?"

"Yes."

"How did she get away?"

Adam took off the canvas belt and sheath. "I had a switchblade with MS-222."

"What?"

"It knocks a shark out faster than anything else."

"You used it to save her?" There was scorn and disbelief in the voice.

"Yes."

"Where is the knife?"

"In the shark." Adam, feeling sick, through with questioning, through with the Cutters forever, started for the door. Typhon Cutter's steel talons shot out and clamped over his arm.

"Wait." A lock of fair hair fell, unheeded, over the older man's forehead. Still holding Adam he asked the doctor, "The arm?"

The doctor shook his head. "Bad. If it were not for the young man and his quick action you would have no daughter at all."

"But what about the arm?"

The doctor shrugged. "There is much damage. A shark's teeth are deadly."

"You're sure it *was* a shark?"

The doctor shrugged again. "I have seen shark bites before. There is no question."

Typhon Cutter, pulling Adam with him, leaned over the bed. "What are you going to do?"

"There is little I *can* do except stop the bleeding and shock. You will have to get her to Lisbon. But even there—" Again the expressive lifting of the shoulders.

Typhon Cutter jerked his head at the manager. "Come." Not relaxing his painful clamp on Adam's arm he went into the corridor. A police officer was waiting outside the door with the hotel detective. Cutter ignored them, although they bowed respectfully, and the detective started to murmur expressions of alarm and concern.

"Get O'Keefe," Typhon Cutter said to Adam. As Adam did not reply the talons increased their pressure. "*I said get O'Keefe.*"

"Why?" Adam asked, beyond caring what he said or did.

"Fool, do you think I don't know that he has worked on human beings in the native village? Go to the telephone. Get him to come. He will do it for you. I will send the helicopter." There was anger in the voice, command in the words, naked pleading in the eyes. Another strand of pale gold hair fell forward, unheeded.

"I'll call," Adam said, "but he may not be there."

"The private line in your office," Cutter snapped at the manager.

They went down the hall, into the elevator, through the lobby: the oily little manager; the uniformed police officer; the detective (still ignored); Cutter, his ponderous body quivering; Adam.

In the lobby the guests were milling around.

"But her arm was ripped off, I saw it—"

"She will bleed to death before anything can be done—"

"Nonsense, it was only a scratch, they said so—"

"It wasn't her arm, it was her leg—"

The police officer shouted for quiet. "Please do not concern yourself. The girl is all right. She disobeyed rules in swimming in the ocean when the lifeguard was not there; she would never have been allowed to go out so far. If you will be sensible there is no danger whatsoever."

The manager echoed him, wringing his hands anxiously. "Everything is all right. There is no cause for alarm. She went out too far." He scurried around to Adam, grasping his hand in an effusion of gratitude. "My *dear* young man—"

"Fool. Come," Cutter said.

The manager put the call through. Charles answered the phone, called his mother. "It's Adam."

"Yes?" Mrs. O'Keefe said. "What is it, Adam?"

"Is the doctor there?"

"No. He's in the village with Poly and Father Tallis. What is it? What happened? Can I help?"

"Kali has been hurt by a shark. Do you know when they'll be back?"

"Some time this evening. I don't know just when. Adam, are you all right?"

The warmth and concern in her voice shook Adam so that he had to lean on the desk for support. But he said, "I'm fine, and I'll be home as soon as I can."

Cutter, who was breathing heavily behind him, said as he hung up, "In the village?"

"Yes."

Cutter snapped at the manager. "Get the helicopter ready." To Adam. "Go to the village and get him."

The police officer held up his hand, speaking to Adam. "There will have to be a statement from you."

The detective finally got in a word. "To absolve the hotel of any blame."

Typhon Cutter's thin voice rose in an angry squeak. "I *am* the hotel. There is no question of blame. She broke hotel rules. *My* rules." Controlling the soaring pitch of his voice he asked Adam, "Why did you have this stuff—whatever it is—on you?"

"You know there have been sharks here. I had the knife with me when Kali and I saw the shark before."

The phone on the manager's desk rang and Cutter pushed the little man aside to reach for it. "Yes? . . . Yes." He put the receiver down. "The helicopter is ready. Bring O'Keefe to her."

Adam said humbly, "I'll try."

"You will do more than try. I will go with you."

"No." Adam's voice was firm. "I'll go alone. Stay with Kali. She may need you."

For a moment Typhon Cutter chewed his lip. "Very well. The pilot is one of my men. If O'Keefe doesn't come he will have my instructions to—"

Adam cut through the threat by walking deliberately past

239

Typhon Cutter and out of the manager's office. Again the procession moved through the lounge, Adam silent, closed in, indifferent to the curiosity, the manager and the detective responding excitedly to the heightening tension of the guests, assuring them that all was well, everything was perfect, the young man was a hero.

The helicopter waited on the roof.

The manager pumped Adam's hand. "Thank you. *Muito obrigado*. Thank you."

As the boy started to climb into the helicopter he paused. "My passport."

Typhon Cutter said, "When you send O'Keefe back."

"No more of that. Now." Adam stood his ground, staring at Cutter's ravaged face. "Do you want Dr. O'Keefe?" The manager, the detective, the police officer murmured. Typhon Cutter reached into his breast pocket and handed over the passport.

Adam climbed into the helicopter. He did not look back. Not in time, not in space. His mind was exhausted to the point where it was bliss to allow it to drift with the noise of the rotors, to relax in the silence of the pilot.

When the helicopter hovered over the village Adam looked down and saw a scurrying of dark shapes. The village emptied, men and women disappearing into the jungle, into the huts. The pilot set the machine down on the greensward in front of the central hut. As Adam climbed out he saw the pilot reaching for his gun, but he felt no fear.

Virbius emerged from his hut, raising his hand in greeting.

Adam, too, raised his hand. "Is Dr. O'Keefe here?"

The old man spoke slowly, tremulously, with great effort. "You—wish—speak?"

"Please."

The old man beckoned and Dr. O'Keefe and Canon Tallis came out of the hut, Dr. O'Keefe bending his tall frame to pass through the doorway. As Adam started to speak Dr. O'Keefe called, "Poly—" and she came out with Temis.

Adam told what had happened, while Poly translated for Virbius and Temis. When the boy had finished Dr. O'Keefe questioned him, then stood, as though still listening. Then he looked at Canon Tallis, and their eyes met for a long moment. Dr. O'Keefe nodded.

"Daddy!" Poly cried. "You're not going!"

"Yes. I will have to see the arm for myself. Then, if it is as bad as it seems, I will have to tell Typhon Cutter of the dangers, and then, if he still wishes me to, I will try."

Poly ran to her father and caught his hands in hers. "But you wouldn't try if you didn't think you could do it, would you?"

"No."

"But why are you going, daddy? Why?"

Canon Tallis drew Poly away from her father. "Ask Adam why, Poly."

But she was silent. They stood, looking, while Dr. O'Keefe climbed into the helicopter, still stood looking, half-deafened by the noise of the rotors, until it had droned away, until the night sounds of the village could be heard again. Without a word Virbius sat on the greensward, crosslegged, looking out to the harbor. Canon Tallis sat by him, gesturing to Adam. The two girls stood together, facing the men. Temis raised her hand, looked at the spread-out fingers, dropped it to her side.

Virbius spoke.

Poly said, "He wants to know if you think daddy did right to go."

"Adam?" Canon Tallis asked.

Adam was silent, looking at the village, at the men returning from the jungle, at the women and children emerging from their huts. Evening was coming quickly. The sun had already dropped with the sudden fierceness of the jungle, and the sky over the island was suffused with great streaks of color: rose, raspberry, deepening to mauve, to indigo. Above a date palm a star began to pulse, at first faintly, then growing in brilliance. In the darkness of the surrounding brush fireflies flickered.

"Adam?" Canon Tallis asked again.

"I think he had to go," Adam said unwillingly. He began to shiver and realized that, like it or not, he would again be able to feel heat and cold, sunlight and moonlight.

At a word from the old man, Temis slipped into the hut.

"But why!" Poly demanded passionately. "*Why* did he have to go?"

Adam was silent while Temis came out and draped a softly woven robe about him. Then he said, heavily, "Because of Joshua."

"But she killed Joshua!" Poly cried. "Why should daddy help her now? I don't want to help her! Adam should have let the shark kill her!"

Adam was silent.

"Father!" Poly cried.

Canon Tallis said quietly, "Suppose it had been Adam the shark attacked?"

Tears began to roll down Poly's cheeks. "But Adam's good, and she's—"

Adam stood up, holding Temis' robe about his shoulders. He could not say what he had to say sitting down. "I killed Joshua, too."

"But—"

"Be quiet, Poly," Canon Tallis commanded.

Adam let the robe drop as he clenched and unclenched his fists. "If I hadn't used the knife, or if we didn't try to help Kali now, it would be justice, wouldn't it?"

Verbius nodded, saying the English word, "Justice," nodding again.

"But Joshua—" Adam said. "Joshua—" he broke off.

"It's Joshua I'm thinking about!" Poly cried.

"It was what he always said," Adam choked out, "about the sparrow. Even Kali would be a sparrow to Joshua. If you're going to care about the fall of the sparrow you can't pick and choose who's going to be the sparrow. It's everybody, and you're stuck with it." He sat down and put his arms about his knees and his head on his arms.

Virbius spoke. When he had finished there was silence until he spoke again, rather crossly, to Poly. She translated.

"He says it is not enough if you pray neither for nor against. He says he will go to his gods and pray. For."

Virbius stood up, tremulously, and went into his hut.

Adam did not know how long he sat there with his head down. When he looked up Temis had gone and Poly had turned away.

Canon Tallis looked at Adam, smiled briefly, but did not speak. Night was coming, but to Adam, as he returned the canon's smile, everywhere there seemed to be light.

At last Poly reached over and took his hand in hers. "I see that daddy had to go," she said. And then, "I love you, Adam."

He held her hand tightly. "I love you, too, Poly."